W9-CQR-725

"Are you always such a martyr?"

"I'm not a martyr," Charlie protested. "I just don't like being indebted to anyone."

"Well, consider yourself indebted," Graham said, with a casual shrug. When she continued to glare at him, he sighed then placed a hand on the bare skin of her shoulder. She gasped at the feel of his hot skin on hers. "Okay, you're not indebted to me, unless…" he said, softly.

His voice trailed off at the same time that his hand tightened on her neck. He leaned closer to her. His gaze dropped to her lips. She felt hot air escape his mouth and caress her lips. Of their own will, her eyes began to close, as she prepared for his kiss. Her body physically ached for his kiss, she needed it. Charlie suddenly knew why women craved men, did things for them, sacrificed for them and forgave them. At this moment, she knew she would do anything just for a taste of his lips….

Books by Tamara Sneed

Kimani Romance

At First Sight

Kimani Arabesque

Love Undercover
A Royal Vow
When I Fall in Love

TAMARA SNEED

was born and raised in the Los Angeles area. She currently is an attorney, practicing civil litigation in Southern California. Her first novel, *Love Undercover* was an instant reader and reviewer smash. Tamara's third book, *When I Fall in Love,* won an EMMA Award for Favorite Romantic Comedy at the 2003 Romance Slam Jam. Tamara has been a lifelong romance reader and writer, and she enjoys stories where brave heroes and heroines laugh their way through life and love. To learn more about her, visit www.tamarasneed.com. Tamara also enjoys hearing from readers at tamara@tamarasneed.com.

Tamara Sneed

At First
SIGHT

KIMANI
ROMANCE

KIMANI PRESS™

ISBN-13: 978-0-373-86014-2
ISBN-10:   0-373-86014-5

AT FIRST SIGHT

Copyright © 2007 by Sekret T. Sneed

All rights reserved. The reproduction, transmission or utilization of this work in whole or in part in any form by any electronic, mechanical or other means, now known or hereafter invented, including xerography, photocopying and recording, or in any information storage or retrieval system, is forbidden without written permission. For permission please contact Kimani Press, Editorial Office, 233 Broadway, New York, NY 10279 U.S.A.

www.kimanipress.com

Printed in U.S.A.

Dear Reader,

Welcome to Sibleyville, California! I'll admit that I'm a dyed-in-the-wool city girl, but a part of me has always wondered what it would have been like to grow up in a small town surrounded by cowboys and blue skies. The best part of being a writer is that I don't just have to wonder about it, I can create it! Enter Sibleyville, California—population 15,000.

I have written about love in big cities like Los Angeles, San Francisco and Washington D.C., but it's now time to give the small-town heroes a chance to shine. I had as much fun creating the flavor and feel of this small town, as I did watching Graham Forbes, native son, and Charlie Sibley, reluctant Los Angeles transplant, fall in love. There is something about clear, smogless skies and wide-open spaces that make the impossible seem possible and the crazy seem logical. Sibleyville may not be real, but hopefully by the end of the book, you will wish it is.

I hope you enjoy this peek into a small town, filled with incredible people, lots of laughter and an occasional flash of Cupid's arrow.

Sincerely,

Tamara Sneed

This book is dedicated to all the sisters out there. A sister is your best friend, your confidante, your toughest critic, your strongest ally and your loudest cheerleader. She can work your nerve like no one else, but, when the chips are down, she alone has your back without question or pause.

To my sister, Alyson, I love you!

ACKNOWLEDGMENTS

As always I must thank my mother, Patricia Sneed, my sister, Alyson Turner, and my two delightful nieces, Lauren and Erin, for their unwavering support in all I do. Whether I accomplish it or not, they are there for me. I also must thank my good friend and fellow writer, Reon Laudat, for always being a calm port in the unpredictable storm that is the publishing industry. In addition, I have to give a shout-out to my agent, Paige Wheeler, whose excitement for this business makes me excited. And, lastly, I must thank Mavis Allen and all the other folks at Kimani Press, who are keeping African-American romance fiction alive.

Chapter 1

"Grandpa Max is trying to punish us from beyond the grave, isn't he?" Quinn Sibley wailed, as she stared at the dilapidated house standing—just barely—in front of her.

Charlie Sibley pulled a bulging black suitcase from the trunk of the silver Jaguar that their older sister, Kendra, had haphazardly parked next to the house, and dropped it on the ground. Dirt billowed around it. She frowned. There was dirt everywhere. Charlie was far from a neat freak, but from the two-lane highway that had branched off the main highway to the small town of Sibleyville, California, to the narrow dirt road that had led to the house, there had been dirt. On the sides of the road, on the road, flying in her mouth when Kendra had allowed her to roll down the window. There was no escaping it.

But, besides the dirt, Charlie had more important things on her mind, like finding her emergency bag of chocolate amidst her sisters' designer suitcases jamming the trunk. Charlie needed that bag. It housed her entire two-week supply of chocolate. And if ever there was a time for chocolate, it was now.

"Have you seen my duffel bag?" she asked Quinn absently. "It's small and dark blue—"

"Look at it, Charlie," Quinn ordered, sounding close to tears. "Look at where we're supposed to live for the next two weeks and tell me that this isn't some form of punishment. Grandpa Max's last attempt to make us suffer."

Charlie followed her sister's command and turned to stare at the house. She had to admit, the house wasn't just bad. It was abominable.

The narrow split-level home had probably once been charming. Now, the white wood was rotting and crumbling at an alarming rate. Portions of the roof hung in jagged edges over the front porch, like a medieval defense system against intruders. What had probably once been a comfortable covered porch that had held a few rocking chairs, now was a death trap waiting to ensnare its next victim, from the rotted steps leading to the porch to the chipped and peeling railing. The blue shutters on either side of the front door hung lopsided as if someone had tried to pull them off, but had grown tired before finishing. Charlie hadn't been inside—and she wished she could keep it that way—but she had a feeling that it would be even worse.

Kendra had disappeared inside the house ten minutes before, and neither Charlie or Quinn had heard anything from her since.

Charlie glanced around the quiet stillness of the country. Cloudless blue skies, free of the smog and towering skyscrapers of Los Angeles, and rolling green hills greeted her. Across the dirt road from the house was a line of imposing redwoods that were so dense that Charlie couldn't see past the first few rows. There was not another house or car or any other sign of civilization in sight. All the trees and stillness and fresh air made her uncomfortable.

Charlie returned her attention to her younger sister and forced a smile. Quinn was dramatic by nature. Being an actress on the popular daytime soap, *Diamond Valley,* didn't help matters. Nor did the fact that Quinn was gorgeous, with the ability to make men do her bidding with one bright smile. She was tall, thin, as most actresses were, had vanilla skin, hazel eyes and long, silky, sandy-brown hair. Quinn would never be caught without makeup or a pair of stiletto heels.

"It's not that bad, Quinn," Charlie lied. "In fact, it's almost…sort of charming. Quaint."

"Quaint?" Quinn repeated, her hazel eyes widened with disbelief.

Charlie nodded vigorously and added, "It just needs a little elbow grease and soap."

"Elbow grease and soap?" Quinn repeated, with the same tone of stunned disbelief. When Charlie smiled, Quinn exploded, hysterically, "The only thing that house needs is a wrecking ball."

Charlie threw up her hands in surrender then turned back to the trunk. She dropped another suitcase onto the dirt and peered into the dark recesses of the trunk for her bag. Her need for chocolate was reaching a critical level. While Quinn, who stood over five foot nine and weighed probably half as much as the shorter Charlie, literally flinched from chocolate like a vampire confronted with garlic, Charlie needed chocolate the way she needed oxygen. And, of course, it showed on her wide hips and thighs.

Charlie grunted from the weight of another bag then threw it on the ground.

"Careful with that," Quinn cried, tearing her gaze from the house at the sound of the suitcase hitting the ground. She wobbled on four-inch designer stiletto heels towards the suitcase. "I have shoes in there."

"You have a whole suitcase devoted to shoes?"

"Of course. Don't you?" Quinn asked, blankly.

Not for the first time, Charlie wondered how she and Quinn could be related.

"This just can't be real," Quinn murmured, shaking her head.

"Shoes don't break, Quinn—"

"Not the shoes. This house. The will. Us living together again, after all these years. It's unreal." She paused for obvious effect then whispered dramatically, "It's as if Fate, that fickle mistress, is punishing me for my success."

Charlie knew it wasn't the reaction Quinn was looking for, but she bit her bottom lip to restrain a burst of laughter. She had watched Quinn whisper that same phrase, with that same expression of overplayed guilt, on *Diamond Valley*. At the time, Quinn's character, Sephora, had been wracked with guilt because her husband's brother had jumped off a bridge after Sephora had ended their affair. Of course, his body had never been found, so there was always a possibility that Sephora was not out of the woods.

Charlie sighed then said, "Grandpa Max is not punishing you, and although I can't speak for Fate, I also doubt that she's punishing you."

Quinn stared at Charlie and asked, in a hoarse voice, "Then why would he sentence me to two weeks in this hellhole?"

"It's his childhood home, Quinn. He was born and raised in this town. The town is named after him, after us. Maybe Grandpa Max wanted us to see where he came from, what we come from. He didn't always live in a mansion in Beverly Hills, and maybe he wanted us to know that."

"Couldn't he just have said that then?" Quinn protested, nearly screeching. "I, personally, don't need the up-close-and-personal history lesson."

The torn screen door opened with a creak that echoed across the yard. Their oldest sister, Kendra, stepped onto the porch. The disgusted expression on her flawlessly made-up face told Charlie everything she needed to know. The inside of the house matched the abandoned and neglected exterior.

The screen door flapped closed behind Kendra and promptly one side of the lightweight wire crashed to the floor. Quinn flinched in surprise, while Charlie laughed at Kendra's expression. She wiped her hands on an immaculately tailored dark skirt and looked over her two younger sisters with the mask of calm disdained boredom that she had perfected in junior high school.

She coolly eyed Quinn then said, "I heard your complaining all the way in the house, Quinn. Feel free to leave at any time. No one will stop you."

Charlie groaned and raked both hands through her chin-length hair. It seemed to have doubled in size from the heat and stress of the past few hours since the sisters had left Los Angeles and driven four hours into California's heartland to Sibleyville, population fifteen thousand. Quinn and Kendra had been at each other's throats for the entire four-hour drive. Actually, Quinn and Kendra had been at each other's throats since birth.

"You would like that, wouldn't you?" Quinn shot back, with narrowed eyes. She tossed her long hair over her shoulder in a move worthy of Sephora and said, "Of course, if I left then you wouldn't get any of the money. Remember that part of Grandpa's will, Kendra, the part where the three of us have to remain in this house together for two weeks or else all three of us lose our inheritance. Do you still want me to leave?"

Charlie pleaded, "You guys, come on. It's been a long day—"

"Why did you even agree to this, Quinn?" Kendra demanded, ignoring Charlie's plea for peace. "You're a big actress, if one could consider what you do acting—"

"You're just jealous," Quinn shot back. "You've always been jealous."

"Of what?" Kendra asked, with an amused laugh.

Kendra's smile would have been gorgeous if Charlie had thought for one second that she was sincere. Kendra was a few inches shorter than Quinn, but still taller than most women. Instead of being tall and thin like Quinn, or short and curvy like Charlie, Kendra was like a gazelle: lean muscles, athletic grace and awesome power. She was mocha-chocolate, with bone-straight midnight-black hair that she wore in a straight bob to her shoulders. Her razor-sharp bangs would never dream of not hanging how Kendra wanted them to.

"That I have a life. Friends. Lovers. People like me, they want to take a picture with me. Who wants to be around you, except old men because you make them rich?"

Kendra's remained calm as she said, in a bored tone, "People don't want a picture of you. They want a picture of your breasts. Those two things are more famous than you are."

Charlie inwardly groaned as Quinn's mouth dropped open in shock. She really should intervene, before the two women came to blows, but Charlie had learned long ago to stay out of their way when they started an argument. It had been almost two years since Charlie had been in the same room with both of her sisters, and Charlie wished it could have been another two years.

But, their grandfather—the man who had raised them after their parents' death—had died, and decreed in his will that his three granddaughters spend two weeks in his childhood home as a condition to inheriting an undisclosed sum of money that could possibly number in the millions. Max Sibley had built Sibley Corporation from the ground up in his twenties and had been worth over millions of dollars at his death. Kendra had estimated that they should each receive over ten million dollars a piece after taxes.

"Just go away, Kendra," Quinn ordered, pointing her finger towards the road.

Kendra rolled her eyes then said, "I'm not going anywhere, and neither are you. For some reason, the old man thought it would be a riot to throw the three of us together in this dump. If we don't survive, then we'll never see a penny of our inheritance and all of the Sibley millions will go to some charitable organization that probably wants to save the whales or grasshoppers or something. I have my own money—a lot of my own money, but I will rot in hell before I allow the Sibley millions to be wasted like that."

"At least we agree on something," Quinn said, begrudgingly, while crossing her arms over her ample breasts.

"So, for the next two weeks, I intend to pretend that you don't exist and that I'm living in the lap of luxury on a small, deserted, primitive island," Kendra continued as if Quinn had never spoken. "I suggest you do the same."

"I don't need or want your suggestions," Quinn said, with a snort.

"Will you two stop it!" Charlie exploded. Both women turned to her with identical expressions of shock and a little guilt.

As usual, they had forgotten that there was a third Sibley sister.

"I've listened to you two argue and complain since six o'clock this morning, and I'm sick of it," Charlie screamed, as tears of frustration, fatigue and chocolate deprivation filled her eyes. "I don't know why Grandpa Max did this, but he did and we're stuck here for the next two weeks. So, maybe we should try to use this time as an opportunity to get to know each other again. We *are* sisters. And with Grandpa Max dead, the three of us are *it*. There aren't any more Sibleys. I don't know about you two, but that scares me."

Her sisters' expressions grew guarded, and Charlie knew it wasn't because she was waving the white flag. It was because she was close to crying, and the Sibley sisters did not cry, especially in front of each other.

In a characteristically un-Charlie Sibley move, she screeched in frustration and kicked the Jaguar's rear tire.

She screamed in surprise as the heel on one of her shoes snapped, and she fell to the dirt in a heap of swirling dust. Both her sisters appeared frozen in place. Neither made a move to assist her. Not that Charlie had expected them to. She cursed, more from her annoyance with them than pain, even though her right foot was beginning to throb.

"That hurt," Charlie muttered.

"Remind me never to make you angry," drawled a deep, amused voice.

Charlie prayed that the owner of the voice did not look as gorgeous as he sounded. Judging from Quinn's and Kendra's slack-jawed expressions however, her prayers were not to be answered. She looked over her shoulder. And gulped.

Her gaze traveled from the dirt-covered genuine cowboy boots to the worn, well-fitted jeans that emphasized long, muscular legs. She gulped again at the slight bulge in his pants at the zipper then at the white T-shirt that settled over his flat stomach and emphasized finely muscled cinnamon-colored arms.

He wore a cowboy hat. A large charcoal-gray cowboy hat that shadowed the sharp lines and angles of his face. He had full lips, a strong nose and piercing brown eyes that were focused intently on her. His profile had probably been chiseled on a African coin.

Charlie wanted to kick the tire again because she realized that despite her supposed cynicism and analytical mind, she had just fallen in love at first sight. And judging from the sudden come-hither smiles that were fixed on Quinn's and Kendra's faces, she didn't have a snowball's chance in hell.

Chapter 2

"Are you all right, ma'am?" the man spoke again in a deep, rumbling voice that slid down Charlie's body to lodge like a ball of lead in her stomach.

When she didn't respond, he took a step toward her, as if to help her stand. Charlie quickly stood to her feet, ignoring his outstretched large hand. The embarrassment flooded her face so quickly that she thought her body would incinerate. That would have been preferable to being subjected to the man's direct, unflinching stare.

She averted her gaze to his right shoulder and noticed the black pickup truck parked at the mouth of the driveway. He must have driven up while she had been screeching at her sisters. Charlie was a twenty-nine-year-old grown woman who had a master's degree in Art History, and who regularly gave lectures and presentations on varied subjects as a curator for the privately owned African-American Art Center in Los Angeles. In other words, she was an intelligent, successful, professional woman who shouldn't have cared that a cowboy had seen her melt-down, but her heart slamming against her chest ignored her reasoned lecture and continued pounding.

"Charlie, you're a mess. Let me help you," Quinn said soothingly, as she quickly ran to her side.

Charlie watched in numb surprise as Quinn brushed the dirt off Charlie's gray slacks. When Charlie saw the look Quinn sent the cowboy, Charlie wanted to strangle her.

"My poor sister is just frazzled after our long drive here," Quinn said, with a flirtatious smile at the man, who Charlie noted with annoyance, sent a flirtatious smile back at her.

Not to be outdone by Quinn, Kendra stepped towards the man, her hand outstretched.

Kendra actually smiled as she purred, "Please tell me that you're a resident of Sibleyville and not just a visitor."

The man directed his thousand-watt smile at Kendra as he shook her hand. Charlie's mood darkened when she noted that they held on to each other's hands far longer than was appropriate.

"I'm a resident…for the moment. I live down the road," he said, with the trace of a sardonic smile that made Charlie's heart clog in her throat. He looked from Quinn to Kendra, skipping over Charlie. "I'm Graham Forbes, and you lovely ladies must be the Sibley sisters."

"At your service," Quinn murmured, as her gaze greedily drank him in from head to toe.

Charlie would have been embarrassed by Quinn's

boldness if she hadn't been wishing she had the nerve to do and say the same thing.

"We heard you ladies were coming. Your grandpa's lawyer asked us to turn on the power and lights, and we cleaned up the place as best we could…" His voice trailed off. Then he asked with a perplexed expression, "How long are you here for?"

Kendra took a few steps closer to the man. She planted her shapely legs in a wide stance and cocked her hip to one side like the pose of a glamorous model at the end of a catwalk. It would have been comical if she hadn't looked so damn sexy.

"We're here for two weeks. By the way, I'm Kendra Sibley, the oldest."

Quinn quickly stepped next to Kendra and slightly bent forward, exposing the tops of her exquisite vanilla-tinted breasts. "And I'm Quinn, the youngest."

Charlie knew it was her turn to step forward, but her legs felt too unsteady to consider operating them right now.

Besides, as with most men who stood within radius of the three sisters, Graham Forbes had forgotten that Charlie Sibley—the middle one, as she was more often known—existed.

"I didn't expect you ladies to actually stay here, not with the state of this place. For a long time, we all thought that your grandpa had forgotten it," he said, while nodding towards the house.

"Apparently, he did," Kendra said, darkly, then flashed a smile at Graham. "But, we're staying here. If it's good enough for our grandfather, then it's good enough for us. After his death, we figured what better way to feel closer to him and to understand him than to come to his childhood home. If it was just me, I could handle the dirt and rodents—I've dealt with worse vermin on Wall Street, but I don't think my sisters can handle it. They're not as accommodating as I can be."

Charlie didn't miss Kendra's emphasis on the word *accommodating*. Judging from the amused and interested glint that entered Graham's eyes he hadn't either. Charlie wanted to smack them both.

"Kendra's right. I'm not as hardy and masculine as her," Quinn said, loudly, drawing Graham's attention. Her voice softened to a bedroom whisper, as she said, "I'm more soft and open."

Charlie couldn't withhold her snort of disbelief. Apparently, it had also been a loud snort because all three turned to her. Charlie's face burned with embarrassment once more as she tried to withstand the laser-sharp gaze of Graham Forbes. Against her will, her gaze dropped to his full lips. His lower lip was slightly more plump than the upper one.

She actually had to fight the urge to cross the dirt lot and take his lip between her teeth.

"So, you must be the middle sister," Graham said, his tone polite and neighborly. One corner of his mouth lifted as he added, "Judging from the beating you gave that tire, you're the one I should watch out for in a bar fight, right?"

Quinn and Kendra laughed, while Charlie just stared at him. His voice was so deep and warm. It reminded her of molasses, or grits or something hot and Southern.

The baritone sound poured into her body and curled into something warm and welcoming.

Then she realized that she had been rendered mute by a cowboy. It was humiliating. When she still couldn't force her mouth to open, she averted her gaze again and instantly spied her chocolate-laden bag in the trunk.

She grabbed it, murmured a choked "Excuse me," and limped towards the house as fast as she could with her foot throbbing with pain and her dignity in shreds.

Chapter 3

"As members of the city council, it's your job to look out for this town's best interests. And the best interests of this town…"

Graham Forbes blocked out the rest of the speech being given by Mayor Boyd Robbins. He had heard it all before during the six months he had spent on the Sibleyville City Council, a position he was still trying to figure out how he had gotten. The issue might change, but Robbins always found something supposedly in the town's best interests that usually involved either he or his two sons profiting in one form or another.

Graham felt an ache growing at his temples and rubbed his forehead to soothe the pressure. He glanced around the small cramped meeting room in city hall. As usual, all the windows were shut tight, even though it was the middle of summer and the old building had never been upgraded to air conditioning. As usual, Robbins' long-suffering wife, Alma, sat in a chair in the corner of the room, taking notes of everything Robbins said, although she usually stopped writing whenever anyone else spoke. And, as usual, the four other city council members managed to look intrigued, as if they had never heard this exact same speech before. And since the other four had gotten elected to the city council around the same time the telephone had been invented—and Robbins had been making the same speech about that long—Graham knew they must have.

Graham was the youngest person in the room by about three decades, and considering he was thirty-two years old, he wasn't exactly young, and he was feeling older by the second. He wondered how his father had done this, year after year. Not only this, but everything else that came with living and operating a ranch in Sibleyville. Yet now Lance Forbes was finding it difficult even to endure the physical therapy that would get him back on track after a heart attack six months ago.

What had started as a three-week vacation to visit his father and help his mother with the farm had turned into six months and a city council position. Graham had started avoiding the increasingly insistent calls from his job, because he didn't know what to say. His father was still playing sick and his mother's eyes lit up every time she saw Graham walk into the house. The guilt was unbearable, but Graham had vowed to return to Tokyo after planting season ended. There were only three weeks remaining in the season, and given the long hours he and the workers had been putting in over the last month, Graham figured the farm was ahead of schedule.

"We have to get Max Sibley's girls to see what a great place Sibleyville is, or they could sell the land right from under us."

Graham snapped out of his brooding at the mention of the Sibleys. He hadn't been able to get Quinn and Kendra Sibley out of his thoughts since leaving their property an hour ago. There definitely weren't women like those two in this small town. The women were gorgeous and sophisticated, like the women he dated in Tokyo.

He had to admit there was no one like the other Sibley sister either. She had looked nothing like Quinn or Kendra. She had been thicker than the other women, more curvy than Kendra and less silicone-assisted than Quinn. Her thick brown hair had hung in limp waves to her shoulders.

Also, unlike her sisters, she had looked at him as if he were evil personified. Graham vowed to stay away from her. Bringing his attention back to the meeting at hand, he demanded more sharply then he intended, "What are you talking about, Robbins? The town owns the land." Robbins glared at him. The two men had a mutual distrust and dislike for each other.

As six pairs of shocked eyes swung to him, Graham grimaced. He had forgotten his rule of not speaking at the meetings.

"We had a small problem in the seventies, Graham," Velma Spears explained, her oversized eyeglasses obscuring half of her wrinkled, kind face. Velma told every citizen who came to speak at city council meeting that their speech was "lovely." And she meant it.

"Small problem." Boyd Robbins snorted at Velma's understatement. "We had some real issues in this town. If you haven't noticed, Forbes, this ain't Tokyo—"

"I've noticed," Graham muttered, dryly.

Boyd's red face grew even more red. Boyd had been in the military for thirty years and it showed in his ramrod-straight posture, buzz-cut graying brown hair and constantly clenched jaw. He was in his late fifties, but after a lifetime in the sun, he looked closer to seventy. His skin was constantly a shade of red or maroon, and just looking at Graham sometimes made him turn purple.

"Boyd means that when we fall on our hard times, we can't rely on tourist dollars or exports to hold us until times get better," Angus Affleck, Graham's father's best friend, chimed in from the seat on Graham's right. "The seventies were tough for all small towns. A lot of people left for big cities like San Francisco and L.A. We almost had to shut down the local elementary school. And without residents, we didn't have a tax base or a consumer base. Main Street was almost shut down, not to mention the problems we had selling our crops. We needed help, and Max helped us."

"He bailed out an entire town?" Graham asked, surprised.

"At a steep price," Boyd said, his voice echoing in the small room because of his close proximity to the microphone on the table. As if he needed it. "He wanted the deeds to all the stores on Main Street."

"He let us keep our ranches, Boyd," Velma said, softly.

"Because he knew we'd stuff his lawyers down his

throat, if he tried that," Paul Robbins, Boyd's brother and loyal supporter, chimed in from his seat on Graham's left.

"Although his bank damn near owns half the ranches in town anyway," Boyd grumbled.

"He made a lot of improvements to Main Street. We wouldn't have the clock tower or the movie theatre without Max," Velma continued, her voice becoming more insistent.

"Some people think throwing around money will buy them respect. Max Sibley was a rat." Boyd's face had gotten so red, he looked on the verge of imploding.

"From what I understand of those Sibley girls, they're just as bad as Max," Paul said, taking over for his brother, who was too overcome with anger to continue. "One of them is even an actor on one of those soap operas."

"*Diamond Valley,*" Angus offered, cheerfully. Graham looked over in surprise at the grizzled rancher and part-time sheriff of the town, whose skin was like well-worn leather after decades in the sun.

"I don't care about the name of her stupid show," Paul snapped, sending Angus an annoyed glance. "The point is, she's an actress, and we all know what those people are like. We don't want an actress in charge of the future of this town, nor the other ones. One is a stockbroker in New York—"

"I bet she had something to do with Enron," Boyd interrupted, suspiciously.

Paul continued, "And the other one works at some Black museum… Oh, excuse me, Graham, African-American museum."

Graham ignored the dig and concentrated on the Sibley sisters. Judging from Kendra's conservative dark suit, tight enough to display that she worked out on a consistent basis and could probably kick a grown man's ass, Kendra was the stockbroker. Quinn's almost luminous glow obviously meant that she was the actress. That left the mute one as the museum worker. It figured.

"A bunch of liberals," Boyd summarized his brother's lecture. "We're looking at our town being controlled by a bunch of female liberals. What are they even doing here? Those girls live in the lap of luxury all of their lives and now they willingly move into a shack that hasn't been inhabited by anything more than raccoons and snakes in over fifteen years? By any means necessary, we have got to get those girls to give us back our town before they cause irreparable damage."

"On that cheerful note, how about we conclude this meeting for the night and go our separate ways to think about how we're going to swindle the Sibley sisters?" Graham said.

"I second that," Angus said, smiling proudly at him.

"Wait, we're not finished—" Boyd started.

"All in favor say 'aye,'" Graham said. A murmur of "ayes" followed his statement, besides Paul's tentative "no." Graham pounded the mayor's gavel and announced, "This meeting is adjourned. Until next week, folks."

He stood, took a few moments to make certain that Velma had a ride home, avoided Angus's attempt to get his attention, ignored Boyd's poisonous glares and slipped out of the claustrophobic town hall.

He breathed in the fresh night air as he strolled towards his truck parked in one of the marked spots on Main Street. The nights in Sibleyville were like nowhere else that Graham had ever been, and he had been all over the world as an executive with the conglomerate, Shoeford Industries. There was something about the mixture of dirt, mountains, green trees and water that combined to make Sibleyville smell…smell like something comforting and inviting.

Graham stopped his thoughts. He was standing on Main Street in a town that had one stoplight, one movie theatre and where the big social event of the year was David Markham's Fourth of July hoedown. There was nothing in Sibleyville that made him want to stay. Graham could not survive in this environment, after having spent the last fifteen years living in major cities around the world. He needed excitement, luxury, glamour. And not even Boyd could lie and say that Sibleyville had that.

"I'm sick of you railroading me in city council meetings, young man," came Boyd's angry voice behind him.

Graham inwardly groaned. He remembered his grandmother's old phrase: *Speak of the devil, and he'll appear.*

Graham turned to face Boyd. Graham was tall at six foot two, but Boyd was probably stronger and showed no signs of allowing age to slow him down.

Graham nodded a greeting to Boyd's wife, Alma, who cowered behind him. As large and intimidating as her husband was, she was small and petite. Graham tried not to think about it, but he still wondered how they… Well, they had two big sons, so they must have figured out a way.

"Good evening, Alma," Graham said, smiling politely.

Alma smiled shyly in response.

Boyd grumbled, then said, abruptly, "I got your number. I know what you're doing."

"What am I doing?" Graham asked, curiously.

"You're trying to bring your big-city ideas here. This isn't New York City," Boyd informed him, while drawing out "New York City" as if he was saying "Sodom and Gomorrah." "You think you're so special because you have a few stamps on your passport. I've been to all of those places, too, with the service, and there's no place like Sibleyville, U.S.A."

"I'm not trying to do anything, Boyd. I just don't think threatening the Sibley sisters is going to make them hand back the keys of the town. They either will or won't, but it's their decision to make."

Boyd's eyes narrowed then he poked a gnarled finger in Graham's face and warned, "I'm watching you. You get in the way of this town's progress, and I'll rip you a new one."

Boyd stomped off towards his town car. Alma smiled apologetically at Graham then raced after Boyd. Graham shook his head in disbelief then laughed. He had spent the last ten years working and living in almost every major city around the world, and the only time he had been threatened with bodily harm was by the mayor of Sibleyville.

Chapter 4

For one glorious moment when Charlie woke up, she thought she was back in her apartment in Los Angeles. She smiled and stretched her arms over her head. She couldn't wait to walk to the deli down the street. She loved the tuna sandwiches there, and the canolis. Delicious cream bursting from the delicate shell, all covered in gooey chocolate. Her mouth watered just thinking about it.

Then she felt her sweat-soaked nightgown plastered against her skin. Something else was wrong…. That smell. Usually, she got the ocean breeze, but now all she smelled was dust and…and fresh, country air. *Country*. Charlie gasped and opened her eyes. The first thing she saw was a large brown water stain at the corner of the white ceiling. And then she heard the sound of glass breaking followed by Kendra shrilly berating Quinn.

Charlie placed an arm over her eyes, as it all came rushing back. The long drive to Sibleyville, Kendra and Quinn and—even worse—the gorgeous cowboy. It hadn't been a nightmare. Charlie seriously contemplated remaining in her bed for the rest of the two weeks, but she suddenly noticed the bedspring poking into her back and rolled out. Her feet hit the hardwood floor and the dust that lay on the floor like a carpet billowed around her.

Charlie glanced around the bedroom that she had been given by default last night. Quinn and Kendra had both claimed larger—and coincidentally cleaner—bedrooms upstairs. Charlie had been stuck with the only bedroom on the ground floor. It had one squeaking bed, an antique dresser with a cracked mirror and a window that was covered with a faded, daisy-covered sheet. She shuddered in disgust at the filth in the room. The night before, she had willed herself not to notice the dirt and had simply unrolled a sleeping bag on top of the bed and climbed in. But, now, in the sunlight that streamed unimpeded through the sheet, she saw everything. Goosebumps raised on her skin. She could not believe that she had slept in this room. It was disgusting.

Charlie heard more screaming in the kitchen. She slipped her bare feet into her tennis shoes and stood up from the bed, groaning at the protesting ache in her back. She wiped the sleep from her eyes then shuffled down the hallway into the living room.

She could hear chaos behind the door to the kitchen. Since she couldn't avoid her sisters forever, Charlie took a deep breath and pushed open the swinging kitchen door.

Black smoke was curling out of the brand-new silver toaster on the counter that Charlie had brought from home. Quinn stood in a sheer white minidress with her arms crossed, glaring at Kendra, who wore skin-tight, black workout pants and a black sports bra. Both of her sisters looked showered and refreshed, and Charlie reminded herself to check their bathroom first.

"What in the world is going on?" Her sisters turned to her and both began speaking at once. Charlie instantly held up her hands for silence. Surprisingly, Quinn and Kendra both fell silent. "First, I need coffee. And, second, I need to find the closest Wal-Mart so we can start disinfecting this place."

"Wal-Mart?" Kendra gasped in horror at the same time that Quinn whispered in dismay, "Disinfecting?"

"If we're lucky," Charlie muttered. "There may not be a Wal-Mart around here, which is great for the local small businesses, but very bad for us."

Charlie shuffled to the coffeemaker that she had also brought from home. Kendra wordlessly handed her a coffee cup with the name of her alma mater, Harvard, emblazoned on the side. Charlie smiled gratefully then filled the mug with the steaming liquid. She usually liberally sprinkled sugar into her coffee, but since she knew neither of her sisters would think to pack something as caloric as sugar, she just gulped it down and cringed.

"You're not actually expecting us to clean this place, are you, Charlie?" Quinn asked, nervously. "We don't have the skills for this—"

"Skills," Kendra snorted. "We're just cleaning, Quinn, not launching a space shuttle."

"But, there could be rodents or something," Quinn said, with wide eyes. She rubbed the back of her neck, as if brushing something off her skin. "Can't we hire someone to do this?"

"I hate to admit this, but I actually agree with Bimbette here," Kendra said to Charlie. Ignoring Quinn's glare, she continued, "We need this entire house cleaned from top to bottom, and I'd rather not get buried alive if it collapses, so we need to have someone secure the frame and foundation. And then I need to contact the office—"

Charlie interrupted her, "We're not allowed to use our personal bank accounts, call friends or boyfriends, or to work—"

Kendra's eyes turned cold, and Charlie fought to hold her gaze. Kendra could be intimidating when she wanted to be, and she usually wanted to be. "You don't seriously expect us to live by the draconian conditions of the will?"

"We agreed," Charlie replied, simply.

"I can't disappear from my job for two weeks, Charlie," Kendra snarled.

"Then you shouldn't have agreed to come," Charlie said, quietly. She focused on the dust bunnies in the corners of the room and said, "If we're going to live here for the next two weeks, we need to clean this house. We also need food, besides coffee."

"I should have known you would be Ms. Rules," Kendra said in a tone that told Charlie she was not complimenting her.

"Stop being a baby, Kendra," Quinn finally chimed in. "Charlie's right. We agreed to do this Grandpa's way. And that means no cleaning ladies, no Internet and no contact with our real lives. No one in our lives or in this town is supposed to know the reason we're here. And, considering the fact that this town benefits if we fail, we should definitely stick to the strict-confidence policy."

Charlie stared at Quinn surprised. She had never heard Quinn sound so forceful or serious. Then Quinn added, with a giggle, "Besides, how will I be able to ask the cowboy to show me his barn if I'm stuck out here?"

Charlie choked on her coffee, but neither woman noticed as they squared off like two old-time cowboys.

"He's mine, Quinn. I saw him first," Kendra retorted angrily.

"Whoever saw him first won't matter once I work the Quinn Sibley magic on him," Quinn challenged.

Kendra laughed, while Charlie finally was able to swallow unimpeded. Kendra crossed the kitchen to stand in front of Quinn.

"Are you actually considering going head-to-head with me on the cowboy?" Kendra asked Quinn, one finely arched eyebrow raised in disbelief.

"If you're not too scared to go head-to-head with me," Quinn responded, mirroring Kendra's expression.

Kendra shook her head, obviously amused. "Well, this should add some excitement to our time here. You're on, Quinn. We both go for the cowboy and he decides."

"He has a name," Charlie blurted out, before she could stop herself. Her sisters turned to her and Charlie averted her gaze when she saw their identical curious expressions. She poured herself another cup of coffee, hoping her sisters didn't notice her trembling hands. "I just…You're both being childish. He's not some toy or a— He's a person."

Kendra tilted her head to one side and studied Charlie. "You can try for *Graham,* too, Charlie," she finally said, placing emphasis on his name.

Charlie felt her face burn in embarrassment, while Quinn grinned and bobbed her head excitedly. Charlie had spent most of the previous sleepless night dreaming about Graham. She still wanted to tie him to a bed and just look at him for an hour, but now it seemed gross that that Kendra and Quinn obviously had the same feelings.

Charlie squared her shoulders and said, "I won't *try* for him, like he's some kind of…of carnival prize."

Kendra shrugged then said, "All right, but I don't want to hear your mouth. There was nothing in Max's will about not trying to make things a little exciting around here. Give me a few minutes and we'll head into town and find something to clean the house with."

Quinn looked down at her spotless white dress then back at Charlie. "I'm going to get really dirty today, aren't I?"

Charlie ignored Quinn and looked down at her nightgown. She needed to shower, brush her teeth and get dressed, but then there was her refusal to share the shower with the fungus growing at the bottom.

"You're right, Quinn. We're going to get really dirty, so there's hardly any use changing clothes," Charlie said, with a relieved sigh.

She had been saved once more.

It was one of those perfect summer days that only exist in Smalltown, U.S.A. Cloudless blue skies, birds chirping in the distance, children running down the sidewalks and young men standing at the town water fountain watching young women walk past. If Graham wasn't dead-set on leaving all of it as soon as possible, he would be appreciating this scene right now.

Instead, Graham ignored the scene around him and steered his truck to a stop in front of the town's all-purpose store. One thing that Graham could admit to feeling grateful about was that there was always convenient parking downtown. He got out of the truck then slapped on a pair of headphones. The soothing sound of a cultured voice speaking Japanese filled his ears.

His Japanese had gotten rusty in the six months he had spent in Sibleyville. He had never been that good to begin with, but if there was one thing Graham could say about Sibleyville, the small-town afforded him plenty of time to practice, when he wasn't working.

"Afternoon, Graham," Velma called out from the entrance of her clothing boutique.

"*Konnichiwa*," Graham greeted in return, with a slight bow.

"*Ogenki-desu-ka?*" Velma returned.

Graham stopped in mid-stride, took off the headphones and gaped at the older woman. Velma speaking Japanese was about as likely as…as Graham speaking Japanese.

Velma winked at him then turned back into her boutique. Graham laughed to himself and shook his head.

"Don't you have anything better to do, besides stand in the middle of the street, grinning like a fool?"

Graham grinned at the sound of Wyatt Granger's voice. Graham had known Wyatt almost as long as he had known himself. Their families had been the only black people in Sibleyville, when the two had been growing up. And it had remained that way until the arrival of the Sibley sisters, who had increased the African-American population in town by a full thirty percent.

"What are you doing out and about? Business slow as usual at the funeral home?" Graham asked then winced when he noticed Wyatt's honey-brown skin turn a light shade of gray at the mention of anything related to his family's funeral parlor.

The Grangers had been Sibleyville's only morticians for the last three generations, and Graham had a feeling that Wyatt would have put an end to the family business if he could have. But Wyatt's father had died five years ago, and his mother had never recovered from her husband's death, which had left Wyatt to continue the family business.

"No one has died in Sibleyville since Ted Gravis. Business is slow," Wyatt replied.

"I hear Ron Walker had a severe case of heartburn last night," Charlie said then winced again when Wyatt narrowed his eyes at him. "I'm just trying to help you out."

"That's real funny, Graham," Wyatt responded dryly.

"I just don't want you to pass out again when someone asks you about the embalming process."

Wyatt's jaw twitched before he protested through clenched teeth, "I did not pass out. I told you, I just hadn't had a lot to eat that night and my blood sugar was low and then the heat—"

Graham patted Wyatt on the shoulder and said, somberly, "Your secret is safe with me, Wyatt."

"What secret?"

Graham hid his smile and changed the subject, "Do you want to grab some lunch? I'm supposed to be getting wood to fix a fence on the east end, but a man has to eat, right?"

Wyatt smiled instantly and said, "It's Thursday, and you know what that means, right?"

"No."

"Pot roast at Annie's." Wyatt's wide grin made Graham shake his head with regret.

He didn't know which was more pathetic: the fact that he was probably just as excited as Wyatt was at the idea of forking down some of the delicious pot roast at the diner in town, or that this time last year, he had been eating in some of the best restaurants in Tokyo, ordering caviar, champagne and other delicacies.

"Pot roast, it is," Graham said, with a resigned sigh.

The two men started the short walk towards the diner on the other end of Main Street.

Graham nodded in greeting at other residents they passed on the sidewalk, while Wyatt was glad to shake everyone's hand and have boring conversations about the weather and the predictions for the fall harvest. A few minutes later, the two men settled in their regular corner booth at Annie's, where the eponymous Annie was taking orders from another table. Annie's husband stood over the grill visible through the open window behind the counter.

"I heard you met the Sibley sisters," Wyatt said, while passing Graham one of the plastic menus on the table. "What are they like? No one around here has seen them yet."

"I just met them. Did a carrier pigeon spread the word?"

Wyatt shrugged, noncommitally. "Hey, what do you expect? This is Sibleyville. So, tell me about them. Please let one—at least one—be somewhat decent-looking. The pickings around here have gotten pretty slim since the Hodgkin girls moved back to Oregon."

"The Hodgkin girls are forty-three and forty-four years old, respectively," Graham deadpanned.

Wyatt shrugged again. "I take what I can get."

Graham rolled his eyes in exasperation. "Why do you stay, Wyatt?"

"It's my home." Graham stared speechlessly at Wyatt: to him it was really that simple. To Graham, *nothing* was that simple. "So, you haven't told me about the Sibley sisters, which must mean they're as ugly as a pimple on a horse's butt."

"Not quite," Graham said, smiling.

In fact, there was nothing remotely ugly about any of the sisters. Quinn had marvelous breasts that would make a grown man weep, Kendra had a body that could make a grown man beg and then…Well, and then there was the third sister. Whatever her name was—he couldn't even remember now. She had…Graham couldn't really remember what she had because he had been so transfixed by Quinn's breasts and Kendra's rock-hard body.

"You're smiling," Wyatt noted. "That's a good thing. Please tell me that's a good thing."

"Let's just say you won't be disappointed."

Wyatt grinned then prodded, "Tell me more. Details. Stats."

"Words don't do them justice. Two of them, at least. Probably about thirty years old and twenty-six years old. Then there's the third sister. She's the middle one. She's different, I think—"

"Different how?" Wyatt demanded, sounding worried again.

"She's not like her sisters. She's…different." The look of distaste that had crossed her expression as she had glared at him floated through his mind again. He abruptly smiled and said, "She kind of reminds me of Mrs. Smythe."

"Our fourth-grade teacher you had a crush on?"

Graham frowned at his friend. "I did not have a crush on Mrs. Smythe."

"Do not try to stick me with that one," Wyatt said, cringing in distaste, ignoring Graham's annoyance. "I always get stuck with the plain ones."

"I did not have a crush on Mrs. Smythe," Graham repeated to make certain Wyatt heard him. When Wyatt only shrugged in response, Graham muttered, "Don't worry. Her sisters more than make up for her."

"Did you get anything out of them about why they're here?"

"I didn't ask. As the saying goes, don't look a gift horse in the mouth."

Wyatt's grin nearly spilt his face. "That good, huh?"

Graham remembered the come-hither look in Kendra's eyes as she had grinned at him. "Better."

Wyatt whooped like the cowboy he sort of was, then laughed as the other diners glanced curiously at them. Wyatt waved at them then turned back to Graham.

Graham laughed then added, "Besides, Boyd thinks they're here to settle their grandfather's business with the town. He has ordered each of us on the city council to roll out the red carpet. Butter them up. I initially thought this whole thing would be another one of Boyd's idiotic ideas, but the more I think about it…and them…the more I think he might not be so dumb."

"About rolling out the red carpet, or about their reason for being in town?"

"The red carpet, Wyatt," Graham said, impatiently. "I don't care about their plans for this town."

"So, when are we going out with them?" Wyatt asked, eagerly.

"Out? Out where?" Graham asked, frustrated. "Maybe the hoedown next week or the next four-wheel-drive tailgate at the lake?"

"Yeah," Wyatt said excitedly, obviously missing Graham's sarcasm.

Graham rolled his eyes, annoyed. "Wyatt, these women… These women are not like the women around here. We can't take them to a hoedown. They're used to lobster and champagne, not hot dogs and beer."

Wyatt's grin disappeared before he said, matter-of-factly, "Well, while you're trying to find five-star restaurants and champagne, someone else in this town is going to invite them to that hoedown or a tailgate, because what you seem to be forgetting, my friend, is that regardless of what these women are used to, they're in Sibleyville now."

Graham mulled over his friend's words then

muttered, reluctantly, "I guess I'll be stopping by their house to invite them for a night of Sibleyville revelry."

Wyatt smiled, satisfied, then signaled to Annie that they were ready to order.

Chapter 5

"Graham, is that you? Did you get the wood for the fence?"

Graham inwardly cringed as his father's booming voice echoed through the house the moment Graham stepped inside. He closed the front door and glanced around the familiar foyer of the house. Nothing ever changed in his parents' house. It was all wood and comfortable furniture, and it always smelled like lemons.

His father's charcoal drawing of the view behind their house still hung framed in the hallway leading to the living room on the right and the kitchen on the left, even though Lance had done many sketches and paintings since then. The charcoal drawing had apparently been the first gift Lance Forbes had given his young bride.

The same Navajo rug that had lain on the entry floor

when Graham had been in junior high school still remained on the floor—faded and almost threadbare from many washings. His parents did not like change. The perfect day for his parents was to do the exact same thing that they had done the day before. Graham didn't know how in the world he came to be so different from his parents, because he longed for change. He didn't just want to read about South Africa, he wanted to go there. And he had. He had been everywhere else on his wish list, and now… Well, now, Graham's goal was to become a vice president in Shoeford Industries—if he could ever get back to his job. Then he'd think of something else to do.

"Yes, Dad," Graham called back to his father, who was no doubt upstairs in the study that overlooked their lands with his binoculars watching the farmhands. Lance would stay in the study, alternating between working on the computer and using his binoculars to spy on the work in the field until Graham and the farmhands quit for the day. Then, during dinner, Graham would be treated to a fifteen-minute evaluation of every move he had made.

"Did you check the corn?" Lance called back.

Graham struggled for patience. He loved his father, but the man did not know how to be an invalid.

"Yes, Dad, I checked the corn," he called back through clenched teeth.

He heard his mother's soft laughter behind him. Graham turned to her, taking in her amused expression and glowing brown skin. Her short black hair was liberally sprinkled with gray, but she still had a smile that could light a room. No matter how much Graham wished and hoped and dreamed to get the hell out of Sibleyville and return to his life, he also could admit that he would miss his parents. Especially his mother.

Eliza Forbes was not a Sibleyville native. She had met Graham's father in New York thirty-five years ago, and after dating long-distance for three months, she had married him and moved to California. And, as far as Graham knew, she had never looked back, despite the disdain and shock of her decidedly east-coast family. But Eliza might as well have been a Sibleyville native. She could out-ride and out-shoot most men, and seemed to thrive on the sometimes extreme weather and rigorous farm life.

"He's driving me crazy," Graham muttered, motioning up the stairs, where Lance no doubt sat with his binoculars.

Eliza smiled in understanding, but said, "You know he loves having you around."

Graham felt that flash of guilt he always felt whenever his parents expressed their joy at having him near after years of his living overseas and only visiting during the holidays.

"And I like being here," he murmured, then added, "But, Dad is driving me crazy. Either he has to let me do the planting my way, or he can limp out to the fields and do it himself."

"I heard that," came Lance's voice as he teetered down the stairs with the aid of a cane.

Graham rolled his eyes, but couldn't restrain his grin. His heart had momentarily stopped when his mother had called him with the news of his father's heart attack. After rushing home and standing over his father's hospital bed, Graham had finally realized that his father was only human. Graham had never fully recovered from the idea of losing his father. That fear—along with a fair amount of guilt—had kept him in Sibleyville for six months. And his father knew it. The old man was as healthy as a horse now, and Graham swore Lance needed his omnipresent cane as much as Graham did. But he just wouldn't own up to it.

"I also checked the soy beans, the animals and I lassoed the moon, so it would shine specifically on our house," Graham added.

His mother smothered a giggle while Lance's eyes narrowed.

"You're a real smartass, y'know that?" Lance muttered, as amusement twinkled in his eyes.

"I wonder where he got it from," Eliza teased Lance, caressing one of his stubble-covered cheeks. Lance smiled down at his wife and for a moment Graham knew that neither of his parents remembered that he was in the room.

Graham was used to their moments of total immersion in each other. A small part of him wanted to ask his parents how they did it, but that would have led to too many hopeful questions on their part. Graham was thirty-two years old and their only child. He knew their grandparenting biological clock was clicking.

Eliza turned back to her son and said, "Someone called for you earlier. I took down the message in the kitchen."

Graham left his parents to their secret caresses and walked into the kitchen. His mother's kitchen looked like every television or movie kitchen set in the country. Warm, shades of yellow, sturdy wood furniture and even a cookie jar shaped like a cow on the counter. He took a still-warm chocolate chip cookie from the jar then grabbed the telephone mounted on the wall. He read his mother's elegant handwriting on the notepad next to the phone and smiled to himself. He should have known. He quickly dialed the international number.

"Speak," greeted the male voice on the other end of the telephone.

"Do you answer all your calls that way?" Graham demanded of his best friend and financial day trader, Theo Morgan.

"Only when they come from area codes belonging to some godforsaken small town in the middle of nowhere," came the prompt reply.

"Glad to know you haven't become all warm and cuddly in the six months I've been gone."

"Warm and cuddly? Not in this life," Theo grumbled. "Hold the phone a second, Forbes."

Graham heard the muffled sound of Theo ordering people around and then the rapid-fire sound of computer keys being struck. Graham felt a brief pang of jealousy. While Graham was rotting away in Sibleyville, Theo was in Tokyo. Living. Graham and Theo were the same age, but Graham had several more years of experience at Shoeford than Theo and was eligible for the next promotion while Theo was not. That, Graham suspected privately, drove the competitive Theo insane. However, the two men had become friends, or as close to friends as one could be with Theo.

"Forbes, I will deny it to my dying day, but things just aren't the same without you here," Theo said, coming back on the line, without preamble. "I feel like the lone Black man on the planet. When are you going to stop playing John Wayne and get back to work?"

Graham leaned against the wall and stared out the window over the sink at the pasture and trees growing unimpeded in the distance. There weren't views like that in Tokyo. Whether that was a good or bad thing, Graham still hadn't decided.

"I'm in farm country, Theo. *I* am the lone Black man on the planet," Graham retorted.

"You have a point," Theo responded. His voice lowered to a whisper as he said, almost desperately, "Seriously, man, when are you getting back here? How long does it take to find a private nurse for your father and a guy to temporarily run the ranch? I mean, it's one ranch, Graham. We make in ten minutes what that ranch probably puts out in a year."

"Breathe in deep, Theo, because I'm about to tell you something that may rock the foundation of your world," Graham said, then waited a beat, before whispering dramatically, "Sometimes it's not about money."

"Now, you're truly talking crazy."

"This ranch has been in my family for five generations. We don't turn it over to strangers."

"Depp is retiring," Theo said flatly.

Graham widened his eyes and tried to speak, but no sound came out. Depp Shoeford was the brother of the CEO and owner of Shoeford Industries. He also happened to be two hundred pounds of dead weight, whose only contribution to the company was to help usher in Casual Friday. But, his brother loved him—or, at least, pretended to in public—and Depp had been one of four vice-presidents approved by the Board of Directors.

"I'm sure you know exactly what this means," Theo said. "The Board is voting on the new VP in two weeks. You have to get back here for the vote…like yesterday."

"Jude wouldn't dare appoint anyone else. It's mine. He knows it. The Board knows it. Everyone knows it," Graham said, but even he heard the doubt in his words.

"Big words coming from a man in a small town," Theo shot back. "While the secretaries may swoon over your dedication to hearth and home, it hasn't won you any fans in corporate."

"I'm trying," Graham muttered, frustrated, while running a hand down his face.

"Try harder," Theo snapped. "Kent is trying to snatch this thing from under your feet. And you know what they say—out of sight, out of mind."

Graham cursed and tried not to strangle the phone. He should have known. He and Dennis Kent had been competing for the same raises and promotions since they had started at the company ten years ago. Fortunately for Graham, Kent had the personality of a wet rag. Unfortunately for Graham, Kent had the work ethic of an indentured servant. He took the assignments no one wanted, he worked weekends and holidays and made certain the right people knew it and he puckered up whenever the powers-that-be were around.

"Kent would never get it. He's a yes-man, not a VP."

"You know that. I know that. But, I'm not sure if the people who make the decisions know that."

Graham itched to slam down the phone, rent a charter plane to Los Angeles and catch the first thing smoking to Tokyo.

Instead, he took a deep breath and murmured, "I'll talk to my folks."

"That's not good enough, Forbes."

"It's the best I can do."

"The best you can do?" Theo sputtered in disbelief. "Do you want this thing or not?"

"Of course, I do… Wait. Why do you care?"

"I am hurt by your implication," Theo said, and actually made a good attempt at sounding wounded. "Aren't we brothers, man? Compadres? Friends—"

"Ahh, I get it. You think if I make VP, I can promote my brother, compadre and friend, right?" Graham said, more amused than offended that Theo had an ulterior motive. He should have guessed immediately. With Theo, there was always an ulterior motive. Plus, Graham would have been thinking the same thing if he had been in Theo's position.

"Hey, each one teach one, isn't that another thing they say?" Theo said, the self-satisfied grin obvious in his voice.

Graham rolled his eyes in disbelief. "Suddenly, you're Black Power?"

"We brothers have to stick together."

Graham shook his head in amusement, despite his sick feeling about the impending destruction of his career.

Theo continued in an urgent tone, "And because, my brother, I cannot afford to let you pass up the opportunity that will eventually mean opportunities for me, I'm coming to that flea-bag town tomorrow and I'm dragging you back to Tokyo whether you like it or not."

Graham felt a surge of panic at the idea of Theo Morgan in Sibleyville.

"Theo, I don't need you to come here—"

"Too late. A car is waiting downstairs to take me to the airport. I should be in Nowheresville by tomorrow at eleven o'clock. I was told that there is no airport in Sibleyville, so that I have to fly into a town called Bentonville. Trying to get to your town was more difficult than getting to Sri Lanka last year. I have three connections... Anyway, be on time, Graham. I'd hate to imagine what would happen to a Black sitting alone in the middle of the country for too long."

Without another word, Theo hung up. Graham inwardly groaned, then hung up the receiver. He leaned his forehead on the kitchen wall. Theo Morgan in Sibleyville was not a good idea.

Chapter 6

Whenever Graham and Wyatt wound up at The Bar—capital *T* and capital *B*, thank you very much—the only place that could remotely meet the definition of a club in Sibleyville, they usually sat at the bar, joked around with people they had joked around with since childhood, and flirted with the same women they had flirted with since childhood. There was a certain charm to The Bar that even Graham couldn't deny. It sat just outside the border of Sibleyville on a remote stretch of Highway 2 and attracted farmers and ranchers from over one hundred miles since it had the only live entertainment in the area and the cheapest beers.

Usually, there was a band on stage, with a male singer groaning about heartache and being in love, the place would be packed and the cement floor would be sticky with spilled beer and peanut shells. The Bar's charm was not necessarily its cleanliness.

The only difference between this night when Graham and Wyatt walked into The Bar versus any other night was that every man in the bar was on one side of the room, every woman in the bar was on the other side of the room and Kendra and Quinn were dancing in the middle. Not just dancing, but… Was striptease too harsh? Both women wore short tight clothes and underneath the bar lights they looked like two goddesses, granting the men of The Bar a special performance.

Wyatt grinned like a man who had found heaven, and stared transfixed at the Sibley sisters. Graham scanned the crowd in search of the other sister. He didn't see her, not that he would have expected her to be wearing a short skirt in a bar and gyrating next to her sisters, but still… Graham laughed at the roar of male approval as Kendra took her moves to the floor, until she was practically sitting. The singer onstage actually stopped singing to stare transfixed at her.

Meanwhile, Quinn, not to be outdone, was moving her hips in some semblance of an X-rated belly dance while she waved her hands over her head. The only problem—or not problem—was that her already short skirt kept creeping farther and farther up her thighs until… Graham's eyes widened. A black G-string. The men in the building roared again, while several women stalked out the bar.

Wyatt clamped Graham's shoulder and his voice was unsteady as he said, "Graham, please, please, please tell me that those are the Sibley sisters."

Graham grinned, just as the two women turned and spotted him. Both waved energetically, motioning for him to join them. Quinn's gaze remained on him as she licked her lips and ran her hands over her breasts then down to her slim hips, making no secret of the fact that she wanted his hands to follow the same route. Kendra stepped in front of Quinn, drawing Graham's attention, and went low to the floor again while gyrating her hips.

Pretending not to notice the looks of pure hatred and envy from the other men in the room, Graham casually waved to the women.

He yelled to Wyatt over the loud music, "Those are the two Sibley sisters I was telling you about. Kendra and Quinn."

Wyatt cursed softly in appreciation. "Which is which?"

"Kendra is the one who just did the splits. Quinn is the one shaking her behind. Apparently, Quinn is on television."

"Diamond Valley," Wyatt said automatically, his gaze still on the women.

"How do you know that?"

Wyatt shrugged in response and seemed no longer capable of conversation. Graham shook his head, realizing that Wyatt was a lost cause, then glanced around the bar once more. Even though the building was packed and the noise level was near deafening, Graham knew he would have spotted the other sister if she had been there. Maybe she had stayed home. Graham frowned at the idea of her staying alone in that death trap she and her sisters had insisted on living in for their visit.

Graham glanced back at Kendra and Quinn. Both

women were still watching him. He smiled nervously, suddenly understanding how cows must feel when ranchers stared at them before leading them to slaughter. Both women began to motion to him to join them on the dance floor.

Wyatt gripped Graham's shoulder and choked out, "One more question, man. Please tell me that you're taking me out there with you to dance with them."

"Go out there now, and tell the ladies I'll be right there with drinks."

Wyatt actually looked as if he wanted to kiss Graham. Instead, he briefly hugged him then practically ran onto the dance floor. Graham laughed and every other man in the place looked shocked as the women started dancing with Wyatt, whereas before they had turned their backs on all other comers.

Graham walked towards the bar to order a round of drinks and scanned the bar once more. He stopped himself. He had two gorgeous women waiting for him on the dance floor. And, if he played his cards right, he could actually get lucky—something that hadn't happened, God help him, in six months. And, instead of running onto the dance floor, he was searching for a woman who clearly did not like him, if her look of disdain in the driveway had been any indication.

Graham had just signaled the bartender, when out the corner of his eye, he saw a brown-skinned woman walk out of the bar. Since there were only three Black women in Sibleyville who would have been at The Bar, and two were doing a burlesque number on the dance floor, Graham could guess who she was. Before he even made the decision to follow her, he was making his way through the crowd and towards the exit.

Graham pushed open the door and walked into the cool night air. It was too dark to see much, besides the outlines of the trucks and cars in the parking lot. There was one dim light bulb over the door, but that cast barely enough illumination to see fifty feet in front of him.

Graham finally saw a woman standing on the outskirts of the parking lot, next to a large stallion that had been tied to the wooden fence. The huge horse meant only one thing—Earl McPhee was nearby. Except Earl—all six foot five inches and two hundred and sixty pounds of him—wasn't just nearby. He was standing in front of Charlie—that was her name!—who was screaming at him, obviously having no idea that she was facing the meanest, cruelest sonofabitch in town. A man that even Boyd Robbins had the good sense to give a wide berth to whenever Earl made one of his rare appearances in town.

Graham muttered a curse and wished he'd had the good sense to stay inside the bar to watch the Kendra-and-Quinn show. Instead, he was about two seconds away from having his ass handed to him on a platter.

"…you have no right to treat this animal that way!" Charlie was screeching at Earl, as Graham reluctantly walked closer. Her breasts were heaving inside the plain white T-shirt she wore, her caramel face was flushed red and her eyes glinted with fire. It was a very inopportune time to notice, but Graham realized that the third Sibley sister was actually decent-looking.

Earl, on the other hand, was even bigger and more frightening than Graham remembered. His forearms were easily the size of most men's biceps.

"Get out of my way, lady," Earl growled, towering over her more than the horse did. "That is my horse. I'll do with him whatever I want."

"You will not leave this parking lot with this horse," she responded with such deadly calm that Graham believed her.

Earl, on the other hand, laughed. Or, at least, Graham thought it was a laugh. It sounded so evil that the horse even shuffled his feet in an attempt to get away.

Earl leaned down until he was almost nose to nose with Charlie. "And who is going to stop me? You?"

As Charlie's eyes widened with fear, something ugly coiled in Graham's stomach. Graham was not a fighting man. In fact, he couldn't remember the last fight he had been in, but as Earl towered over Charlie, every one of Graham's fighting instincts propelled him across the parking lot.

"Charlie, I see you made a new friend," Graham said, with as much casualness as he could muster, as he inserted himself between Earl and Charlie.

The relieved look she sent in his direction nearly made Graham change his characterization of her from "decent-looking" to "kind of pretty." He forced himself to turn to Earl, who had impossibly bulked up even more since Graham had crossed the parking lot. He gulped as he remembered whispers years ago about Earl having stabbed a man in a bar fight in Boise.

"Good evening, Earl," Graham greeted, keeping his

tone light. "I haven't seen you since I've been back in town. How have you been?"

Earl growled, "Talk to your woman, Graham. I want my horse, and I want him now."

"Never," Charlie retorted, over Graham's shoulder. She turned to Graham, grabbing his arm. Her grip was a little too tight, but for some reason, Graham didn't mind. Her eyes were huge and shining in the moonlight as she said, "I saw him…abusing this horse, Graham. He kicked him in the side and then punched him in the face. I will not allow any creature—man or horse—to be abused in my presence. We cannot send this horse home with this monster."

Graham barely restrained himself from raising his eyebrow at her use of the word *we*. He also wondered if Charlie should have been the actress, instead of Quinn. She certainly was dramatic enough. Sure, everyone knew that Earl was not the nicest guy around, but even Earl wouldn't be stupid enough to abuse an animal that he had to rely on for his livelihood.

"Now, Charlie, I'm sure you didn't see what you thought you saw," he said, in what he hoped was a soothing voice. "Just give the man back his horse, and we can straighten this all out in the morning. I'm sure Earl would let us come to his ranch and see in the sunlight that this horse has suffered no abuse—"

"Like hell," Earl spat out, directing his rage at Graham.

Graham was glad that at least Earl was no longer looking like he wanted to throw Charlie across the parking lot. Instead, he looked like he wanted to throw Graham across the parking lot.

Graham focused on Charlie again and fought hard not to be affected by the silent pleading in her eyes. Had any woman ever looked at him like that? Obviously trusting him to do the right thing, to support her?

His hand caressed her cheek before he even realized that he had moved. Her skin was soft. Like a rose petal or something…something really soft. He lowered his voice to a whisper, "It's his horse, Charlie. We have to give him back."

Disappointment swam in the depths of her eyes. Graham hesitated. Her disappointment made him hesitate.

"I don't have time for this," Earl snarled. "You have five seconds to give me my horse."

Charlie continued to stare at Graham. Then she bit her bottom lip, chewed on it actually, drawing his attention to how plump and sweet it looked. *She* looked. That was it. Graham silently cursed again then turned back to Earl.

"Look, Earl, Charlie's upset and you're upset. Why don't we let her take the horse home tonight and, in the morning, I'll personally deliver him to you. And I'll throw in a case of beer. Deal?"

Earl's eyes narrowed with rage. "You've spent your whole life trying to talk this town into doing one thing or another, but I'm not falling for it. You don't control nothing out here, Graham Forbes. I don't care if you're on the city council, or if you're the mayor himself, but I will clean this parking lot with your ass if you don't get out the way.

"And then after I've beaten you into a bloody pulp, I'm going to teach your girlfriend here some manners.

I don't know where you found this one, but you should have taught her that we do things different here in Sibleyville. And little girls do not become involved in grown men's business."

Graham stared at Earl for a moment, as anger warred with rage, making him incapable of speech at that moment. He didn't care that Earl had insulted him. Graham had heard better insults in three different languages. The rage came from the lascivious glare he had sent Charlie when he had talked about teaching her "manners." If anyone was going to teach Charlie Sibley manners, it was going to be Graham, and he hoped she would love every minute of it.

"You've terrorized people in this town long enough." Graham said, then tried not to laugh at his own canned speech. He had watched one too many Jet Li movies. He could have come up with something a little more clever, or, at least, funny. He didn't want to get into the first fistfight of his adult life with that corny line hanging in the air.

Charlie's grip on his arm tightened even more as she rose on her toes to whisper in his ear, "What are you doing? He'll kill you."

Graham stopped his glaring contest with Earl and glanced down at her. "Thanks for the vote of confidence."

"I'll give him the horse, Graham. I don't want—"

"You said you would never give him the horse."

"I know, but I can call the animal cruelty society tomorrow—"

"There is no animal cruelty society out here."

"Have you conferred with your girlfriend long enough?" Earl demanded, rolling up his shirtsleeves.

Graham turned to Earl and silently cursed again. It was obvious that Earl knew exactly what to do in a fight in a dark parking lot. Graham felt a brief flash of nerves. He had been taking boxing lessons in Tokyo before he had to come to Sibleyville, but he had a feeling that Earl would not pull punches the way the trainer at the exclusive health club had.

In fact, as Earl's fist slammed into Graham's jaw, Graham realized that his trainer had been treating Graham like a two-year-old. Graham barely managed to stay on his feet as white-hot pain flashed in his jaw.

Charlie screamed then dropped the reins and ran towards the bar. Graham mentally thanked her for leaving him to this humiliation in private. He spat out a bit of blood swimming in his mouth and briefly wondered if his jaw was broken. That pain hadn't felt natural. He managed to duck Earl's next compact swing at his face and then get off a swing of his own.

There was a satisfying crunch as Graham's fist connected with Earl's chin. Earl mildly shook his head, but to Graham's utter disbelief and horror, seemed relatively unfazed. And then Graham felt the pain in his own hand from the punch. He barely managed to hold back his own scream. That didn't happen on television when the good guy hit the bad guy.

Graham heard several female screams. Charlie was running out of the bar followed by her two sisters and every other patron. Graham's distraction ended as Earl plowed a fist into his stomach followed by another one. Charlie screamed his name and Graham felt a burst of energy as he gave up trading punches and talked Earl to the ground.

Earl and Graham rolled around as the men from The Bar began hollering and whistling, forming a circle around them, just like kids in an elementary schoolyard. Graham deflected Earl's powerful blows and landed a few of his own that at least slowed Earl down a little bit. The two men scrambled to their feet and Earl managed to land a few more punches. The crowd cheered in approval as one of Graham's fists plowed into Earl's nose and blood spewed in one direction. Earl stumbled several steps backwards, prompting a round of applause. For the first time since the fight began, Earl hesitated.

The sound of sirens suddenly rang in the air, and Graham caught a glimpse of the town's two police cars speeding towards The Bar. Like cockroaches, people began to scatter. Graham held up his fists, prepared to continue, as Earl looked from the approaching police to Graham. Wyatt suddenly ran to Graham's side, and Graham refused to acknowledge the relief he felt that he wouldn't have to face the giant by himself again.

"Graham, what the hell is going on? I go to the bathroom and come out to find the bar empty…" Wyatt's voice trailed off, as he followed Graham's glare in the direction of Earl and cursed. "Your first fight in twenty years and you pick Earl McPhee?"

Earl abruptly ran towards a parked truck filled with a group of men who looked at each other with horror at the thought of giving Earl a ride. Graham didn't lower his fists until Earl ordered the driver to drive and the truck sped down the road, away from the police cars. Graham released the breath he hadn't known he was holding, then collapsed to his knees, drawing in the air that he had been deprived of during the last several seconds.

"Graham, my God, are you all right?" Quinn screeched, running to his side.

"He'll live. It's just a few scrapes," Wyatt muttered, sounding suspiciously annoyed as he watched Quinn check Graham's injuries.

"Scrapes, my ass. That man could have killed him," Kendra chimed in, running to his other side.

Graham never thought it would have been possible, but he barely noticed the two women as he stared up at Charlie, who stood next to Wyatt. She sent him a small smile then walked towards the horse. And dammit if that wasn't all Graham needed to see to make the whole thing worth it.

Chapter 7

"I don't know about you all, but last night at The Bar confirmed two things for me," Quinn announced the next morning, as she massaged sun block onto her shoulders then settled onto the lawn chair for optimal sun coverage of her bikini-clad body.

Charlie looked down from her perch on the ladder where she was attempting to repair the roof trim that had come loose. Charlie had become handy with a hammer from the constant small repairs that needed to be done around the African-American Art Center, despite the fact that the budget didn't allow constant small repairs. But even Charlie had to admit that the repairs needed on this house went beyond her mediocre skills.

She had spent most of the morning scrubbing and disinfecting every inch of the house. She had gone through one whole bottle of disinfectant on her bathroom alone, but at least now she didn't feel as though she had to put a toilet liner on the seat before sitting down or needed to take a shower with her bathing suit and flipflops on.

She grimaced as she almost hammered her thumb instead of the nailhead. After she dealt with the hammer, she still had ten cans of paint waiting on the porch for her. She was going to kill herself before this was all over.

"What was confirmed for you last night, Quinn? That you're a bad dancer and that I'm a better dancer?" Kendra grunted from the front porch in midpush-up. Sweat gleamed off every taut and toned inch of her dark skin.

While Charlie had been cleaning, Kendra had been stretching, pulling, exercising and generally driving both Charlie and Quinn insane.

"You are not a better dancer than me, Kendra," Quinn said, obviously insulted.

"If we're having a contest over who can dance like a stripper, then you're right, Quinn, you'd win hands-down. But, if we're talking about real dancing, then you know *I'd* win hands-down," Kendra shot back as she flipped onto her back to begin a dizzying assortment of sit-ups.

"What did you learn last night?" Charlie asked, interrupting Quinn's retort to keep the fragile peace.

Quinn glared at Kendra one moment longer then looked at Charlie and said excitedly, "Graham Forbes is the most gorgeous man in this town, and I think we've seen them all, between the group that followed us when we went into town yesterday and the group at The Bar. I chose well, and I'm going to be very, very happy when

I win our little contest. Did you see those muscles? There's nothing like a man after a fight. All that testosterone and wounded male ego. Sephora and Niles, her third husband, had one of their best love scenes after his fight with his bitter rival, Milan."

Charlie steadied herself on the ladder as her mouth became dry and her heart began to pound at the mention of Graham's name. She had noticed Graham's muscles. She had noticed everything about him. Just when she had written him off as another pretty face, as someone she would never deign to talk to even if he actually paid attention to her, he had stood up for her. No man, besides her grandfather, had ever defended her, and even then Grandpa Max had done it reluctantly.

Of course, afterwards, Graham had eagerly turned to Quinn's and Kendra's arms for their ministrations after the fight. Maybe Graham wasn't the jerk she had thought he was, but he was still a normal red-blooded man. Unfortunately, that knowledge hadn't stopped Charlie from dreaming about Graham for another night in a row. Vivid, erotic dreams that she usually only had after watching a Henry Simmons *NYPD Blue* episode.

Kendra paused mid sit-up to mutter, "I have to agree with you, Quinn."

"That she's going to win the bet?" Charlie asked, surprised, snapping from her daydreams.

"Of course not," Kendra said, with a snort of disbelief. "I agree with her that Graham is the best product this town has. I'm going to have so much fun with him. All of that cowboy manliness and aggression…" Kendra visibly shivered in delight, then murmured with a grin, "I may even have to take him with me back to New York."

Charlie pounded the next nail a little too hard and the sound echoed through the yard. Both of her sisters glanced at her.

"Are you all right, Charlie?" Quinn asked, concerned. "That ladder looks a little unsteady."

"I'm fine," she muttered.

"Charlie, you were outside when the fight between Graham and Andre the Giant started. What caused it?" Kendra asked curiously.

Charlie pretended to focus on the trim as she murmured, "I don't know."

"You don't know—" Kendra's question was cut off by the sound of a truck roaring down the driveway towards their house.

Charlie twisted on the ladder to see who the unexpected visitor was. Her palms became damp with sweat and her chest felt tight as she recognized Graham's profile behind the steering wheel of the truck.

Quinn immediately positioned her body to the best advantage, while Kendra quickly dotted the sweat off her face with a towel. Even Charlie tried to smooth sweat-dampened clumps of hair back towards her ponytail. But, considering she had been working and sweating all day, there wasn't much she could do in five seconds to make herself look presentable.

Graham parked the truck and stepped out. Charlie couldn't help the sigh that escaped her lips. He wore his ubiquitous cowboy hat, jeans and another T-shirt. And his sexy smile. He was dangerous.

Quinn jumped to her feet as Kendra walked down the stairs. They reached him at the same time.

"Graham, your face," Quinn gasped, as Kendra asked, "Does it hurt?"

Charlie swallowed the lump in her throat. He had a reddish-purple bruise on his right cheekbone and along his jaw, but otherwise he was no worse for the wear. In fact, his bruises hardened his almost too-perfect features, coincidentally enough, making him look more perfect. More manly.

"It only hurts when I breathe," he replied, grinning at Kendra and Quinn. Or, more appropriately, grinning at their breasts, which were pushed forward for his display. Charlie narrowed her eyes as each woman pressed a kiss against his cheek and Graham didn't seem to mind.

"You were very brave to take on that awful man," Quinn cooed. "He could have killed you."

Before Graham could respond, Kendra asked, "What in the world possessed you to take on that freak of nature? If you want to wrestle with someone, all you have to do is say the word. I'll even let you win."

Graham laughed, while Quinn glowered and Charlie gripped the hammer a little tighter. Graham stared across the yard at Charlie for the first time. His smile instantly disappeared.

"Charlie, that ladder doesn't look steady," he said, gruffly. "Get down from there before you break your neck."

Charlie gritted her teeth at the flash of anger. Kendra and Quinn got grins and kisses, while she got a dismissive order. She had been killing herself all morning, trying to make the house remotely habitable while her sisters had sat on their butts, and they got Graham's smiles and she got an order? She suddenly wanted to slap his too-perfect face.

"I've been on this ladder all afternoon. It's fine," she responded stiffly then turned back to the house.

Except she turned too fast. Suddenly, the ladder was wobbling and Charlie was wobbling. Her stomach sank as she realized that she was about to fall and break something. She dropped the hammer to hang onto the ladder with both hands, but instead her shifting weight caused the ladder to tilt farther to one side. She screamed as the ladder balanced on one stem for a moment then began to fall. She was propelled into the air.

But instead of hitting the porch, Charlie slammed into a just-as-hard but distinctly fleshy surface. Graham. Before they hit the ground, Graham's strong arms wrapped around her and he twisted so that he hit the porch first, taking the brunt of the fall. She slammed onto his body, as the ladder fell harmlessly to one side. Just when she thought the worst had passed, she felt the spread of thick, warm paint spreading across her back and neck and, unfortunately, onto Graham, who was beneath her.

Silence covered the porch after the screams and collapse. Charlie did not want to open her eyes, but she did and stared straight into Graham's enraged expression. His face, neck and shirt were covered with white paint, which looked ridiculously funny.

Charlie knew it would only make matters worse, but a giggle slipped past her lips. Graham's eyes narrowed at her bubbling laughter and that instantly terminated all of her amusement.

She tried to scramble off him, and, instead, accidentally dug her elbow into his stomach. He winced in pain.

"Charlie, you're killing him," Quinn cried, running up onto the porch.

"Sorry," she said, frantically, as Quinn and Kendra practically pulled her away to get to Graham. Charlie felt a sinking sensation in the pit of her stomach as Graham, with paint dripping off him, limped to the railing of the porch.

"Do you need water or something?" Kendra asked, wiping paint off his face, which only worked to smear it into a war-paint decoration á la *Braveheart* cowboy.

"I think she knocked the breath out of you when you two went down," Quinn said, worriedly, then asked Kendra, "Should we call an ambulance?"

Graham ignored her sisters and kept his laser gaze on Charlie. She picked up one of her discarded rags on the porch and hesitantly approached him. She moved to wipe paint off his arm, but he abruptly snatched the rag from her hand. He was more angry than she had thought, and that made her angry. Accidents happened. They seemed to happen more often when he was around, but it was just an accident.

"You're a menace, lady," he abruptly declared. "An honest-to-God menace. You could have killed yourself."

"It was an accident," she shot back through clenched teeth. After all, she was covered in paint, too. It would take her an hour to wash the paint out of her hair.

"Was last night an accident?" he shot back. "At the rate you're going, I'll be dead in another week."

"What happened last night?" Kendra asked, surprised.

Neither Charlie nor Graham spared her a glance. Charlie informed Graham, icily, "I didn't ask for your help last night. And I didn't ask for your help now."

Graham's mouth flapped open in disbelief and outrage, and Charlie inwardly cursed because, even covered in paint and acting like an ogre, the man made her knees weak.

"You were about to run screaming into the night before I showed up," he growled through clenched teeth.

"I don't run from anything, including men like Earl McPhee or men like you. I dealt with Max Sibley for twenty-eight years. Believe that dealing with you two is a piece of cake," she retorted.

His nostrils flared in anger as he said in a low and dangerous tone, "Are you actually comparing me to Earl McPhee?"

"Of course not," she said, annoyed. "But, I didn't ask you to step in last night, and I didn't ask you to step in just now."

Graham snorted in disbelief then threw the rag on the porch. He cast a quick glance at her sisters and said tightly, "Kendra and Quinn, always a pleasure."

He shot Charlie another venom-filled look then stormed off the porch. He climbed into his truck and slammed the door so hard that Charlie briefly wondered if the glass would break. The truck kicked up dirt as it fishtailed then righted before Graham sped from the yard.

Tears coated Charlie's eyes, and she blamed it on her stinging elbow that she had bumped on the ladder on her way down. Graham's obvious dislike for her had absolutely nothing to do with it.

Quinn and Kendra suddenly moved in front of her, with identical expressions of murder on their faces.

"If you've run off Graham, I will never forgive you," Quinn announced, then gingerly stepped over the paint puddles to walk into the house.

"Do you have to do everything in your power to alienate the one decent-looking man in this town?" Kendra asked, angrily. "I'm not even going to ask what happened last night because I don't want to know, but you better make this right, Charlie. If I have to spend the next two weeks with just you two for company, things are going to get real unpleasant around here."

Kendra jogged off the porch and down the road. Charlie sighed then looked at the paint-splattered porch. She should have stayed in L.A. She didn't belong here. That much was clear.

Graham sped down the highway towards Bentonville. After his detour to the Sibley house, and then the return trip to his house to shower and change, he was running an hour late to pick up Theo from the local airport in Bentonville. Graham had turned off his cell phone fifty miles back after Theo's sixth call demanding to know where he was. Theo and his Armani suits would not be able to tolerate the Bentonville airport for long, although *airport* was too nice a term for the one-room building with three chairs and a counter for the guard, Old Man Harris, to sit at and read the paper.

Graham knew exactly who to blame for the complaining he would have to endure from Theo during the one-hour drive back to Sibleyville. Charlie Sibley. He had not been exaggerating. The woman was a menace. Practically every time he was around her, he ended up with a bruise somewhere.

Graham refused to feel the slightest bit of guilt as her hurt expression swam through his mind. Okay, maybe he shouldn't have screamed at her, but his heart had leaped into his throat when he had seen her balancing on a wooden ladder as old as he was. Graham had stopped at their house to ask them to dinner that night, but he had gotten distracted by Charlie. First, he had noticed her very nice-looking legs in a pair of shorts, then he had noticed her obvious plan to break those gorgeous legs. He had envisioned her tumbling from the ladder and breaking her neck, and that thought had shaken him, which had made him more curt than usual. And then the little fool had fallen.

His hands tightened around the steering wheel. He refused to dwell on the sight of her falling off the ladder. It was too disturbing.

Graham cursed again because he remembered the feel of Charlie on top of him. He usually liked his women slim, sophisticated and lethal, like Kendra, but he had momentarily forgotten that when Charlie's softness and curves had been pressed against him. His one thought at that moment had been to hold her as long as he could. And maybe that was why Graham had become so angry at her. Yes, she was a menace and didn't know her right hand from her left, but…there was something there.

Charlie shook his head at his thoughts. He had always been honest with himself and the idea of plunging in between her thighs and getting his hands on those luscious breasts had been his one driving thought since he had dodged Earl's first punch. All of his dreams, or, more appropriately, porn-star fantasies last night had been about her—that is when the aches and pains from the fight weren't enough to keep him awake.

The one-room Bentonville Airport came into view around the next bend. It wasn't really an airport. It was just a building that local pilots used to hang out in while refueling. Graham pulled into the parking lot and bit his bottom lip to keep from laughing.

Theo sat on the sidewalk curb, next to one large designer suitcase. Old Man Harris's beagle sat next to Theo, or actually on top of Theo, his nose close to Theo's crotch. Graham could not picture Theo willingly allowing a dog to come near his designer suit, but then again Graham could not picture Theo anywhere near Sibleyville.

Theo was fastidious about his appearance and his surroundings. Three-piece suits and wingtips were not just part of his professional appearance, but a way of life. Graham would bet that Theo did not own a pair of jeans or tennis shoes. Nike and Adidas did not exist in Theo's world. Theo's ruthlessly short black hair was neat to the point of obsession. His chocolate-brown skin always gleamed, and his teeth were sparkling white and even.

Theo stood when he saw Graham get out of the truck. He whipped off his designer sunglasses and crossed his arms over his chest.

"If you had come five minutes later, I would have had

to ask this dog to marry me," Theo announced, as he carried his suitcase towards the truck. "Where the hell have you been?"

"Don't ask," Graham muttered. Theo lifted the bag into the cramped confines of the truck cab. Because Graham wasn't spending the next hour with Theo's suitcase poking him in the shoulder, he grabbed it and threw it into the truck bed.

"That is Louis Vuitton," Theo protested. He stared into the truck bed and obviously saw dirt, mud and other bits and pieces of the field matted on the bottom. He didn't touch the suitcase, but said, simply, "You owe me one Louis Vuitton suitcase, Forbes."

"Graham," Old Man Harris called, limping towards the entrance of the airport. His dog instantly limped up to the old man and sat at his feet. Graham didn't know who was older—Harris or the dog. "How are your folks?"

"Good, sir," Graham responded. Theo climbed into the truck and slammed the door, shooting Graham impatient glances.

"I thought you'd be long gone by now," Harris said, then spat a wad of tobacco in the exact spot where Theo had been sitting. Graham wondered if Theo had noticed the other dried tobacco stains. He would wager not.

"When you flew in six months ago, you told me that you were only going to be here for a couple of weeks."

"The best-laid plans and all that," Graham muttered in reply then waved. "See ya, Mr. Harris."

He sat in the truck and started the engine. He pulled away from the airport and started down the two-lane highway to Sibleyville.

"Is that country music?" Theo asked in disbelief, looking at the radio as if he had never seen one.

At the unmistakable sound of fiddles and guitars, Graham grinned. "This the only music they play in these parts."

Theo shook his head in disbelief. "How do you stand it?"

"Hello to you, too, Theo. It was no problem leaving in the middle of the day during planting season to drive an hour away to pick you up," Graham said, dryly.

"It took you damn near long enough," Theo muttered, while fiddling with the vents on the truck dashboard. "Can we get some damn air? It must be ninety degrees."

"The air conditioner is broken."

"Why doesn't that surprise me?" Theo muttered, then leaned back in the seat, practically sticking his head out the window to take advantage of the hot air.

Graham glanced at Theo and felt a slight twinge of sympathy. Theo had come from the air-conditioned modern buildings of Tokyo, where his dark suit was the norm, rather than the exception. Graham wasn't certain if Theo even ventured outside in Tokyo.

"I have some water under the seat. You look a little red," Graham said, noting the sweat dripping off Theo's dark skin and soaking the collar of his shirt.

"And you look like someone used your face for a punching bag," Theo snapped, while reaching for a bottle of water. "I hope the bruises will fade before we leave for Tokyo. What the hell happened to you?"

"Bar fight."

Theo looked more worried than angry as he muttered, "Where the hell am I?"

"I didn't tell you to come here, Theo," Graham retorted, annoyed. He could talk about Sibleyville, but he'd be damned before Theo could. "In fact, it would have done us both better for you to stay in Tokyo where you could watch Kent. With you here, I have no way of knowing what he's up to."

"Since you seem to be unable to leave on your own, I had to fly down here to drag you, by force if necessary, back to Tokyo."

Graham rolled his eyes at Theo's dramatics. "I told you that I planned to be back in another two weeks, after planting season.

"And how many times have I heard that?" Theo demanded, sounding surprisingly right.

"Let's talk about this later, Theo," Graham said, annoyance creeping into his voice. "I had a rough morning."

"A rough morning?" Theo barked in disbelief. "I've been on one airplane after the other for the last twenty hours. And I arrive in this town to a fat old man who kept trying to sell me life insurance and his flea-wielding mutt who humped my leg for five minutes. The dog humped my leg, Graham. My Armani-clad leg."

Graham tried hard not to laugh, but he failed. "Mr. Harris is the local insurance agent."

"I figured that much out," Theo muttered dryly then demanded, "You still haven't told me where you were."

"I got tied up."

"Tied up?" Theo murmured then said, flatly, "This must involve a woman."

Graham snorted in disbelief. Yes, Charlie was a woman, but *walking cyclone* was a better description for her. Or a walking red-neon stop sign.

"It involves a woman, but not like you're thinking. Let's just say it began with me telling the harebrained idiot to get off a ladder and it ended with a gallon of paint on my head." Graham was too busy fuming to notice Theo's appraising gaze immediately. When he did, he demanded. "What are you looking at?"

"Nothing," Theo murmured, that same strange look on his face.

"Spit it out," he ordered.

"All right. I just haven't heard you this passionate about anything in a long time. If we can redirect—"

"I'm not passionate about Charlie," Graham said, gritting his teeth. Except his body chose that moment to relive the feel of her in his arms that morning. Her soft flesh, the way her eyes had widened and her lips had slightly parted, as she sprawled on top of him. Graham decided that it was hot in the truck, and he fiddled with the vent then cursed, but of course, it was broken.

"Is that her name?" Theo asked, knowingly.

"You're really starting to piss me off."

"You pissed me off when you left Tokyo to come down here and play cowboy," Theo shot back, all amusement gone. "If I find out that my future as a VP has been destroyed because of some woman—a woman with a man's name, no less—I will not be a happy financial analyst. And an unhappy financial analyst is a poor financial analyst. My financial death will be on your shoulders. Do you want that, Graham?"

"Save me the doomsday scenarios," Graham said, amused despite himself.

"I just hope this woman is worth it," Theo muttered then snorted in disbelief and added, "Although, how a woman from this hellhole can compare to the women we were scoring in Tokyo, I can't imagine."

"She's not from here," Graham replied, automatically. At Theo's knowing look, Graham cleared his throat and said, "I mean…Charlie has nothing to do with anything. She just got into town yesterday. She and her two sisters are the granddaughters of the man the town is named after. Since she's been here—two full days—I have had the crap kicked out of me and paint lodged in every orifice of my body. Trust me. Charlie Sibley is not the reason I'm staying in Sibleyville. In fact, if anything, she's the number-one reason I should get the hell out of here before I wind up in a coma or castrated or something. There's no telling what in the world could happen with her around."

Theo appeared slightly appeased as he pulled his cell phone from the leather briefcase at his feet. He paused while dialing then cursed, staring at the phone in disbelief. He frantically searched in his bag then pulled out his BlackBerry.

"I don't have any reception," he said, awed. He turned to Graham, his eyes wide with alarm, and repeated in a hoarse whisper, "I don't have any reception."

"Welcome to Sibleyville," Graham said with a flourish.

"How am I supposed to survive…? How can I…? You're actually living in a place where there is no cell phone reception or BlackBerry reception? How do you people talk or plan anything or—"

"It's just a cell phone, Theo. The human race survived hundreds of years without them. You'll survive a few days without yours. Besides, not every area has a dead signal. You might get something."

"I have us two tickets first-class back to Tokyo next week. If you want to salvage your career, you better be on that plane with me," Theo warned. He glanced around at the fields of wild grass on either side of the highway. There were no cars behind or in front of them. No houses or buildings were in sight.

Theo slammed on his sunglasses back and slumped against the seat. "Wake me when we get to civilization… Oh, I forgot where I was for a moment. Wake me when we get…somewhere…else."

Graham glared at Theo then focused on the road again.

Chapter 8

Charlie tried to withhold her moan of delight as she bit into the chocolate bar. Then she remembered that she was alone in Kendra's Jaguar. For the first time in forty-eight hours, she was truly alone. She didn't have to hide anything.

She licked the smudge of chocolate off the tip of one finger then forced herself to concentrate on the road. Unable to handle her sisters' disapproving looks, Charlie had volunteered to make the drive to Bentonville, the slightly larger town an hour's drive from Sibleyville, which apparently had a Wal-Mart. Charlie had stocked up on groceries, cleaning supplies, protein shakes for Kendra and coffee for Quinn. And, of course, she had replenished her own supply of chocolate.

Charlie directed the car off the highway and down the

road that led to the Sibley house. She spotted the trucks parked around their house and the beehive of activity from a few miles away. She pressed harder on the gas, wondering what in the world was going on. They had met a few men at The Bar last night, but no one who Charlie expected to visit them. But, then again, there was no denying the attraction of Kendra and Quinn to the opposite sex.

Charlie pulled into the drive and parked, noting the construction paraphernalia arranged around the front yard and the various men walking around, consulting papers and measuring things. One man was on a ladder on the porch, nailing in the trim that she had tried to fix earlier that morning. A few men were on the roof hammering. She even heard men stomping around inside the house.

Charlie stood back from the car and looked around for her sisters, but she only saw men. Men, who thank God, appeared to know how to use a hammer much better than Charlie did.

A tall, handsome man with a dimpled smile and dark curls walked over to Charlie. She recognized him from last night at The Bar. He had been standing with Graham, watching Kendra and Quinn dance, with a dazed expression on his face.

"You must be Charlie," he said, stopping in front of her. His smile was so warm and open that Charlie couldn't help but smile back. "I'm Wyatt Granger, Graham's friend. He told me that you ladies might need some help fixing up this place."

Charlie stared amazed as a short man with a balding

head opened a can of paint and began to paint the porch frame that she had abandoned after the accident.

"Graham…" Charlie's voice trailed off, as her gaze darted from the house to Wyatt. She was trembling, overwhelmed. She managed to ask, "Graham is responsible for all of this?"

Wyatt nodded and turned to the house, proudly. "With all of the guys pitching in, we should have everything at least livable within the next three hours. I thought I was going to have to do the job myself, but as soon as word got out that I was coming here…" Wyatt's voice trailed off then he laughed said, "Let's just say, half of the town would have been here, if I hadn't put a limit on the number of men I would take with me. I didn't want to scare you ladies with a bunch of nosy farmers and ranchers milling around your house. After putting in a long day on their fields, you ladies are some attraction for the men to come out here and work for another few hours."

"Graham is responsible for all of this?" she repeated, since it seemed to be the only question she could ask.

Wyatt studied her for a moment then asked, curiously, "What happened here this morning? Graham didn't exactly ask me to come over, he used everything he's ever done for me as leverage and ordered me to come over today, for fear that 'that damn woman'—and that's an exact quote—was going to break her neck. He wouldn't have been talking about you, would he, Charlie?"

Charlie's mouth flapped open and closed as she looked at the men working in and on top of and around the house. Graham had done all of this for her. It didn't make sense. No, he must have done it for Kendra or Quinn, and the fact that she wouldn't have to climb up on any more faulty ladders was just an added benefit. That made sense.

Wyatt's eyes narrowed before he said, "You were also outside with Earl McPhee and Graham before their fight, right? I've known Graham my entire life. He's like my brother, and I know Graham wouldn't tussle with a lunatic like Earl McPhee just because of a few insults. Something serious happened. Graham still hasn't told me what started the fight. Maybe you can tell me."

Before Charlie could respond, Quinn walked out the house. She had wrapped a colorful sarong around her hips in some nod at modesty, but considering how short and sheer it was, it was a false attempt. She blessed a few of the men with smiles, and they began to work harder and pound faster, then she sashayed across the yard to Charlie and Wyatt.

"Isn't it wonderful, Charlie?" Quinn exclaimed, while sweeping her arms towards the house. "You should see what they're doing inside. New showerheads and faucets. Kitchen cabinets. Even new doorknobs, Charlie. We may actually have some water pressure when this is all said and done."

Charlie noticed that Wyatt's smile had disappeared and he suddenly became interested in poking at a clump of grass with the toe of his boot. It was obvious that he was studiously avoiding looking at Quinn. And it was just as obvious that Quinn was studiously avoiding looking at him.

Quinn's smile disappeared as she abruptly grabbed

Charlie's arms and said, somberly, "You owe Graham an apology. He not only saved your life, but he made all of this happen. We couldn't have done this on our own, not if we had had two years."

"Where did all of this come from?" Charlie whispered, more to herself than to Quinn.

"Graham paid for everything," Quinn said, simply.

"He can't afford this—"

Quinn abruptly grabbed Charlie's arm. "Do not ruin this. We are being treated the way we should have been treated since we first got into this godforsaken town. Just accept it."

"But the will—"

Quinn groaned in exasperation and rolled her eyes. "We didn't ask for this. They came over without our knowledge. Even Grandpa Max's blood-sucking lawyers couldn't fault us for this."

"Why?" Charlie whispered, confused, staring past Quinn to Wyatt.

"Because he likes me," Quinn answered, obviously thinking Charlie was speaking to her.

Charlie ignored Quinn and told Wyatt, "We'll pay you. We don't have much money for this," she said, thinking of Grandpa Max's stipulations, "but we'll figure something out—"

Wyatt's smile returned full bloom as he shook his head. "If you offer these men or me one cent, you'll insult us. Pride is all most of us have, but it's a mighty thing."

Quinn sighed in frustration then grabbed Charlie by the shoulders and spun her around to the car. She gave her a not-so-gentle push towards the car. "Go. Now."

"Graham went to Bentonville this afternoon. I doubt he's back yet," Wyatt chimed in, still not looking at Quinn.

Quinn kept her gaze on Charlie as she said, "Then Charlie can wait at his house to thank him. She owes him that much."

Charlie stared from Quinn to Wyatt then, with a defeated sigh, got back into the car. She sped down the road and crossed a small crest before the Forbes's spread came into view. Graham didn't live far from their house at all and for some reason that made her lick her suddenly dry lips.

As she drove closer to the white dot down the road, she realized that Graham's house looked just like a farm in a movie. A paved driveway led from the road to circle around a manicured patch of grass and a blooming flower bed to the front door of the neat white split-level house. There was a wraparound porch and white lace curtains in the front ground-level windows. Fifty feet to the right of the house there was a corral, where Charlie recognized Earl McPhee's horse standing in the middle, nibbling at the grass. A few feet from the corral was a large barn that was red, again, just like in a movie. There was a large grassy field behind the house that ran into rolling hills. In the far distance, beyond the hills, Charlie could see neat row after neat row of packed dirt.

Charlie forced herself to stop admiring the house and get out of the car. She just hoped that Wyatt was right and Graham was still in Bentonville. She needed more time to think about what he had done, what it meant. Her breathing became shallow as she thought of Graham calling his friends to fix her house, so she wouldn't break her "damn neck." Maybe it wasn't expressed in the most romantic, politically correct way, but at least he had thought of her. He had thought of her.

Charlie clung to that as she forced herself to walk up the porch steps to the screen door. She gulped over the lump in her throat when she noticed that the wooden door was open behind the screen door. She could see straight into the house, which meant someone was home.

Charlie hesitantly tapped the screen door. "Graham, are you here? It's Charlie." No answer. "Graham," she called, more loudly.

"Come on in," came back the soft female reply from somewhere within the house.

Charlie froze. A woman. Graham lived with a woman. Her face flushed with the heat of humiliation. Of course, Graham would be living with a woman. Why hadn't she or either of her sisters thought of that? They didn't know anything about him, besides the fact that he was gorgeous and sexy.

The woman rounded the corner and opened the screen door. Charlie laughed in surprise and relief as she took in the older woman's dark skin, silver hair and eyes that reminded her of Graham.

"You're his mother," she blurted out. The woman smiled, but Charlie saw the confusion in her eyes. Charlie grinned and shook her head. "I'm sorry. I'm Charlie Sibley—"

"Our new neighbor. Graham has told me about you," the woman exclaimed, with a delighted smile. Charlie liked her voice. It was soft and welcoming, with just a hint of a slow, happy life. The woman held out her hand.

"I'm Eliza Forbes. Welcome to Sibleyville. I'm so sorry I haven't been by sooner. I wanted to bake an apple pie and introduce myself the proper way. Are you here alone or are your sisters with you?"

Charlie couldn't help but warm up to Eliza. Besides the fact that she was Graham's mother, there was such kindness in her eyes that Charlie couldn't help but want the woman to like her.

"I'm here alone."

"I still owe you girls a pie. However, I did make some chocolate chip cookies yesterday. Would you like some? I'll give you a plate to take home." Eliza opened the screen door wider and beckoned for Charlie to come inside, without missing a beat. "I'm just chattering away while you're standing in that hot sun…please come in and join me in the kitchen. I'm right in the middle of making lunch for the men."

Charlie's heart skipped a beat at the mention of "men." It was pathetic how even the offhanded mention of Graham made her skin hot.

She walked into the house and followed Eliza across highly polished wood floors through a formal dining room and into the wide, sunlight-bright kitchen. The rich, hearty scents of meat and potatoes filled the air.

"I hope you can stay for an early dinner," Eliza said, as she rummaged in the refrigerator.

"I don't want to be a bother. I just came—"

"Oh, don't be silly," Eliza admonished cheerfully, as she pulled out a pitcher of lemonade and poured a tall glass for Charlie. "I cook for ten men a day. Adding one woman's name to the pot won't be a bother at all."

"I really shouldn't," Charlie said, shaking her head, even as she longed to stay. It would have been nice to share a meal with Eliza, instead of her sisters with their sniping and insults, but she could imagine Graham's reaction if he sat down and saw her at the table. He would run screaming in the opposite direction. "I just came to see Graham. Is he around?"

Eliza abruptly stopped flitting around the kitchen and turned to openly study Charlie. Nerves made Charlie force a smile in response as Eliza's eyes narrowed speculatively.

She murmured, "You're the reason Graham came home with a black eye and Earl McPhee's horse, aren't you?"

Charlie bit her bottom lip and avoided Eliza's eyes. "No."

"I knew it," Eliza said excitedly, ignoring Charlie's answer completely. "I heard in town that Graham had gotten into a fight over one of the Sibley sisters, and I knew it had to be you the minute I saw you. My son has never been shy about protecting those around him."

Charlie shook her head in response. "He wasn't protecting me—"

A deep male voice interrupted her, "Who are you talking to, Eliza?"

Charlie turned to see a tall, older man with rich brown skin standing in the doorway of the kitchen. He looked the part of a rancher with jeans, cowboy boots and a plaid shirt. Instead of a cowboy hat, he wore a Chicago Cubs baseball cap that had seen better days.

Graham may have gotten his eyes from his mother,

but everything else—his height, his confidence, his movie-star handsome looks and the devilish twinkle in his eyes—had come from his father.

Eliza walked across the kitchen to place a hand on his arm. "One guess who she is."

The man looked back at Charlie then said, firmly, "The woman our Graham got a black eye over."

"Exactly," Eliza said, laughing, at the same time that Charlie said, "Not quite—"

The man stepped forward and offered his hand to Charlie. "I'm Lance Forbes, Graham's father. Welcome to Sibleyville."

"This is Charlie Sibley," Eliza said, as Charlie once more tried to explain about the horse and Earl and, most importantly, that Graham didn't even like her, let alone want to protect her.

"One of the infamous Sibley sisters," Lance guessed, as he sat on the stool next to her.

"Infamous?" Charlie croaked.

"Lance," Eliza admonished, returning to her pots and pans.

"Well, it's true," Lance said, stubbornly. "You girls appear out of nowhere, insist upon staying in that condemned shack and keep to yourselves. That qualifies for infamy around these parts."

"This is only their second day here, Lance," Eliza said, with a long-suffering sigh.

"You girls should be introducing yourselves around here. No one knows you and we should. You're practically family."

"Well, that's *our* job," Eliza said, excitedly. "We

should have a party in their honor, Lance. Invite the town. We haven't gotten together in a while. This will be fun."

"Will the invite list include Boyd Robbins?" Lance asked, with an expression that conveyed what he thought about Boyd Robbins.

"Of course it does. We can't have a party and not invite the mayor," his wife responded, with a censuring look. Lance cursed under his breath. Eliza ignored him and looked at Charlie excitedly. "This will be perfect. We should grill. Have a barbecue. We'll do it the day after tomorrow."

Charlie was getting a headache following the couple. They were too…too lively. She didn't know people like them in Los Angeles, people who were so openly welcoming and kind.

"There's something I should explain," Charlie said quickly, before either one started talking again. Both looked at her expectantly, and she almost lost her nerve. She knew it was childish, but she wanted Graham's parents to like her. "Graham didn't get a black eye over me—"

"Isn't that Earl McPhee's horse in our corral?" Lance demanded, looking at her exactly the way Graham looked at her—as if she was a strange creature that amused him and confounded him all at once.

"Yes, it is."

"And Graham ended up with the black eye because he took the horse from Earl?"

"Right."

"Because of you?" Lance concluded.

"No," she answered, a little too emphatically. For the first time since she'd entered the kitchen, Eliza and Lance both gave her their full attention. "I mean…Earl was abusing that horse and Graham stopped him. It had nothing to do with me, except I pointed out to Graham what was happening. Except I didn't mean for it to get violent, or for Graham to get hurt, and he did. And then…" She forced herself to stop talking then added, uncertainly, "So, you see, Graham didn't get in a fight over me."

She didn't like the look the Forbeses exchanged. With a strange expression, Eliza gently patted Charlie's hand and said softly, "Of course, dear. Whatever you say."

"Like hell," Lance said gruffly, drawing another censuring glance from his wife. He stared at Charlie closely and said, "I know my son. He likes animals well enough, but he would not take on Earl McPhee just because of a horse. He would talk to McPhee, buy the horse from McPhee, but fight him…? Nope. There was more involved."

Charlie shook her head in disbelief. Of course, she couldn't explain to Graham's parents that he was in serious lust with her sisters and wouldn't waste breaking a sweat over her. They wouldn't understand. No one understood until they saw the Sibley sisters together.

"Lance, make yourself useful, and take plates out to the table," Eliza ordered. Lance pouted, but stood to his feet and limped to one of the highly polished wood cabinets over the sink.

Charlie smiled at the older woman gratefully and stood as well. "Is there something I can do to help?"

"Good God, no," came a familiar, wry voice from the doorway.

Charlie's body reacted before she turned and saw

Graham lounging against the door frame, looking gorgeous and clean. Her entire body came alive, as if it had just been waiting to be near him again. Her thighs clenched and her stomach tightened. She would never become accustomed to her reaction to him. A reaction that obviously wasn't reciprocated, considering the slight trace of annoyance on his bruised face.

"Whatever you do, Mom, don't let her near the stove. I would hate to think of the consequences of allowing this woman anywhere near an open flame," Graham said, his eyes on Charlie.

He took his time looking over her body. His gaze lingered a little too long on her hips and then moved to her breasts. Charlie barely withheld a sigh. She really should be upset or something that he was studying her breasts with an intensity usually reserved for her gyne-cologist, but instead heat seared through her body and seemed to center in the places his gaze touched. Then his gaze lifted to meet hers. She tried to smile. He frowned.

"Is that how you sweet-talk all the women you meet?" Lance admonished Graham then said to his wife, "And you wonder why he's still single."

"She's a walking disaster," Graham said, with a shrug, as if that was explanation enough.

Despite the heat rising in her body at his mere presence, Charlie felt the anger bubbling in her throat. He might be beautiful, but he was definitely trying her nerves. She bit her bottom lip to restrain herself from insulting him in front of his parents.

"Charlie is wonderful," Eliza said, firmly, as she stirred a pot of something that smelled delicious on the stove.

Charlie laughed in embarrassment, as Graham snorted. Eliza continued cheerfully, "In fact, we're having a party in her honor. I haven't decided on the menu, but Lance is going to grill."

"If my health allows it," Lance reminded his wife, his voice suddenly weak and soft.

"The party is for my sisters and me," Charlie felt the need to clarify to Graham. Graham hadn't taken his eyes off her since he had walked into the kitchen. He was making her nervous, and a part of her knew he was doing it on purpose. She had come into his private sanctuary, a place where she was not invited and didn't belong.

No matter how welcoming Lance and Eliza were towards her, Graham did not want her there. She had never felt more out of place in her life.

"You could have told me that there was no air conditioning anywhere in this town, Graham…." came another male voice from behind Graham.

A tall, dark-skinned man wearing an obviously expensive pin-striped suit stepped around Graham and into the kitchen. From his highly polished—and dust-covered—expensive wingtips to the gold watch on his wrist and the designer sunglasses pushed high on his head, everything about him screamed money. And misery. Charlie had a feeling that her sisters would find a kindred spirit in the man because he seemed as horrified to be in Sibleyville as Kendra and Quinn were.

"You must be Theodore," Eliza said, with a warm smile. "Welcome to our home."

"Please call me Theo," he said, with a smile much warmer than Charlie would have imagined. He seemed too handsome, too slick and too perfect to have a smile that warm.

"Things must be dire at work for you to fly all the way out from Japan to talk to Graham," Lance said, suspiciously, as he shook Theo's hand.

"Something like that," Theo murmured to Lance shooting Graham an inscrutable look. Charlie noticed that Graham avoided Theo's eyes.

Graham motioned to Charlie and said to Theo, "This is our neighbor, Charlie Sibley." He grumbled to Charlie, without quite meeting her eyes, "Charlie, this is Theo Morgan. He and I work together in Tokyo."

Charlie was surprised about Tokyo because she had assumed that Graham lived in Sibleyville, but, instead, she smiled at Theo. Something about his return smile made Charlie guess that he had heard her name before. She could only imagine what Graham had told him.

"Charlie, it's a pleasure," Theo said, taking her hand in his. "Really," he added, as if he normally didn't mean it. He bent over slightly and placed a kiss on the back of her hand.

Charlie laughed at his obviously manufactured civility, while Lance snorted in disbelief. Graham only glowered.

"It's nice to meet you, too," she said to Theo, ignoring the Forbes men.

"All right," Graham said abruptly, glaring at Theo. Theo made a great show of reluctantly releasing her hand. Graham walked farther into the kitchen to place himself between Charlie and Theo, and grunted at Charlie, "What are you doing here?"

"Graham," Eliza gasped, staring at him concerned,

while Lance was the one to glower at Graham this time from across the kitchen.

Graham ignored his parents and crossed his arms over his chest as he continued to stare at Charlie expectantly.

Charlie tried to control her temper. Usually, she had no problem doing that. She was the serene Sibley sister, but between Graham's nasty mood and her own discomfort and urge to reach across the kitchen to touch him, she no longer could claim to be serene. She was hot, confused and horny.

She said through clenched teeth, "I came here to apologize to you and to thank you for sending Wyatt and the other men to our home, but you're making that very difficult to do. In fact, you're making me wish for another can of paint."

Graham ignored her last statement said smugly, "You came to apologize. Well, that's a start."

"Graham, don't be an ass," Eliza said, firmly. "And, Charlie, don't take it from the likes of him. A Forbes man can try a woman's patience. Believe me."

"Hey, how'd I get involved?" Lance wailed, helplessly.

Eliza rolled her eyes at him and pointed towards the cabinets. "Aren't you supposed to be getting plates for lunch?"

Graham groaned in exasperation then motioned for Charlie to follow him out the kitchen door. She squared her shoulders, sent one last look at Eliza, who nodded encouragingly, then followed Graham out of the house. Graham had already stalked off the porch and towards the corral that stood behind the house. The large horse from last night stood in the middle of the wide, fenced-in circle.

Graham leaned against the fence, his back to the horse, facing her, his elbows propped on the top rail. The brim of his hat partially shadowed his face, but it was clear that all of his attention was focused on her. She stopped a few feet in front of him.

"You were saying?" he prodded.

Her temper snapped again. "Why are you making this so difficult?"

"Because torturing you is fun, and I haven't had fun in a long time," he drawled, lazily.

She stared at him, surprised by his blunt honesty. He returned her gaze, his expression amused. He was confusing the hell out of her, but she did owe him an apology.

She took a deep breath then said, "I didn't mean to fall on you—"

He waved away her impending apology and said, with a shrug, "No permanent damage."

She narrowed her eyes and crossed her arms over her chest. "Are you usually this confounding, or do I just bring it out in you?"

He actually smiled, and her body felt as though she had been drenched in a vat of extreme heat at the sight. He tipped back the brim of his hat and said, "I think you bring it out in me."

She turned to leave, speechless at more of his blunt honesty, then whirled back to face him. He continued to watch her, a small smile lifting the corners of his mouth. She didn't know whether to be insulted or angry…. And was he flirting with her, or just being a jerk?

She should leave. She had ice cream and meat in the trunk of the car that would spoil, if it hadn't already. And

Graham was playing with her because he could. She was no match for him. That much was obvious from the fact that she could barely string two sensible sentences together, and Graham was clearly enjoying her bewilderment. Yes, she should definitely leave.

Except, instead of leaving, she said, "I didn't know you had worked in Tokyo."

He answered, "I *work* in Tokyo."

"What do you do?" she asked, fascinated, in spite of herself.

"I work for an international conglomerate. We merge companies, find companies that need merging, increase profits for shareholders."

"You're a corporate raider."

He grinned and her stomach dropped as if she had just shot down a roller coaster and left it at the top. "Some people call us that."

"I thought you were a cowboy…or a rancher or something?"

"I don't know why. I never told you that," he shot back.

Charlie resisted the urge to snap back at him. For some reason, he enjoyed baiting her. She reminded herself that she should be leaving. But, once more, she remained rooted in place. Graham continued to assess her, as if he could sense her internal struggle. Charlie guessed that he had been in this exact position many times—snarling at a woman who just stood there and took it because he was so gorgeous.

She struggled for patience and asked, "Are you here on vacation?"

"Not quite," he snorted. "Six months ago, my father

had a heart attack while riding a horse. He fell off the horse and broke his leg. I took a leave of absence to come home and help my mother with the ranch while my father recovered."

She moved to stand next to him as worry for the grumpy but loveable old man made her momentarily forget her annoyance with Graham. "Is Lance all right?"

"All right?" he repeated, with a small laugh. "The man is healthier than a horse, but he won't admit it. The doctors have given him the okay, Mom has told him to stop faking, but he refuses. He thinks that keeping me here will make me fall in love with the farm."

"If you're only here temporarily, why are you on town council?" she protested, still apparently unconvinced.

"That's what I ask myself every Wednesday when I'm sitting in the council meeting, trying not to bang my head against the desk," he muttered. "I had been back in Sibleyville for about two weeks, when a bunch of folks came out to the farm and told me that I should throw my hat into the race for the open council spot— the old town council member, Merv Lowe, had moved to Seattle to be near his daughter and grandkids. The townspeople could only hold off Tom Robbins—the mayor's son, whom I'm sure you'll have the pleasure of meeting soon, and I use the word *pleasure* as in run if you see him coming—to fill the vacant spot by calling for an emergency election. I told everyone I talked to that there was no way I would be a council member. I had a job in Tokyo. I have a life, and I wasn't planning to stick around long enough to serve out the term."

"It didn't work," she pointed out.

"Write-in votes," he answered simply. "Ten thousand three hundred and thirty-seven write-in votes. It would have been ten thousand three hundred and thirty-nine write-in votes, but two were discounted because Mr. and Mrs. Duckworth, who have never been able to remember names, wrote 'Hank and Nina's oldest boy.'"

She laughed and shook her head. "And you've been in purgatory ever since?"

"If purgatory means hell, then yes."

"So, you're planning to leave?"

"As soon as possible," he confirmed. "Theo is here to apply a little pressure since a promotion I've worked long and hard for is on the verge of being mine... assuming I can get back to the company in time to fight for it. And it's a little hard to fight when I'm thousands of miles away."

She heard the frustration in his voice and felt a strange sense of sympathy for him, even though she didn't want to. She wanted to think of him as a gorgeous man who was a jerk, just like all gorgeous men were jerks, except he was making it harder and harder for her to do that.

She said abruptly, "Look, Graham, I shouldn't be telling you this. You almost deserve what they're doing, but you've been so nice... Or, maybe *nice* isn't the right word, but you did help me last night and today at the house... And then having Wyatt..." Her voice trailed off as she realized that he was staring at her with an amused and confused expression. She cleared her throat then blurted out, "You're a bet."

He frowned in confusion. "What?"

"Kendra and Quinn bet each other on who could score you first."

"Score me?" he murmured, sounding more amused than insulted.

She continued, ignoring his amusement, "My money's on Kendra, although Quinn has always been the dark horse. I shouldn't have told you, but you don't deserve to be some stupid object and you've helped me in the last two days more than any other man ever has tried to, or wanted to…" Her voice trailed off as she realized that she had revealed too much about herself.

Silence weighed between them and Charlie chanced a glance at him, wondering how his male ego would take the news.

Instead of looking devastated, he looked intrigued. "So, what's the grand prize for bagging me?"

She rolled her eyes in annoyance and raked a hand through her hair. Of course, he thought it was a joke. "I don't think they've thought that far ahead. Besides the prize doesn't matter, it's the chance to one-up each other. Ever since we were kids, they've been competitive with each other. Boys, clothes, grades. It was exhausting watching them."

"What about you?"

She was surprised by his question. "What about me?"

"Are they competitive with you?"

Charlie laughed in disbelief and shook her head. "Of course not. They don't even consider me in the same league."

His gaze drifted to her breasts again, and Charlie stiffened. Her breasts stiffened. She swallowed the sudden lump in her throat and averted her gaze when he finally looked at her.

His voice was low and soft, as he asked, "So, I'm guessing you're not taking part in the bet to score me?"

Her mouth dropped open in indignation. "I would never… Never—"

"Don't get all self-righteous on me," he soothed, with a small laugh. "I was just thinking if there was some sort of grand prize, we could rig it so you could win and we'd split the profits."

Charlie didn't know if she could handle this smiling, flirting Graham. The scowling, angry Graham had just been bearable. This Graham was dangerous.

"You think this is some kind of joke," she demanded, angrily. "Kendra and Quinn are not women to be toyed with."

"Maybe they just haven't come across the right toy yet," he said, with a shrug.

Charlie rolled her eyes then laughed. Her first real laugh in a day or two. "It is going to be so fun watching them take you apart."

"Have some faith in me, Charlie. I can handle Kendra and Quinn."

"Famous last words," she murmured.

He grinned then turned to face the horse in the corral. "What are we going to be name him?"

Charlie stared at the horse, watching his sleek muscles glide smoothly under the dull coat. She didn't know much about horses—actually, she didn't know anything about horses—but this horse seemed like a good one. He just was a little neglected and scared. She frowned because she realized that maybe she had saved the horse because it reminded her of herself.

"Name him?" she repeated, dumbly.

"We can't just keep calling the horse *it*. I'm no horse whisperer, but I'd have to think that would be a drag on his self-esteem." When she only continued to stare at him in confusion, he said, with a sigh, "I'm going to buy him from Earl."

"You can't do that," she gasped in surprise. "It must be expensive—"

"I can handle it."

"What if Earl won't sell?"

Something dangerous flashed in Graham's eyes as he said, grimly, "He'll sell."

She wracked her mind for some other solution, besides Graham being stuck with her mistake. She tried again, "But…Graham, I didn't mean for you to be stuck with a horse that… Surely, there must be something else we can do."

His voice was gruff as he said, "I looked the horse over this morning. There are signs of abuse." He took that moment to look at her and she could tell that despite his big talk last night, Graham would have taken on Earl if he had seen him strike the horse, with or without her prodding. It was becoming apparent that Graham Forbes was a softie. And Charlie fell in love a little more.

"Then *I'll* buy him," she said, suddenly.

Graham's eyes narrowed as he studied her. "Do you even know how to ride a horse?"

"No. I must have missed the part where knowing how to ride a horse was a prerequisite to owning one," she said, her chin lifting at his condescending tone. His eyes narrowed in response and she quickly continued before he could interrupt, "I appreciate your efforts last night. Really, I do, despite what I said earlier today, but I don't want you to have to pay for it. This horse is my problem, not yours. I made the decision to intervene, and I will take care of him. Maybe when I get back to L.A., I'll find a proper owner for him. He deserves it."

Graham rolled his eyes in a mixture of exasperation and amusement. "Are you always such a martyr?"

"I'm not acting like a martyr," she protested. "I just don't like being indebted to anyone."

"Well, consider yourself indebted," he said, with a casual shrug. When she continued to glare at him, he sighed again then placed a gentle hand on the bare skin where her shoulder and neck met the strap of her tank top. She gasped at the feel of his hot skin on hers. He appeared oblivious as he held her gaze, and said softly, "We can use the horse, Charlie. You're not indebted to me…unless…"

His voice trailed off at the same time that his hand tightened on her neck. He leaned closer to her. His gaze dropped to her lips. She licked her lips, and his eyes narrowed. She felt hot air escape his mouth and caress her mouth. Of their own will, her eyes began to slide closed, preparing herself for his kiss. Her body physically ached for his kiss. Needed it, when she had never needed anything from a man before. Now, she knew why women craved men, did things for men that she had though she wouldn't do for anyone.

Then Graham abruptly released her. He appeared

more confused than she felt as he took several steps from her, nearly stumbling and kicking up dust all around him. He cursed, steadied himself on the corral then stared at her with an unreadable expression.

"I have food in the trunk. I should go," she said, abruptly. She hesitated for a moment, wanting him to stop her.

He continued to stare at her as if he didn't know who she was or how he had gotten to be alone with her. She took several unsteady steps towards the front of the house.

"Charlie," he said, quietly. She stopped then slowly turned to him. The strange expression in his eyes had been replaced with something stronger and more foreign. Maybe even desire. He sounded hesitant, as he murmured, "It was nice talking to you."

Charlie murmured a half-hearted response then abruptly turned on her heel and stumbled to the car. She could feel his eyes boring into her back the entire way.

Chapter 9

The next morning, Graham hammered a wooden stake into place in the fence that surrounded the Forbes's property. He had been putting off replacing the temporary frame on the border fence for three months, but this morning, the only thing he wanted to do was hit something.

Still, the physical activity did not stop him from thinking about Charlie, or the way her lips had parted for him. He had almost kissed her, and she had almost let him. Just the thought of that momentary bout of insanity had Graham pounding on the nailhead harder. He had been standing there having a surprisingly good time teasing her and the next thing he knew he had been on the verge of taking her, outside his parents' house and in front of an emotionally and physically abused horse. It certainly had not been his finest moment.

He had taken one look at her lips, which had looked so damn welcoming and lush and full, and… He had to admit it. The way he had been feeling, it would not have ended with a kiss. Not when his hands had been trembling and he had felt as though he had just run a marathon.

Graham cursed as the hammer missed its mark and, instead, glanced off his left thumb that had been holding the nail in place. He instantly dropped the hammer and rose to his feet. He shook his hand violently, as if to shake away the pain, then quickly glanced around to make certain no one had seen him make such a novice mistake.

He had been hammering nails since he could walk; to do something so stupid… Of course, it would happen while he was thinking of Charlie. Even when she was nowhere near him, she was dangerous. At this rate, Graham could picture himself in a full body cast by the end of the week.

He was safe. No one else was around. His stallion, Sid, glanced up from grazing at the grass a few feet away, but otherwise didn't care that Graham was cursing and talking to himself. Graham had ridden to the far north end of the pasture and was surrounded by nothing but rolling hills, grass and country sky and a beaming sun. It was barely nine in the morning and it was already hot enough to fry an egg on the sidewalk.

If Graham didn't know himself better, he would think that he was trying to work off some type of frustration. He refused to think that had anything to do with Charlie.

"Hello, Graham," came a throaty, seductive voice behind him.

Graham turned in surprise to find Kendra, with her feet planted wide and her hands resting on her barely clad hips.

She apparently had been running. Sweat gleamed on every toned inch of her body, and there were plenty of inches available for his inspection, considering the exercise clothes—or, at least, Graham thought they were in the exercise category—she wore. Lingerie would not have been a stretch either.

Not that Graham was complaining. As a red-blooded heterosexual male, he couldn't help but appreciate her long, dark legs, flat, muscled abdomen and the barely there black sports bra that was the only thing between him and a flash of her breasts.

While Graham liked to think he was a little discreet about his own appraisal, Kendra openly studied him, her gaze raking from his bare chest to the worn waistband of his low-riding jeans. He suddenly felt uncomfortable. Hell, it was downright disconcerting. God help him, he liked aggressive women, but he could tell instantly that Kendra Sibley was her own breed.

"Hello, Kendra," he greeted, subconsciously tipping the brim of his hat.

She grinned in return, her gaze lingering on his right nipple. Graham resisted the urge to reach for his shirt that he had tossed aside earlier under the intense sun. Then she licked her lips. Forgetting pride, Graham quickly pulled on his shirt.

"I just went for a ten-mile run to town and back. What a great workout," she said, slowly and deliberately stretching her arms over her head as she stuck out her chest.

Graham kept his gaze trained on her face and away

from her breasts as he said, "You must have taken a wrong turn somewhere. You passed your house. Your place is in between ours and town."

She lowered her arms and lifted one finely arched eyebrow in challenge as she said bluntly, "I didn't take a wrong turn, Graham."

Graham coughed over the sudden catch in his throat. Kendra definitely was not subtle.

"I was looking for you, Graham," Kendra continued, taking a step closer to him. Graham resisted the inclination to turn and hightail it out of there. Her eyes gleamed as she said, "Don't you want to know why?"

He forced himself to relax against the fence. "Why?"

"I love how I feel after I run. Hot and invincible. I don't like to waste that feeling—"

The sound of a beeping horn caused both of them to turn towards Graham's pickup hurtling across the field towards them. Graham barely held back his sigh of relief. Whatever invitation Kendra had been on the verge of issuing him would have been foolish for him to pass on, and Graham knew that he would have. Not because of Charlie, but because… Well, just because.

The truck stopped a few feet from them, sending small clouds of dust to circle around the air, and Theo hopped out. In deference to his surroundings, Theo had changed from his suit into a pair of dark, expensive slacks, a button-down starched shirt and another pair of highly polished wingtips that were being covered with dust as Graham watched. At least Theo had not worn a tie. Although, Graham suspected it was killing Theo not to.

"I've been here a day and I'm going crazy with

boredom," Theo announced, stalking towards the couple. He immediately stopped when he noticed Kendra.

Graham smiled to himself as Theo gave Kendra a few lessons in open appraisal. When Theo's gaze remained a little too long on Kendra's breasts, Kendra shifted her weight and placed her hands on her hips to glare at him. Theo finally stopped staring at her breasts and lifted his gaze to hers. He smiled, and Graham wanted to tell Kendra to run. He had seen that look in Theo's eyes before.

"As much as Graham has gone on ad nauseam about this town, he has never mentioned you," Theo murmured, his eyes once more dropping to her breasts.

"Theo, this is Kendra Sibley. She's Charlie's sister," Graham introduced, barely able to conceal his laughter at Theo's open ogling and Kendra's growing annoyance. "Kendra, this is Theo Morgan. He and I work together in Tokyo."

Whatever Kendra had been on the verge of saying to Theo was gone, as she turned to Graham in surprise. "You work in Tokyo?"

He smiled, remembering Charlie's surprise. "I was born and raised in Sibleyville, but I don't live here anymore. I work in Shoeford Industries' Tokyo office."

"Shoeford Industries," she murmured, appreciatively. "I'm a stockbroker with Franklin Financial Group. You tried to acquire us last year."

"We don't *try* anything. We either do it, or we don't," Theo said, with a snort of derision. "We decided not to acquire FFG because it's small change and would not have been cost-efficient in the long run."

Kendra's eyes narrowed as she turned to Theo. "I see

you're that rare man who can cause a woman to despise you upon first sight."

Graham swallowed his laugh, while Theo's mouth tightened into a straight line. "Not usually," Theo said.

"It's a gift, Mr. Morgan. You shouldn't deny it," she continued. "Your ability to ogle a woman and then insult her three seconds later…it's dizzying."

"Well, as my grandmother always says, if you don't want someone looking, you shouldn't advertise," Theo said, with a distinctly non-Theo shrug.

Kendra's expression turned murderous, and Graham quickly said, "Wow. Look at the time. We should all head out—"

"What exactly do you think I'm advertising?" Kendra demanded, her gaze focused on Theo with enough heat that Graham wondered if his friend would combust.

Theo once more lazily looked over every inch of her body. Kendra endured his perusal with an expression that went from murder to pure rage. Graham discreetly closed his toolbox, in case she got any ideas.

"What does a woman usually advertise when she's wearing clothes not fit for public consumption?" Theo replied with another shrug.

Graham shook his head in disbelief. Theo never did know when to shut up. Kendra marched across the distance that separated them and stopped mere inches from Theo's surprised face. She jabbed a finger into his chest and said through clenched teeth, "Whatever I am advertising, *you* will never have to worry about being the recipient of the message."

Graham winced at the direct hit then forced a smile as

Kendra turned to him. She sent a smile filled with enough passion to make him uncomfortable again. She purred, "Charlie told me about the party. I'll see you there."

She turned back to Theo and demanded in a gruff voice that was nothing like the sex-kitten whisper she had used on Graham, "Will you be there?"

Theo nodded then shot back, "Disappointed?"

"Hardly. I make it a rule never to allow myself to be disappointed by jackasses." She sent a flirty wave in Graham's direction then took off at a jog down the field towards her house.

Graham watched in appreciation as all of her parts bounced in the right way then turned to Theo, who was watching the same scene with a little less appreciation on his face. In fact, Theo looked pissed.

"Typical," Theo spat out.

"What?"

"A woman who looks like that. A stockbroker, no less. She would have to be a ballbuster."

"You were ogling her as though she was onstage in a strip club," Graham couldn't help but point out.

Theo directed his anger at Graham. "So what? If she chooses to dress like that, she shouldn't get all prickly because a man looks at her. It's what men do. We look. I bet even a paragon of virtue like you can't resist on occasion."

Graham laughed dryly, as he thought of the X-rated images that had floated through his head when he had stood at the corral with Charlie. He could admit to himself that he hadn't just wanted to kiss her. He had wanted to drag her to the barn, pull down both their jeans and plunge into her. He had wanted her on her back with her feet in the air, screaming his name. Graham stopped himself and took off his hat to wipe the sweat off his forehead.

"I am hardly a paragon of virtue," he muttered, more to himself than to Theo.

"What party is she talking about?"

Graham hid his smile at Theo's disgruntled expression. "You're going to be there, remember?" Theo glared at him and Graham took pity on him. "Mom is throwing a party at the house to welcome the Sibley sisters to town. I'm guessing that everyone will be there, once my mom and her quilting circle get the word out."

Theo was still for a few moments as he looked after Kendra, who was now a small dot down the road. He abruptly stalked back to the truck. "Tell your father soon, Forbes. This town is growing old fast."

Theo jumped in the truck and kicked up dirt and grass as he turned and headed back to the house. Graham shook his head then laughed. Theo Morgan had finally met his match.

"What should I wear to the party?" Quinn mused, as she stood in front of a clothes rack in her bedroom.

Charlie lay across Quinn's lumpy bed and studied her sister. Ever since she had told her sisters about the party at the Forbes's house, Quinn had been in a frenzy. She had painted her toenails and fingernails, waxed her legs and rolled her hair in rollers the size of staplers.

She had spent the last twenty minutes studying each and every outfit that she had brought with her.

And she had brought a lot, along with four collapsible clothing racks that had fit into her suitcase like CIA-developed, micro weapons. The small room that Quinn had claimed now bulged with clothes racks and shoes. The only other things in her room were the bed—now overlaid with clothes—and an antique chest of drawers that was covered with makeup and— what else?—clothes.

Charlie should have been painting the back porch, or cleaning the living room, but she couldn't concentrate on anything at that moment. She would never admit it to Quinn, but she was just as excited as she was about the party. Not that she had a reason to be. Charlie had no delusions about tomorrow night; she would be the fifth wheel as Kendra and Quinn enacted Operation Graham and Graham enacted his own sting. But, that still didn't stop her from looking forward to the party.

"What do you think of this?" Quinn asked, turning to Charlie, while holding up a piece of blue cloth that involved a few buckles and belts. Charlie murmured non-committedly, and Quinn frowned. "You're right. It's too much for this party. I have to think Sephora at her father's house in the country, not Sephora at the Diamond Valley annual fundraiser."

Charlie didn't bother to hide her smile as she asked hesitantly, "Don't you think you're taking this a bit too seriously, Quinn? It's supposed to be just a casual thing. A chance for us to get to know the people in this town."

Quinn shot her a look as if Charlie had just announced that her daytime Emmy had been a mistake. "Charlie, I am Sephora Wilkins Deveraux Tritt McGuire

Jackson. When people see me, they see Sephora. I cannot let my public down," Quinn explained patiently.

"I doubt that anyone in this town even watches the soap—"

Quinn straightened her back and said, in a regal tone usually reserved for Sephora's put-downs, "The *soap*, as you insist upon calling it, is watched in over millions of households. Sibleyville is precisely the type of place where it is watched. How do you think these women would feel if I showed up to that party in jeans and a T-shirt? It would devastate them. Actresses are held to a higher standard, Charlie. We must always look our best."

Charlie probably could have taken Quinn a little more serious if she hadn't had giant rollers in her hair and pads between her freshly painted toes.

"I'm not saying that you…I just think you're putting too much pressure on yourself," Charlie said, diplomatically. "We probably won't ever see these people again once we've finished the two weeks."

Charlie was surprised by the sting of pain that followed her words. It was the truth. She would never step foot in Sibleyville after the sisters finished the two weeks. She would never see Graham again. It was funny. She had only known him two days and it seemed as though he had always been a part of her life. The prospect of not seeing him again seemed like cruel and unusual punishment.

"That's not the point," Quinn said, sounding exasperated. "I have an image to uphold. I have to protect Sephora's image, and the show's image. I am an actress. and everyone will expect me to look like one. You don't understand what that's like. You go to work and deal with a bunch of dusty paintings and old men. I am dealing with adoring young girls, men and women who are searching for any flaw."

"You're right," Charlie murmured because it seemed easier than arguing about it. If Quinn wanted to spend the next twenty-four hours getting ready for an outdoor barbecue then Charlie was not going to stop her.

Quinn smiled in satisfaction then turned back to the clothes rack. She plucked out a green dress that glittered with sparkles and gold strings. She studied the dress then murmured, "The house seems different…peaceful. I take it the Wicked Witch of the West has flown away on her broom."

Charlie stifled a laugh. Barely. She and Quinn had often called Kendra that behind her back when they had been children. "While you were in the shower, she went on a run."

Quinn glanced at Charlie, with eyes wide with disbelief. "In all this heat and dust? Didn't she go on a run this morning?" Charlie shrugged in response. Quinn placed the dress back on the rack then began to laugh in disbelief. "A run, my ass. Kendra went on a hunting expedition. She went to find Graham. She has no pride."

Charlie tried to hide the panic in her voice as she said, "I doubt that."

Kendra was a force of nature. If she wanted Graham, she would have him, and there was nothing Graham would be able to do about it.

"We're talking about Kendra here," Quinn said, with a snort of distaste. "You know how competitive she is.

It doesn't matter what the prize is, as long as she gets it. Remember when I was sixteen years old and I beat her at tennis at the country club in front of that guy with the big nose that she was dating. She threw down her racket, claimed I cheated and stormed off the court."

"I beat her in tennis, Quinn. Not you," Charlie corrected, wryly.

Quinn waved that hand in dismissal of something so trivial as the facts. "Does it matter who did it? The point of the story is that Kendra did not win and she doesn't handle *not* winning very well."

Charlie decided the best course of action in her attempt to be Switzerland in between her two sisters was not to respond. But Quinn was right. Kendra was competitive, and Charlie had only beaten Kendra at anything once in her life.

"But, I'm not worried," Quinn said, confidently. "What man in his right mind would want Kendra over me? She practically looks like a man herself."

"Quinn," Charlie admonished her, surprised by the bitterness detectable in Quinn's voice.

"Well, I said *practically,*" Quinn mumbled.

Charlie shook her head and said sadly, "You and Kendra used to be so close when you were kids. Now, you two can't stay in the same room together for more than five minutes without arguing and I feel like the UN trying to keep the peace. What happened?"

"Kendra is impossible," Quinn said, as if that was the explanation.

"She's not the only one," Charlie said, pointedly staring at Quinn.

Quinn innocently smiled then waved her hands as if to dismiss the irrelevant subject. She asked excitedly, "So, what are you going to wear tomorrow night?"

"I don't know. I'm still debating if I should go or not. Graham would probably count himself lucky if I never stepped foot in his parents' house again," she said, ruefully.

Charlie knew that she and Graham would never be together in any real sense of the word. The idea was preposterous. But, she had caught a glimpse of what a friendship with him could be like that afternoon, and it had seemed...exciting. More exciting than anything in her life had been in a while. She had never ached for anyone, or anything in her life, but she found herself aching for Graham.

"You know, Charlie, the role of Sephora has taught me a lot about human nature," Quinn said, softly.

"Playing a character who has been divorced five times, shot twice, and temporarily imprisoned in a mental hospital has taught you a lot about human nature?"

"Yes," Quinn answered, apparently missing—or ignoring—the sarcasm in Charlie's tone. Her expression became sympathetic as she gracefully sat on the bed and placed her hands on Charlie's hands. "Do you want to talk about what happened yesterday?"

"Yesterday?" Charlie repeated confused.

"With Graham," Quinn responded, with what Charlie could only guess was a smile Sephora must have used to engender confidence.

"I didn't mean to fall on him, Quinn. It was an accident. I've told you this—"

"I believe you, Charlie," Quinn interrupted her,

patting her hands. "I'm not talking about the accident… although, you should try to be a tad more careful. You could really have hurt him…I'm talking about your attitude towards him."

"I wasn't aware I had an attitude towards Graham," Charlie said, tightly. "I just remember him yelling at me like I was five years old."

"And I think I know why," Quinn continued, ignoring Charlie's response.

"Why?" Charlie asked, suspiciously.

"It's obvious that you have a little crush on him. Kendra and I both see it. I'm sure Graham sees it, too." Charlie's eyes widened as the tell-tale heat of humiliation filled her face. "It's natural to have those feelings for a man like Graham," Quinn continued, with a soothing sigh. "He's a handsome, charming man, and I know you don't run across many of those at *your* job. You've spent most of your adult life acting as Grandpa Max's personal secretary and general slave—"

"No, I didn't," she replied, angrily. "He was my grandfather. I spent time with him because I loved him."

"Of course, dear," Quinn said, with disbelief edging her tone. "I'm just trying to say that I understand why you would instantly fall for Graham. He's probably the most fascinating man that you've come across in a while. But…well, how can I put this delicately…" Quinn's voice trailed off as she stared at the ceiling for inspiration, while Charlie tried to control her bubbling temper. She could not believe that her baby sister was lecturing her about men.

Regardless of the fact that Quinn probably had infinitely more experience with men, Charlie didn't like it.

In fact, she didn't like the direction of this entire conversation. She had not been their grandfather's "personal slave." She had enjoyed spending time around him. He yelled a lot, but his bark had been far worse than his bite. And, truth be told, she had gotten along far better with Grandpa Max and his friends than with people her own age.

Quinn abruptly smiled, as inspiration struck, and she said excitedly, "Graham is like Ralph Robinson. Remember him?"

"The quarterback of the football team during my senior year in high school?"

"Right. The guy you had the huge crush on. Remember you made the carrot cake and invited him to the house to ask him to the prom and—"

Charlie held up her free hand, since Quinn was refusing to relinquish the other one, and said, flatly, "I remember, Quinn."

"And he came to the house and ate the cake and then stared at you in horror when you asked him to the prom. He had thought you were just going to help him with his calculus homework," Quinn felt the need to finish.

Charlie narrowed her eyes and said through gritted teeth, *"I remember, Quinn."*

Quinn grinned, obviously relieved. "Good. Because that's how this is. Graham is like Ralph Robinson. He's a good guy, but he'll never appreciate an honest, sweet woman like you. And, frankly, Charlie, it's for the best. A man like Graham—that handsome, that charming, that smooth—would chew you up and spit you out without breaking a sweat."

Charlie did not normally scream or rant and rave. She left that to her sisters and to her grandfather when he had been alive. But, for the third time in as many days, Charlie wanted to kick something—preferably Quinn's butt.

She yanked her hand from Quinn's supposedly comforting grasp and scrambled off the bed to her feet. Anger made her chest tight and her words choked. "Ralph didn't laugh when I asked him to go to the prom. He didn't do anything, because you took that exact moment to prance outside and dive into the swimming pool."

"Was I not supposed to swim in my own home?" Quinn questioned, all wide-eyed innocence.

"You were topless, Quinn," Charlie screeched.

Quinn at least had the decency to look ashamed before she murmured, "Sweetie, that's in the past. I'm trying to protect you now."

"It's *not* in the past, Quinn. You're the same now as you were back then—unable to handle the fact that someone else may be the center of attention instead of you."

Quinn jumped to her feet, a mixture of confusion and worry crossing her face. "You don't really think that you're the center of Graham's attention, do you, Charlie?"

"Why not?" Charlie shot back. "Why can't—for once—a man be interested in *this* Sibley sister? Is that so difficult to believe?"

Quinn's mouth flapped open several times before she said, helplessly, "Yes."

Charlie didn't think either one of her sisters could hurt her anymore than they already had over the last few years. The unreturned phone calls, the unanswered emails, the missed holiday meals. Charlie had always been an afterthought to them, and now she realized that she was also a joke.

And as much as Charlie did not want to acknowledge it, it still hurt. If she ever wanted to grow up, to live outside her sisters' shadows, she would have to give up on them just as they had given up on her a long time ago.

Charlie shook her head, no longer angry, just tired. She had lasted three days. Grandpa Max would have been disappointed. She was disappointed in herself, in her sisters. But, most of all, she was disappointed at the thought that she would never see Graham again. Because she was going home.

"I can't deal with this anymore," she whispered, more to herself than to Quinn.

"What is that supposed to mean?" Quinn asked, a little too carefully.

"Exactly what I said." She started for the door, but Quinn quickly blocked her path. She glared at Quinn, clenching her hands into fists. She ordered, "Get out of my way, Quinn."

"You can't leave, Charlie. We all have to remain here for two weeks, or, else, none of us will get the money."

"I don't care about the money," Charlie shouted, truthfully.

"You need this money more than Kendra or I do," Quinn pointed out, obviously not believing her. "You need to make improvements to the museum, right? Acquire some famous pieces? You can't do without this money."

"We don't even know how much money we'll get. Knowing Grandpa Max, we could each get ten dollars—"

"He wouldn't do that to us."

"He didn't make us any promises, Quinn. And, frankly, no matter how much it is, I'm beginning to think it's not worth it…" Charlie's voice trailed off as she studied Quinn's desperate expression. Whatever anger she felt was replaced by concern and pity. She whispered, "I don't think I'm the only one who needs this money."

Quinn flinched, but otherwise remained silent. Charlie forced herself to ignore the brief spark of concern and, instead, walked out of the room. She ran down the stairs and into her room. She was a blur of motion, as she yanked open her suitcase and began to throw the toiletries on her dresser into the bag.

Then, just as quickly as Charlie's anger had risen, it dissipated. She plopped onto her bed and buried her face in her hands. She didn't want to leave. She didn't want to fight with her sisters. She lay on her bed and stared at the newly painted ceiling. She turned and stared out the window in the direction of Graham's house. She had never wanted to talk to another person in her life more than she wanted to talk to him at that moment.

Grandpa Max had taught her not to trust anyone, but in a few short days she trusted Graham. And she admitted she had feelings for him—as strange as it was. For some reason, that knowledge made her feel worse.

Chapter 10

Graham scowled as he watched Charlie talking with a group of women he had known since high school. The women had never seemed as interested in him as they did in Charlie. Since Charlie had arrived at his mother's party, Graham could admit that he had spent most of his time watching her. He had noticed that Quinn looked gorgeous as usual in a glittery top and short leather skirt that had drawn the eye of every man at the party, and Kendra looked the picture of original temptation in some tight, short dress, yet Graham's gaze kept returning to Charlie.

He cursed and forced himself to look away from her. It was barely five o'clock, the sun was still high in the sky, and it seemed like half of the town had shown up to join the Forbeses in the expansive field behind the house.

It was a typical Silbeyville party. No one arrived empty-handed. There was one picnic table laden with various pots and pans and plastic containers. Another picnic table was filled with bowls of punch and lemonade and bottles of soda. Still another table was covered with homemade pies, cakes and cookies.

Lance, with help from Wyatt, was manning the biggest grill that Graham had ever seen at one end of the yard, and Eliza was flitting around seeming to be in twelve places at once. Lights had been strung between trees, and a band was setting up their instruments on a temporary stage.

Graham should have been bored by the whole scene. But, as he stood on the porch, surveying people he had known his whole life, he wasn't. Instead, there was something comfortable about it. But, then there were the Sibley sisters.

Graham frowned as he thought of their arrival earlier that evening. Charlie had barely spared him a glance before gushing over his father, who had pretended to be annoyed by the attention, but anyone with eyes could see how much Lance had enjoyed Charlie's warm greeting. Kendra and Quinn had more than made up for Charlie's distinctly cool greeting, but it had rubbed Graham the wrong way. So, he had avoided Charlie for the last two hours. And, dammit to hell, she hadn't even seemed to notice.

As if Charlie knew he was thinking about her, she looked up from her conversation and scanned the yard. Graham told himself to look away, but instead, he waited until she found him. Her gaze collided with his. Graham just stared at her, images of all the things he wanted to do to her flooding his mind, making his breath quicken. Her eyes slightly widened, as if she could read his mind. Even from across the yard, Graham saw the flush cover her latte-colored cheeks. She looked away from him.

Graham shook his head. He was acting crazy.

"Great party, Graham," came Quinn's soft voice, as she walked up behind him.

Graham forced a smile at her. "All the credit goes to my mom," he murmured then studied her. She really was beautiful, almost unnaturally so.

She had flawless skin that glowed in the heat, while other women sweated. Her hair flowed in a mass of loose curls that had that just-got-out-of-bed look that men loved and she had a sweet body that Graham normally would have spent a lot of time trying to see naked. Instead, he looked at this beautiful woman and felt nothing.

"You're too modest," Quinn purred, sliding closer to him. "I know some of this must have been your doing."

Graham forced another smile then found himself once more seeking out Charlie in the crowd.

Following his gaze, Quinn sighed and murmured, "She's always gotten along better with people than Kendra or I have."

Guilty at being caught staring at Charlie, Graham laughed. "You and Kendra are the most popular people here."

"With the men," Quinn accurately noted. It might have been a trick of the light, but Graham thought he saw sadness flit across her expression before she turned to him with a blinding smile. "Save me a dance later? Just the two of us?"

Graham nodded dumbly. Quinn trailed a finger down his arm then walked down the steps to rejoin the party. Graham thought about following her, just to prove to himself that he didn't prefer to find Charlie and force her to talk to him, but his mother waved to him as she extracted herself from a group of women and walked onto the porch.

"Everything is turning out nicely," Eliza said, gleefully.

"You outdid yourself, Mom," Graham said, planting a kiss on the top of her head that came to just below his shoulder.

"You say that every time," she murmured, squeezing his waist.

"And every time it's true."

Eliza smiled up at him, then surveyed the crowd of people in the yard. Her gaze rested on Charlie, who had moved on to another group of people. "The Sibley sisters seem to be making a good impression, especially Charlie. I can't tell you how many people have told me how much they like her."

Graham rolled his eyes as he heard the tone of his mother's voice. Eliza had been polite when had she had met Kendra and Quinn earlier in the evening, but the hug and smile she had shared with Charlie had made it obvious who Eliza favored.

He said, in a warning tone, "You vowed to never become one of those matchmaking old biddies—if I recall your exact words, remember?"

"I haven't done anything," she said, with wide-eyed innocence that didn't fool Graham for one minute.

"I know you. You like Charlie."

"Who wouldn't like her?" Eliza said, with a surprised look. "She's polite, respectful, sweet as an apple pie and so cute. It's a wonder the men in this town haven't beaten down the door of their house to talk to her."

"Mom, stop," he warned.

"How did you feel when you first saw her?" she asked, watching him closely.

Graham rolled his eyes and couldn't help but laugh. "You know I don't believe in that crap."

Eliza sniffed. "I don't know why not. Your father and I are living proof. Your grandparents were living proof. Your great-grandparents—"

"Yes, I know the stories, Mom," he said, amused.

From Red Forbes, who had escaped slavery during the Civil War, to Lance, every Forbes man had supposedly fallen in love at first sight. The period between dating and courtship had ranged from one month—Red Forbes and his wife, Simone—to three months—Lance and Eliza. The myth was that Forbes men loved once and loved forever.

Lance and Eliza had been telling Graham the stories for so long that even though he laughed at the whole thing, he still waited for that spark when he first met a woman. It hadn't happened, and he knew it never would, but that didn't mean that he wouldn't fall in love. Or, at least, serious lust.

"You honestly don't believe that you will fall just as hard as your father and every other Forbes man in this family?"

"No, I don't," he said, leaving no room for doubt in

his tone. "I've been to a lot of places, Mom, and I've met a lot of women. If it was going to happen, it would have happened by now."

Eliza looked worried. "Graham—"

"Besides, you're not supposed to be doing anything, remember?"

"What am I doing?" she asked innocently.

"Charlie is not my type," he said, firmly.

"Tell me, son, what exactly is your type?"

Graham had to laugh at his mother's dubious expression. He decided to spare his mother details that she definitely didn't want to hear and said, "Not her."

"And why not?" Eliza demanded, crossing her arms over her chest.

"Here it comes… The matchmaking," he teased.

"I'm not matchmaking. I'm just noting that an attractive, single woman who happens to be kind and sweet is living down the road from me at the same time that my attractive, single son who also happens to be kind and sweet is home. And if you tried not to growl at her every time you saw her, we might actually get somewhere."

"We?" Graham questioned, amused.

"Yes, *we*," Eliza said, with a playful swat at his arm. Her voice became suspiciously frail as she said, softly, "Your father and I are getting old, Graham—"

Graham groaned and shook his head. "And, here I am, telling my friends that my parents never question me about grandchildren or settling down. That my parents never meddle in my business. Thank goodness, I don't have the overbearing parents that they seem to have."

"We don't pressure you, and I'm not pressuring you

now, but you are our only son, and, therefore, our only chance to have grandchildren."

Graham wrapped an arm around his mother's shoulders and said sympathetically, "You'll get your grandchildren one day, Mom, I promise." She frowned at him, and he added, emphatically, "But, not any time soon and not with Charlie Sibley."

Eliza pushed his arm off her and glared at him. "You still haven't given me a good reason why not. She's wonderful."

Graham gently turned his mother to face the yard and the people. "Notice where your dear Charlie is. Now, notice where the single—and most of the married—men are."

He watched his mother's gaze move from Charlie, who was talking to a group of married couples, teenagers and senior citizens, to Kendra and Quinn who were lounging on a picnic table surrounded by eager men. Graham grinned as understanding dawned in his mother's eyes. His amusement turned to concern when something like disappointment flitted across her expression.

"You're right, Graham. I shouldn't meddle," she said, simply, then patted his arm. "Could you grab the pitcher of tea off the table in the kitchen and bring it to the picnic table for me? It was too heavy for me to lift."

She started down the stairs and Graham abruptly grabbed her arm. His mother looked at him, expectantly. He tried to explain, "Charlie is a great girl, Mom, but…she would expect things. She'd want things. You don't mess with a girl like her unless you're ready."

"Ready for what, Graham?"

"For…" Graham's voice trailed off as he glanced around the yard at the families around him. "For all of this," he finally said.

Eliza smiled then patted his cheek. "No one's ever ready for it, son. You just grab hands with the person you love, take a deep breath and jump."

Graham watched his mother walk down the steps then searched the crowd for Charlie.

Charlie's head ached. Every time she attended a social event her head ended up hurting. Maybe it was all the forced smiles and the small talk, but inevitably, her head would feel as if it was in vise. She glanced around the yard, noticing that at some point the sun had gone down and the lights hung around the yard through the trees had been turned on. The band on stage had stopped singing cheerful songs and had moved on to songs of heartbreak and want, and most of the men and women with small children were going home. Charlie also noticed that most of the men left behind were inching closer and closer to Quinn and Kendra. None had spared Charlie a glance. Well, she had to admit that wasn't true. Throughout the party, she had noticed Graham glowering at her. She could always count on a good glower from Graham.

Charlie definitely needed a break, especially since the night was going in the direction that she had predicted. The music would start, then the dancing. Quinn and Kendra would get asked to dance by every man at the party, while Charlie would find a dark corner and pray that no one noticed that she never got asked.

Charlie bit her bottom lip to restrain the sudden flood

of emotions. She was tired, her head ached, her feet hurt from standing for so long and she hadn't gotten a decent night's sleep due to her lumpy bed.

Charlie scanned the crowd and saw no sign of Graham. For some reason, that made her feel worse. It was official. She was heading back to the shack. Quinn and Kendra wouldn't miss her and, other than maybe Eliza, no one else would either.

Charlie turned to make her escape and nearly collided with a tall, imposing older man. He smiled at her, but the smile didn't entirely reach his eyes. It took Charlie several seconds to realize that a woman stood behind him. The woman wore a brown turtleneck and a pair of blue jeans a size too big, so that almost every inch of her body was covered, except her hands and face. Her skin was pale and her hair and eyes were the exact same color of brown.

"I'm Boyd Robbins, the mayor of this paradise on earth," the man boomed, offering his hand.

Charlie shook his hand and tried not to cringe from his strong grip. She placed him in the category of a man who did not know his own strength. "It's nice to meet you. I'm Charlie Sibley."

"The art curator," Boyd said, with another obviously forced grin that split his weathered, tanned face. "I always tell my wife, the only thing that would make Sibleyville better is a museum. The Robbinses are strong supporters of the arts."

Charlie glanced at the woman who must have been Boyd's wife. Noting her glance, Boyd said, offhandedly, "This is Alma, my wife."

Alma seemed surprised that Charlie offered her hand.

And, after several seconds, she shook it. Her hand felt weak and delicate. Charlie wondered how in the world this delicate woman survived Boyd.

"Tell me, Charlie, how are you enjoying our town?" Boyd asked, while leaning towards her, as if he was on the verge of telling a big secret.

"From what I've seen of it so far, I like it," she lied.

"I've lived here my whole life. So has Alma. We knew your grandfather. If you want to see some of his old stomping grounds or hear some of his old tales, let us know. In fact, I insist that you and your sisters come over for dinner next week. You can meet our sons and their families. Doesn't that sound fun?"

Charlie murmured, "It certainly does." She didn't have to go to the Robbins's house to know that bringing these two people together with Quinn and Kendra would be a huge mistake.

"How about Tuesday?"

"Tuesday?" Charlie repeated, uncertainly.

"Better yet. Let's make it Sunday after church. Alma will make her world-famous meat loaf and apple cobbler. Once you've tasted her cobbler, you'll never want to leave." His eyes glinted with a hardness that made Charlie reflexively step back. "What do you say, Charlie? We do have business to discuss after all, and we may as well do it over a nice slice of apple cobbler rather than in some dusty courtroom."

Charlie sputtered in surprise, "Courtroom?"

"Boyd, I see you're being your usual charming self," came Lance's voice as he walked over to stand next to Charlie. "Good evening, Alma."

Charlie smiled at him, hoping her relief was not too obvious. Lance winked at her in return then motioned to a tall, thin man standing next to him. "Charlie, this is my best friend, Angus. Angus sits on council with Graham. You have any trouble at all with Boyd and Angus will rally enough votes at the town council to censure Boyd."

Angus smiled at Charlie and nodded eagerly. "Just give me a sign, Charlie."

"The town council has no authority to censure me. And even if it did, I doubt it could censure me for talking to someone," Boyd protested.

"Boyd also never did learn how to take a joke," Lance said, sounding almost good-natured, and not his usual grumpy self. "We've known each other almost sixty years, and he still can't tell when I'm joking."

"That's because you weren't joking," Angus explained.

"Oh, that's right, I wasn't," Lance confirmed, causing Charlie to laugh.

Boyd looked ready to explode as he snarled, "The apple doesn't fall far from the tree, Forbes. You have no respect for law and order and neither does your son."

"It's a shame, isn't it? Poor Graham. He never had a chance," Lance agreed, with a poor attempt at looking shameful.

Charlie coughed over her laugh, while Angus made no attempt to hide his own. Boyd fumed, his face turning a peculiar shade of red, visible even under the dim lanterns.

"Charlie, go grab an old man a beer, will you?" Lance said, gently prodding her towards the house.

Charlie smiled at him gratefully then glanced at the Robbinses. "Nice to meet you both."

"We still need to discuss—"

Lance interrupted Boyd, "I'm thirsty, Charlie. I've been standing over that grill all day. Do you want me to collapse from dehydration? Go on."

Charlie shrugged helplessly at Boyd then practically ran towards the house. She walked into the dark house and sighed in relief. It was so blissfully quiet inside the house. All of the windows were open and she could hear the din of conversations and music, but for the first time in hours, she was alone, with no one studying her, watching her, trying to decipher her motives. Now was her chance to escape.

Charlie turned for the front door and walked straight into a hard, unyielding warm body. There was a curse in the darkness and then the sound of something large and plastic clattering to the floor. Cold wetness sloshed against her feet and Charlie screamed. She heard a curse and the room was plunged into light.

Charlie's mouth dropped open as she stared at Graham standing near the light fixture with tea soaking through the front of his shirt, plastering the cotton to his lean, muscled chest. Then she noticed his expression. If he had been a cartoon, steam would have been rising from his face. With exaggerated slowness, Graham wiped drops of tea from his face and flicked it away.

"I should have known," he growled.

Charlie tried hard not to laugh. She really did, but Graham was so…outdone, and it was really kind of funny how accidents always seemed to happen around him. She wasn't usually a clumsy person, but there was something about him that just brought them together like two colliding forces of nature.

The more difficult it became for Charlie to contain her laughter, the deeper and deeper Graham's frown became.

"Oh, dear, what happened in here?" came Eliza's dismayed voice as she ran into the living room.

Charlie instantly stopped laughing as she surveyed the damage. Thankfully, no tea appeared to have touched the leather sofa nearby or the thick rug on the floor, but it had pooled onto the entrance of the living room on the hardwood floor and into the hallway. Not to mention that Graham looked as if he had taken a shower.

"Charlie happened," Graham answered, through gritted teeth.

Eliza glanced from Graham to Charlie and Charlie could have sworn Eliza's mouth twitched before she said, "Graham, go change. I'll clean up down here."

Graham shot Charlie one last glare, then turned on his heel. His heavy footsteps resounded through the room before he began to trudge up the stairs.

"What can I do to help?" Charlie asked, turning to Eliza.

"I'll take care of this. You go help Graham," Eliza murmured, distractedly, as she checked a nearby chair to make certain it was unharmed.

Charlie froze at the mention of Graham. "Eliza, I—"

"Go on," Eliza shooed, still absorbed in her inspection. "Up the stairs. Second door on the left."

Charlie hesitated, then walked out of the room. She climbed the stairs, dreading the confrontation with Graham. He would scream. She would scream. And then she would receive another lecture from Quinn about her attitude. The whole thing was growing tiresome.

Charlie noticed the row of framed family photographs on the wall leading to Graham's bedroom and couldn't help but smile at the various pictures of Graham at different ages. Was it really a surprise that he had been an adorable baby, a cute kid and then a sexy teenager who probably made older women wish they were a little younger?

Charlie stopped in front of his bedroom door and hesitantly knocked. Because she didn't think Graham would welcome her into his room, she opened the door and stepped inside.

The air trapped in her lungs and she froze as she saw Graham standing near a dresser, bare-chested, with a clean shirt in his hands. His chest was… It was beautiful. She had known he was big, but his clothes had hidden how big he was. How strong. An even coat of furry dark hair covered his chest, with the exception of two dark nipples. A network of muscles glided under beautiful brown skin. And all that hair tapered to disappear into the waistband of well-worn, wet jeans that showcased just enough to let Charlie know that he was big all over.

She remembered to breathe and forced herself to stop staring at his chest. She lifted her gaze to his and once more found herself breathless at the darkness that gleamed in his expression.

Graham dropped the shirt and walked—or maybe stalked was a better word—towards her. She took several defensive steps back until she bumped into the

wall. She tried to stand her ground, but it was really hard
when a six-foot man was standing only inches from
her, staring at her as if he wanted to completely devour
her. Desire lit in her stomach and traveled lower, igniting
a flush across her entire body.

Graham moved slowly, as if not to frighten her,
placing his hands on the wall on either side of her face,
effectively trapping her. Not that she could have moved,
even if she'd wanted to.

"I'm going to kiss you now, Charlie," he said, his
voice thicker and deeper than she had ever heard it.

She gasped. Graham couldn't kiss her. He didn't
even like her, except then he was lowering his head, and
Charlie knew that whether he liked her or not, he was
going to kiss her.

Chapter 11

Graham meant to kiss Charlie only once. Just to get the thought out of his head. He had been dreaming about her lips and imagining their taste ever since they had talked at the corral. And all night at the party, he had watched her until he had become more and more aroused. He had spent half the damn party hiding his boner. And now she was in his bedroom, and Graham planned to kiss her just once and go on with the rest of his life, free of this strange obsession with her mouth.

Except, after he had brushed his lips against hers, Graham had the sinking feeling that *obsession* was a mild word for what was happening to him. His hands on the wall clenched into fists as he fought the urge to grab her, throw her on the bed and plunge into the wet warmth that he knew awaited him.

Graham settled his mouth against hers again. A chaste, innocent kiss, fit for two children. Her lips were soft and slightly damp. Addictive. He pressed another soft kiss against her mouth. Graham pulled away from her slightly, staring at her upturned face. Her eyes slowly fluttered open and he became harder at the desire dancing in their dark depths. Her hands were still clenched at her sides. The tips of her breasts were mere inches from his bare chest, and Graham felt like a magnet attracted to their fullness. She was not plump, as he'd first thought. She was voluptuous. Like a Renaissance painting, except in place of the usual pale skin, there was brown beauty.

The two stared at each other for a moment, as their combined deep breaths filled the silent room. Despite the cool air floating into the room through the open windows and open door, the room suddenly felt hot.

Suddenly Graham could not control himself. He dipped his head again and brushed his mouth against hers. She made a strange sound in the back of her throat and he brushed his mouth against hers again. He wanted more. He definitely wanted more, but he was content just to touch her, to taste her. He ran his tongue along the seam of her closed mouth and then gently nipped her lower lip. She sighed into his mouth and Graham used the unspoken invitation to slip his tongue inside her mouth.

Lightning struck in his brain as he tasted her sweet depths. He groaned and stepped closer, pressing his body against her softness. Every inch of their bodies touched, pressed together. He felt one of her hands move onto his arm and then up his back to touch the back of his neck. And that touch did it. Made him lose the restraint he was trying so hard for.

He grabbed her waist feeling warm skin above the waistband of her pants and slammed her against him as he ate her mouth. Tried to swallow all of her sweetness whole. And the best part was that she was giving back just as good as she got. She raised on her tiptoes and met his tongue stroke for stroke, resuming the kisses when Graham tried to leave for air, holding his head in place by his neck, refusing to allow either one of them to retreat. Their tongues battled, then soothed then parried and played. Her breasts pressed against his chest, her nipples beading and pressing through her clothes to act like red-hot irons against his chest.

He settled his hardness against her, and she subtly moved her hips to fit him. It drove Graham crazy. He tightened his hands on her waist, hoping that he wasn't hurting her, but he couldn't let go. He wanted more. More of her delicious mouth. More of her breasts. More of her.

He abruptly wrenched free of her mouth and forced his hands to release her. He stumbled back several steps and stared at her. He almost went to her again. Her lips were slightly swollen, her hair was mussed and her eyes were wide and bright.

Graham took one step towards her, his eyes on her breasts. Charlie abruptly held up her hand and he stopped, staring at her, confused.

"We can't," she whispered, shaking her head. Something like sadness and guilt moved across her face.

"Like hell," he said, indignantly.

She shook her head again and as her hair swung side

to side, Graham realized that he hadn't touched her hair. He hadn't touched her face. He hadn't touched her breasts or those gorgeous legs, or the curls that he knew awaited him between her legs. He had big plans for her.

Then Graham remembered where he was. While probably his adolescent self would be jumping up and down at the idea of taking her in his bedroom, the adult Graham liked to think he had a little more class than that.

"You're right," he said, with a sigh. He dragged a hand down his face then said, "We'll have to go back to your place."

She looked shocked at his suggestion. "What?"

Graham walked over to her again, until she once more backed against the wall. "We need to finish what we started," he growled.

Graham would have been ashamed of his own behavior if he hadn't been so damn horny. Her nipples, still beaded against the thin blue top she wore, were calling to him. He wanted to rip off that accursed shirt and take one into his mouth.

"No," she said, simply.

She easily stepped around him and put more distance between them. Graham turned to watch her behind in the tan capris. She had a great ass. He had noticed that before, but had tried to ignore it. He wanted to fill his hands with her ass, while he… He forced himself to hold off the visions that danced in his head because she had turned around to face him and she was frowning.

"You don't even like me," she said in a confused whisper.

"Apparently, I do." He resisted directing her attention to the proof of how much he liked her at the front of his pants.

She stared at him confused then she said, "What about my sisters?"

"What about them?"

She looked embarrassed as she said, "They want you."

"And?"

"And… You want them, right? I mean, every man usually wants them, especially men like you."

"Men like me?" he said, intrigued, leaning against the wall. "What is that supposed to mean?"

He saw her glance towards the door, as if to break for an emergency exit, and he tried to hide his smile. He could not remember having so much fun while clothed and with a raging hard-on.

"You know what it means," she shot back, crossing her arms over her chest.

"Men like me… Men who are thirty-two years old. Men who are six foot two. Men who—"

"Fine, I'll say it," she interrupted, with a groan of exasperation. "Gorgeous men like you. Men like you who have never had to work for a date or a phone number. Men like you who walk down the street and get to pick and choose who they want. You know you're gorgeous, so don't even try to deny it. Men like you always end up with women like my sisters."

He sobered and moved to her side, unable to handle the distance between them any longer. Did he always feel the need to touch a woman like this, he wondered, as he stroked a thumb down her velvet left check. She held his gaze and he felt something settle in his bones, something that he had never felt before and he wasn't sure if he wanted to feel it now.

"Why can't I be the type of man who ends up with a woman like you?" he asked, quietly.

She regarded him silently for a moment then moved towards the door again. He watched her, uncertain what he had said wrong and wondering why in the hell he had said that to begin with. Charlie abruptly stopped and stared at him.

"I'm not a toy, either, Graham," she said, quietly.

Charlie inwardly cursed as tears filled her eyes. The last thing she wanted to do was cry in front of him. His expression gentled and it made her want to cry even more. He was so perfect that it was a given any woman who came within ten feet of him would fall in love. It wasn't fair. He could have at least come with a persistent case of bad breath or body odor, anything to even the odds and give a woman some chance for resistance.

He promised her things with his eyes, with his mouth that scared her. She was not naive. She had dated men. She had been with men. She had not had sex, but she had never met a man who made her want to have sex. Her sisters thought she was insane, but Charlie liked to think she was just picky. Now, she knew the truth. She had been waiting for Graham. She also knew that he was going to break her heart.

He started towards her, then stopped. His hands hung at his sides, uncertain. "I'm sorry. I didn't mean to come on so strong, but you… You make me do things and say things that I…."

She swallowed hard, but remained silent. He approached her, slowly and carefully, as if she were a wild, wounded animal. Then he placed his hands on her shoulders. Just comforting.

"Are we okay again?" he asked, with a slight smile.

She nodded, while licking her lips. She didn't want to be his friend, but she also wasn't certain that she wanted to move as fast as Graham was moving.

"I'm sorry—"

He abruptly kissed her again, cutting off her apology. A hard, brief kiss that rocked her to her core. He pulled back from her, then shook his head with an apologetic smile.

"Don't apologize to me, Charlie. I don't deserve it, especially since I'm trying really hard here to be noble, but it's kind of hard with you only a few feet from my bed."

Charlie smiled, which made him grin. She walked out the room, her lips tingling and something like wonder blooming in her heart. She quickly shook her head. Quinn was right. Graham was the most fascinating man Charlie had ever met, or probably ever would meet, but there was no future with him. And she just had to work on protecting herself a little better before she went any farther with him. She knew that she would go farther because, for some reason, Graham wanted her, and she was not going to waste this opportunity.

Chapter 12

It had been two days since Graham had kissed Charlie, and she was crawling out of her skin with the need to see him. She wanted to make certain that he wasn't planning any crazy revenge against her sisters, and she wanted to make certain that she hadn't scared him away. She had wanted him to move a little slower, not become nonexistent.

His kisses haunted her dreams. His smile haunted her dreams. She hadn't been able to sleep with thoughts of him in her head.

Charlie had finally given in and decided to act like the lovesick fool that she was. She put on her tennis shoes and jogging pants and a T-shirt and pretended to take a walk that coincidentally led her directly to Graham's front door. Except once she reached the

Forbes's front door and saw how quiet the house was, she was suddenly grateful. Graham obviously had forgotten about their kiss and was probably plotting the number of ways he could make Quinn and Kendra do whatever he wanted.

Charlie glared at the front door and whirled around to stalk back home and bury herself in the pint of chocolate ice cream she had hidden in the back of the freezer. Her sisters could have him. And the next time he came within arm's reach, Charlie was going to do a lot more than dump paint on his head.

"Charlie, is that you?"

Charlie had been so wrapped in her thoughts that she hadn't noticed Lance walking around the house, his familiar Chicago Cubs cap in place.

"Good afternoon, Mr. Forbes," Charlie said, smiling, then lied badly, "I was just taking a walk and I happened to pass by your house and I thought I'd come in and say hi."

"Call me Lance. And I have to say that you Sibley sisters are mighty neighborly," Lance noted, lightly, then added dryly. "And athletic."

"My sisters have stopped by?" Charlie asked, surprised.

She hadn't spoken to either of her sisters that morning or most of last night. Charlie had spent most of the day in her room, reading magazines, because she didn't want to deal with her guilt or their arguments, which she still heard through her bedroom wall.

"Kendra came by yesterday and this morning. Quinn drove over this morning. And I'll tell you what I told them—Graham was out of town on business for the ranch yesterday, and he's at church with his mother today. They even dragged Theo along. The poor fool has just been sitting and staring at all of his electronic contraptions, I guess hoping they'll suddenly come to life, so Eliza thought it would be good to get him out of the house."

Charlie inwardly groaned at what Lance must have thought of her and her sisters. What Graham must have thought. Whether Charlie had thrown her hat in the ring or not, it looked as though she was competing with her sisters.

"I wasn't looking for Graham…" Her automatic protest faded, as she met Lance's doubtful expression. She finally shrugged helplessly, and Lance laughed. She asked, "Why aren't *you* at church?"

He winced as he dramatically massaged his denim-encased right leg. "It's funny how my leg acts up every Sunday morning like clockwork. The injury, y'know."

"I thought it was your left leg," she said, while pointedly staring at his hand massaging the wrong leg.

Lance straightened and threw up his hands. "I'm healed. It's a miracle." She laughed and shook her head. He smiled then said, "That's our secret."

"I won't say a word."

"Come around back with me. There's more shade."

The two walked around the house to the back porch. An easel was set up on the back porch, along with a stool in front of it. Two wicker chairs sat on the other side of the porch, with a pitcher of lemonade on the table between them. Curiously, Charlie glanced at the easel.

It was a half-completed oil painting of a dark, star-studded night on the open range. Mountains towered in the distance, but the focal point was the campfire, with two men crowded up against it. Two Black cowboys, with cowboy hats and horses in the background and the requisite gear neatly organized around the campfire.

It was simple, but haunting. Man and nature. The West and the loneliness of a Black man. Charlie had never seen anything like it. And her skin tingled as she thought of it hanging on the walls of the center.

"Whose painting is this?" she asked, breathlessly.

"It's that bad?" Lance muttered, squinting at the painting.

"Bad?" she repeated in disbelief then walked up the steps of the porch to peer closer. "No, it's… It's wonderful. The technique, the feelings it evokes, the time it captures. A little-known part of this country's in this painting. It deserves to be displayed and talked about." She turned to him and said, firmly, "I want it for the gallery. Who painted it?"

Lance shrugged and stuck his hands in his jeans pockets, studiously avoiding her eyes.

Charlie's eyes widened as she whispered, "You."

"It's a hobby," he muttered, defensively.

"This should be more than a hobby, Lance. I…I never expected to find an artist here. I don't know why not. Picasso lived in squalor in Spain and da Vinci—"

"Picasso. Da Vinci… Come on, Charlie. It's just a few squiggles of paint," he said, but Charlie could hear the excitement in his voice.

"Trust me, Lance. You have talent. You have skill. Are you self-taught?"

"If self-taught means that I picked up a brush and started painting one day then yes."

"You're perfect. This painting is perfect," she said, excitedly. "This will bring wonderful publicity to the center. Because we are a not-for-profit organization, I can't offer you much compensation, but the recognition—"

"What gallery are you talking about?" he asked, curiously, as he walked up the steps and sat at the stool.

Charlie smiled excitedly and pulled up the wicker chair from across the porch. She now saw the paint smudges on the front of his pants and his paint-dotted hands.

"I am the curator of a private museum in Los Angeles. We showcase works by Black artists and works about the African-American experience."

"I didn't know there was a museum like that in Los Angeles."

"Not many people do," she admitted, frustrated. "But I'm trying to change all of that. In the four years I've been working there, our annual attendance has doubled and we're on the verge of acquiring several high-profile pieces. We just received several pieces on loan from the African-American collection at the Smithsonian Institute in DC."

She flushed as she realized that Lance was studying her, as if she had sprouted another head.

"It's your baby," he said, as the understatement of the year.

"It's the first thing I've ever done on my own, and I know if we just had the right pieces, we could become one of the major private art institutions, like the Getty."

"With Max Sibley as your grandfather, you must already have quite an endowment."

Charlie avoided his gaze as she murmured, "Not quite. In fact, if I don't do something soon, the gallery will close."

"I'm sorry to hear that, Charlie," he said, softly.

Before he decided to pity her, which she could not stand, she quickly explained, "Grandpa Max wanted each of his granddaughters to make it on her own. I worked at the corporation with him for years, and when I decided to run the center, he told me that he wouldn't help me, but…I'm glad he didn't. Because it's all mine. The successes, the failures, the bombs. When I took the reins, it was operating in the red. And now we're in the black…just barely, but we're there." At Lance's understanding expression, Charlie told him something she had never spoken out loud before. "It was my father. He was… He was spoiled. Selfish. So was my mother. Before they died in the plane accident, my sisters and I spent more time at Grandpa Max's house than our own. I think Grandpa Max felt responsible for their deaths, that if he hadn't given my father so much, he would have turned out differently."

"Max sounds like he still never gave himself a break," Lance muttered, picking up the paint brush that had been resting in a coffee mug.

"Did you know him?" she asked, surprised.

"No, but I've heard stories. Everyone in Sibleyville has heard stories about Max, including how he black-mailed the town into changing its name to Sibleyville in the sixties," Lance answered then added, bluntly, "And in every story, your grandfather was a bastard."

"We like to say driven," she corrected, politely. Lance

shrugged, but didn't argue with her. She asked eagerly, "Do you have any other paintings?"

He flashed a bashful smile before he murmured, "A few."

"How many are a few? If this partial is any indication of your other work, I want to display as many as I can. I envision an entire Western theme. Blacks were a part of the Wild West, and your paintings will tell their story. We'll have speakers and authors…all about the African-American experience in the West."

"Slow down, Charlie," Lance said, laughing.

"How many do you have?" she prodded again.

"About thirty." At her shocked expression, he muttered, "I've been doing this awhile."

Charlie laughed and felt the strange urge to hug Lance. Instead, she said, "Do you think I could take a look at the others?"

"Sure," he said, obviously trying hard to hide his own eagerness.

"Lance," she said, as they stood. "I think this is the start of a beautiful friendship."

He laughed then said, "Just don't let Graham find out. I don't want him thinking I'm trying to steal his girl."

The smile fell from her face as she remembered the reason she had come to the house in the first place. To see Graham, who apparently was also receiving visits from Kendra and Quinn.

"I'm not Graham's girl," she said, flatly.

"I told you he had some ranch business to take care of in San Francisco yesterday. He didn't get back into town until late last night, and then early this morning

An Important Message from the Publisher

KIMANI PRESS™

Dear Reader,

Because you've chosen to read one of our fine novels, I'd like to say "thank you"! And, as a special way to say thank you, I'm offering to send you two Kimani Romance™ novels and two surprise gifts – absolutely FREE! These books will keep it real with true-to-life African-American characters that turn up the heat and sizzle with passion.

Please enjoy the free books and gifts with our compliments...

Linda Gill

Publisher, Kimani Press

Peel off Seal and Place Inside...

PUBLISHERS
FREE GIFTS
SEAL
THANK YOU

We'd like to send you two free books to introduce you to our new line – Kimani Romance™! These novels feature strong, sexy women and African-American heroes that are charming, loving and true. Our authors fill each page with exceptional dialogue, exciting plot twists, and enough sizzling romance to keep you riveted until the very end!

KIMANI ROMANCE ... LOVE'S ULTIMATE DESTINATION

Your two books have a combined cover price o $11.98 in the U.S. and $13.98 in Canada, but are yours **FREE!** We'l even send you two wonderful surprise gifts. You can't lose

2 Free Bonus Gifts!

We'll send you two wonderful surprise gifts, absolutely FREE, just for giving KIMANI ROMANCE books a try! Don't miss out — **MAIL THE REPLY CARD TODAY!**

www.KimaniPress.com

THE EDITOR'S "THANK YOU" FREE GIFTS INCLUDE:

Two NEW Kimani Romance™ Novels
Two exciting surprise gifts

YES! I have placed my Editor's "Thank You" Free Gifts seal in the space provided at right. Please send me 2 FREE books, and my 2 FREE Mystery Gifts. I understand that I am under no obligation to purchase anything further, as explained on the back of this card.

PLACE
FREE GIFTS
SEAL
HERE

168 XDL ELWZ   368 XDL ELXZ

FIRST NAME	LAST NAME

ADDRESS

APT.#   CITY

STATE/PROV.   ZIP/POSTAL CODE

Thank You!

Offer limited to one per household and not valid to current subscribers of Kimani Romance.
Your Privacy – Kimani Press is committed to protecting your privacy. Our Privacy Policy is available online at www.eHarlequin.com or upon request from the Reader Service. From time to time we make our lists of customers available to reputable firms who may have a product or service of interest to you. If you would prefer for us not to share your name and address, please check here. ☐

® and ™ are trademarks owned and used by the trademark owner and/or its licensee. © 2006 Kimani Press.

DETACH AND MAIL CARD TODAY!

(K-ROM-07)

Eliza recruited him into driving her to church," Lance said, then added, with a knowing grin, "And if I know my son, you will see him tonight, and he'll make up for his absence."

Charlie decided it was best not to argue and, instead, clapped her hands together. "Let's see those paintings."

"Mark my words, Charlie," Lance said, grinning. "Graham will be knocking on your door tonight. Or your window. That's how I saw Eliza."

Charlie forced a smile because he seemed to expect one then said, "How about those paintings?"

"No one ever listens to an old man," Lance muttered then held open the screen door for her to enter the house.

"Is church usually that long and boring?" Theo asked, curiously, as he loosened his tie.

From the passenger seat of Graham's truck, Wyatt laughed then tore off his own tie. Graham shot a look in the rearview mirror at Theo and gave up on censuring him. He had spent most of the service censuring Theo, when Eliza hadn't been. Graham could only be grateful that Theo had waited to unleash that little bit of blasphemy until after Graham had dropped off his mother at one of her friends' homes for lunch.

"I think it was particularly long and boring today," Wyatt said, with a laugh, then glanced at Graham. "Don't you agree?"

Graham grimaced then shot another glare at Theo in the mirror. "Theo, if my mother had heard you say that about her good friend Reverend Hollister, you'd be sporting a black eye right now."

Theo rolled his eyes in response then muttered, "Black women and their pastors."

Graham's retort stuck in his throat when he saw the strange expression on Theo's face. He suddenly remembered that Theo's father was a pastor. He wisely shut his mouth. Besides, Graham had more important things to think about. Like Charlie. He hadn't been able to see her in two long days, and he could only imagine what stories she had come up with, probably ranging from him having a threesome with her sisters to him having already left for Tokyo.

Graham needed to see Charlie. He needed to touch her. Even if she didn't want him to touch her, which he sincerely hoped she did, he just wanted to be around her. Of course, he would never admit that to her or anyone else, except under threat of torture. And it would have to be pretty horrible torture.

"Where are we going?" Wyatt asked, good-naturedly, relaxing in the passenger seat. "Grab some beers and head to Bentonville? Catch a movie?"

"As much as I like you, Dubya, my idea of a pleasant evening is not catching a movie with you in some other godforsaken town," Theo announced. "I need women. Breasts. Hips. Where do you find those, gentlemen?"

Wyatt laughed in response then said, "Not in Sibleyville. Didn't you take a look around at Eliza's party the other night? There are three types of women in this town—too young, too old and too married."

Theo's groan was audible. "I did notice that. How you men survive in this town is beyond me."

"You forgot the fourth type of Sibleyville woman,

Theo," Graham said, quietly, his hands unconsciously tightening on the steering wheel as he thought of Charlie's response to his kisses. "A Sibley sister."

"Hell, no," came Theo's immediate response. "I want a relaxing evening, not one fighting with Kendra the She-Devil."

"Kendra is not that bad," Graham said, but he doubted that anyone in the truck was convinced.

"That's because she retracts her claws when you're around," Theo shot back. "To the rest of us mere mortals, she's dangerous. Like a porcupine. Prickly and liable to drop a bomb on a brother."

"For some reason, I doubt that Kendra would like the idea of being compared to a porcupine."

"Whatever," Theo dismissed. "I'd rather sit back at the ranch, holding the ball of yarn for your mother as she knits… On second thought, after spending about three hours doing that last night, maybe Kendra isn't so bad."

"Kendra is…a lot to handle," Graham conceded. "But she *is* beautiful. You can't dispute that." Theo tightened his jaw, but remained silent. Graham then shot a look at Wyatt, who stared out the window, seemingly in another world. "Are you contemplating jumping? Kendra isn't that bad, is she?"

Wyatt appeared to realize that Graham was talking to him and turned to Graham with a guilty smile. "No…I don't mind Kendra. I talked to her a little bit at the party. She and I don't have much in common, but she seemed nice enough."

"Nice enough," Theo sputtered in disbelief. "Nice enough if you like fire-breathing women."

"We got your dislike for Kendra, Theo," Graham said then asked, casually, "What about the other two?"

"What man wouldn't like Quinn? She's like a PG-13 Playboy Bunny come to life," Theo immediately said. "And Charlie is… She's easy to talk to."

Graham glared at Theo in the mirror. Charlie was a lot more than easy to talk to. She made Graham laugh. She made him want to make her laugh. Not to mention the fact that her mouth tasted like paradise and he had become addicted to the feel of her breasts.

"What about you, Wyatt?" Graham asked, deciding to ignore Theo before he hit him.

"I don't mind one way or the other," Wyatt said, his voice sounding strangely flat. "You know me, Graham, I can get along with anyone."

Graham studied his friend for a moment then turned his attention back to the road. Something was bothering Wyatt. Graham wondered if there was an upcoming funeral or something.

"We'll pick up a six-pack, chocolate and some meat for the grill, and then we'll head for the Sibleys' house."

"Chocolate?" Wyatt questioned, staring at Graham. "Why chocolate?"

"Women like chocolate," Graham mumbled. Maybe he had noticed at the party that Charlie had spent an inordinate amount of time staring at the two chocolate cakes on the dessert table. She had limited herself to only one piece, but the expression on her face when she had eaten the piece had been enough to send Graham into the house before he had stalked across the yard and tried to put that expression on her face himself.

"Quinn doesn't eat chocolate," Wyatt said, quietly. "She barely ate anything at the party."

Graham glanced at Wyatt surprised, wondering if his friend had joined every other man in town and had become starstruck. He wouldn't have thought that Wyatt would be attracted to Quinn, but it seemed every man was attracted to Quinn... Except Graham. No matter what he told his body, he wanted Charlie.

"We need playing cards, too," Theo chimed in. Graham shot a look of surprise over his shoulder and Theo shrugged, "Well, it's not like I have a choice in the matter."

"Should we call to ask them if we can stop by?" Wyatt asked, worriedly.

Graham thought of Charlie's reaction if they called first. He had scared her the night of the party. She probably wasn't ready to see him again. It was too bad that he couldn't go another day without seeing her.

He smiled and said, "Definitely not. We'll surprise them."

"If there's one thing I have learned in my thirty-two years on this earth, it is that women do not like surprises, unless there are diamonds involved," Theo said, with a warning note in his voice.

Graham shook his head in amusement. He did not doubt that Charlie would leave him to Kendra and Quinn if he arrived by himself, but with Theo and Wyatt in tow, Charlie would have no choice but to remain with them. Graham was not allowing Charlie to get away. At least, not until he left for Tokyo. So he would do something that he hadn't been forced to do in a while—court a woman.

Chapter 13

Graham glanced at his two friends, laden with paper bags, then took a deep breath and turned to the door of the Sibley shack. He was not worried about Kendra's and Quinn's reaction to their surprise visit. If Charlie had told the truth, both women would welcome him with open arms and probably open other parts of their body that it was best for Graham not to think of. Charlie's reaction to their visit, on the other hand, was likely going to be a little more unpredictable.

To stall for more time, he took a moment to admire the newly painted and repaired house. He turned to Wyatt with a grin and said, "You guys did a great job."

Theo abruptly reached around Graham and knocked on the door. Graham glared at him and Theo responded, "It was either stand here all night, while you think about knocking, or one of us knocking and getting the show on the road."

Graham's retort was interrupted as Charlie opened the door. Her mouth dropped open in wordless surprise as she looked from Wyatt to Theo and finally her gaze rested on Graham. Graham grinned, suddenly glad that Theo had knocked. This was exactly where he should be. She looked delightfully tousled in a pair of black shorts and a tank top that loosely hung on her body, but draped against her breasts.

Graham wondered what she would do if he grabbed her and planted another kiss on her open mouth. Before he could see for himself, Theo and Wyatt walked around him.

"We bring gifts," Theo said, cheerfully. "Food. Beer. Chocolate. And playing cards."

Charlie's surprise turned into a delighted smile as she looked from Theo to Wyatt. "Chocolate…come in."

The two men walked into the house, leaving Graham alone on the porch. He smiled at Charlie, which made her frown.

"What are you doing here?" she asked, keeping her voice low.

"You heard Theo—food, beer and chocolate. Oh, and playing cards."

"You're here to torture Kendra and Quinn," she said, suspiciously.

Graham didn't know why she made him smile so much, but she did. He stepped closer and leaned down until their lips were close enough to touch. "The only Sibley sister I plan to torture tonight is you."

A high-pitched scream interrupted her reply. Graham

brushed past her to run into the house. He stopped in his tracks when he saw Quinn, screeching in outrage, as she attempted to cover her ragged robe and rolled-up hair from Wyatt's and Theo's stares.

Kendra, who wore a jogging suit, and sat on the sofa, rolled her eyes and said, "Instead of screaming like a bad horror movie victim, go change, Quinn."

Quinn screamed once more and ran up the stairs. Theo and Wyatt glanced at Graham, who shrugged, then took off his suit jacket. "All right, ladies. Who's up for burgers, beer and a little Texas Hold 'Em."

"You're on, Forbes," Kendra said, grinning. She grabbed the playing cards from Theo's hands and twirled the box around her hand as she looked at Graham. "We could always play strip poker."

"I vote for not seeing Graham or Wyatt naked, but if you want to strip every time you lose a hand, feel free," Theo said.

Kendra glared at him, while the others tried not to laugh. Charlie moved to take the bags from Wyatt and Theo.

"You all get started playing, and I'll get the food ready," she said.

"Oh, no," Graham said, smoothly taking the bags from her arms. "The boys and I brought the food, so we're going to cook it."

"Graham, really, if Charlie wants to—"

Graham cut off a panicked Theo and said to Charlie, "We're cooking."

She held his gaze for a moment then nodded. "If you insist."

Graham glanced at his friends and said, "You guys set up the game. Charlie can show me around the kitchen. We'll be eating Forbes's world-famous chili-cheese-bacon-wrapped dogs in no time."

"Chili-cheese-bacon-wrapped dogs?" Kendra said, sitting straighter on the sofa.

Graham would have laughed at the distress across her face, if he didn't think Charlie would hit him for that. He bit his bottom lip to keep from laughing, then said, "Yeah, every woman I've ever dated has loved my dogs. My last girlfriend could eat three in one sitting. I don't think any other woman has gained my respect more."

Charlie's eyes narrowed, while Kendra looked decidedly crestfallen.

"Come with me, Graham," Charlie said, grimly.

He followed her into the kitchen, staring directly at her behind. As soon as the door swung closed, Graham dropped the bags on the table, grabbed her around the waist and slammed his mouth on hers, swallowing her shocked gasp.

It was amazing how one kiss could make everything seem right. Graham's fatigue, irritation and frustration washed away. Graham's entire being focused on Charlie's soft mouth and pliable tongue and the way her body perfectly fitted against his.

He tasted her and devoured her and claimed her all at once. Graham became insatiable. Every time she tried to pull away, he followed her, capturing her lips, plunging his tongue into her mouth over and over again. He forced himself to pull away so that he could breathe, and he dipped in for another kiss when he saw her dazed eyes. He wanted to keep that expression on her face through the night and the morning.

"I can't stop kissing you," he murmured, against her mouth, just before he nipped her earlobe and then ran his tongue along the rim of her ear. He moved back to envelop her mouth in another searing kiss that left her breathing hard and him just hard.

"Kendra and Quinn are just outside the door," she sighed, her hands clinging to the front of his shirt.

"You taste so sweet, Charlie," he whispered, as he captured her lips again. "I know I'm supposed to be going slow, but—"

"Someone's coming," she whispered, panicked, pushing against her chest.

He abruptly released her as he heard heels slapping against the hardwood floor towards the kitchen. Quinn walked into the kitchen. Graham blinked in surprise at Quinn's rapid transformation. She had gone from hair in rollers, lounging at home in a bathrobe, to Hollywood glamour in about two minutes flat. Her hair gleamed in soft waves past her shoulders and she wore a tight, lime-green dress that played to the undercurrent of green in her eyes. Her face shone brightly with expertly applied makeup.

"Graham, I didn't even see you at the door," Quinn said, regally.

"I walked in right around the time you were screaming and running out of the room," Graham said, helpfully.

"I felt underdressed since you all are in suits," Quinn mumbled then asked, brightly, "What are you boys doing here?"

"We've come to fix you dinner. My family's world-famous chili-cheese dogs."

Graham almost thought that Quinn would faint at the mention of the dogs. "Chili…and cheese," she choked out.

"And I'm going to insist, Quinn, that you eat at least two," Graham said. "At the very least."

"Two," Quinn repeated, turning a distinct shade of green.

Kendra burst into the kitchen, with Wyatt and Theo close on her heels. Graham inwardly groaned and looked at Charlie, who now stood out of his reach across the kitchen and was looking at everyone, but him. So much for private time with Charlie.

"What's going on in here?" Kendra asked, staring suspiciously from Graham to Quinn.

"We're about to start cooking," Graham answered. "And did I mention that we brought the ingredients for a chocolate cake?"

Kendra gasped in dismay, Quinn looked ready to faint and Charlie looked at him as if he were a hero. All in all, it was turning into a great night.

Charlie had to admit it; she was having a good time. Theo was hilarious. Wyatt was charmingly sweet, and Graham…Graham was Graham. When no one watched, he gave her searing looks that sent heat to the tips of her toes. Even Kendra and Quinn seemed to be enjoying themselves. Both had devoured chili-cheese dogs in a bid to gain Graham's favor and to one-up each other. Charlie knew that she shouldn't have taken secret pleasure in watching them stuff their faces with pure fat, but she couldn't help it. She was only human and, therefore, slightly petty.

After eating the hot dogs, demolishing the cake and drinking through the case of beer, night fell and the six sat around the lopsided coffee table, playing cards. Before Graham had appeared on the porch, Charlie had envisioned another night locked in her room, ignoring her sisters and her sisters ignoring each other. Instead, she had been kissed like the most desirable woman in the house and she sat across from Graham, who as the night progressed didn't bother to hide that he wanted her alone again.

"So, tell us about Hollywood, Quinn," Theo said, before taking a quick draw from his beer bottle. "What's it really like?"

Quinn gave Theo a real smile and said, simply, "It's wonderful."

"The paparazzi, the scrutiny, the pressure to be perfect… How could that be wonderful?" Wyatt asked, his voice tight.

Quinn's smile faded and her expression tightened. Charlie noticed that Quinn refused to look at Wyatt, which surprised Charlie. Quinn was self-centered and a self-admitted snob, but she was never purposely rude.

"Most actors act because they love it," she said, quietly, finally looking at Wyatt. Charlie studied her sister and Wyatt, wondering why she felt as if both had forgotten there were other people in the room. "Most of us start out waiting tables, going on auditions, enduring every manner of humiliation… But we do it for the potential of being on the movie screen, making little boys and girls dream like we did once. It's not about the fame or the money. It's about the craft."

Kendra's snort of disbelief was loud and partially fueled by alcohol. "Spare us the craft speech, Quinn," Kendra slurred, while waving around a can of beer. "Your most well-known-and-only role to date is on a soap opera. And I've seen your show. You're hardly working on your craft with that drivel."

Charlie felt her own cheeks sting with embarrassment as Quinn's eyes filled with unshed tears.

"Lots of great actors get their starts on soaps," Theo quickly said to fill the sudden, awkward silence.

"Oh, please," Kendra said, sarcastically.

"There's nothing wrong with daytime television," Wyatt said quietly and with such conviction that Charlie believed he really meant it.

"How touching," Kendra said, with an attempt at a soothing noise. "Wyatt and Theo rush to be Quinn's white knight, while her big sister picks on her. Believe me, boys, she doesn't need it. While Quinn is not a very good actress, she *can* act, and she's pulling the wool over all of our eyes. While she's spouting about the craft and the sacredness of acting, she won't even look at a part that offers less than six figures. Isn't that right, Quinn?"

"Kendra, that's enough," Charlie said in a low, warning voice.

"You don't know what you're talking about, Kendra," Quinn said, angrily.

"As a matter of fact, I do," Kendra continued. "I know that you were offered the role in that independent movie that Regina King received an Oscar nomination for last year, but you refused to do it because they couldn't meet your salary demand."

"Shut up," Charlie ordered, conscious of Graham's concerned gaze on her.

Kendra's smile was nasty as she focused on Quinn. "I also heard some other juicy gossip before I was sent here."

Even Theo's smile had disappeared as he said, "Kendra, you've had too much to drink. Let's make some coffee and sober you up."

He stood and pulled a protesting Kendra to her feet. She tried to push him away, but Theo didn't budge. Kendra swayed on her feet then focused on Quinn once more.

"I heard that your character was being killed off in *Diamond Valley* because the fans are bored with you," Kendra announced. "The fans are bored, the writers are sick of your tantrums and demands and your co-workers can't stand to work with you. I even heard that it's going to be an open-casket funeral. And we all know what that means in Soap World. That means, you're not coming back—"

"Kendra, go get your coffee," Wyatt said. He didn't raise his voice, but there was something in his voice that made Kendra immediately stop talking and look ashamed.

A thick silence fell across the room then Kendra yanked away from Theo. With a half-choked, "Excuse me," she ran out of the house.

Theo stared helplessly at Charlie, and she shrugged at his unspoken question. He looked like he wanted to run after her, but instead, he stuffed his hands in his pockets.

"I'm really tired," Quinn said, in a subdued voice.

She didn't meet anyone's eyes as she stood. "Thanks for the dinner and the company. I had a good time. Really."

She walked out of the room and Charlie heard the quiet click of her bedroom door upstairs.

Charlie forced an apologetic smile at Graham, Wyatt and Theo and said, with an awkward laugh, "Another quiet night with the Sibley sisters."

She felt Graham's eyes on her, but ignored him as she gathered the empty beer cans on the table.

"Theo, can you give Wyatt a ride home?" Graham asked. "I'm going to help Charlie clean up."

"Of course. Thanks for a... Good night, Charlie," Theo said. Wyatt muttered something akin to that and the two men walked out of the house.

Graham didn't move until he heard the truck's engine fade into the night. He placed his hands on Charlie's arms and made her set the beer cans back on the table. She couldn't resist any longer and looked into his beautiful eyes. And she wished she hadn't because it was as though he understood everything she was feeling. The loneliness, the dread about the future. Everything.

"It's too hot in here. Let's go outside," he said, in that deep voice that she couldn't argue with.

He led her through the house and to the darkness of the back porch. The serviceable porch swing, repaired by Graham's friends, rocked softly in the night breeze. She and Graham sank onto the swing. He didn't allow distance between them and pulled her into his arms.

Charlie sank against the solid warmth of his chest and stared into the moonlit fields behind the house. She felt strangely safe in his arms. Like she belonged.

"I'm sorry you had to witness that," she said, breaking the silence between them.

"You have nothing to apologize for."

"Yes, I do," she said, with a dry laugh.

"You're not responsible for your sisters."

"I know, but… You wouldn't understand."

"Try me," he said, his eyes boring into hers.

Charlie wanted to trust him, wanted to tell him everything, about the will, the money, but instead she shook her head. "Just your usual dysfunctional family."

"You're the only thing that holds Kendra and Quinn together."

"I know, and it scares the hell out of me," she admitted. "I don't know what's going to happen to us, when we leave here. We always had Grandpa Max to act as the anchor for all of us, but now that he's gone… I don't know what I'm going to do. I can't keep them together on my own, and I don't want to. They left. They moved away to have their lives, knowing that I was there to take care of Grandpa Max. I did it. I'm done trying to heal other people. It's my turn to be selfish."

"You're not being selfish, Charlie."

She lowered her voice to a whisper as she said, "Sometimes I think that when we leave here, I never want to talk to them again."

Graham squeezed her, as if he realized how difficult that was for her to admit. He was silent for a moment then asked, "What are you going to do after you leave here?"

She sighed and linked her hand with the one on his lap. She studied his calloused, large hand. It bespoke of his strength and his hard work. She traced the length of each finger as she said, softly, "I'm not sure. The museum will probably close by next month, unless a miracle happens. I guess I'll have to look for another job."

"What else would you do?"

"I don't know, probably one of the executives at Sibley Corporation would give me a job."

"Is that what you want to do?"

"Art is my life. Bringing new artists to the community, opening up a child's eyes to the art world, telling our history... That's my passion, but like most people, I have to accept that living your passion does not pay the light bill."

When his arms tightened even more, she raised her head to meet his concerned gaze. She smiled at the worry obvious in his face.

"You don't have to worry about me, Graham. I'm a Sibley. We always land on our feet."

"I'm not worried about you, Charlie... Okay, maybe I am a little bit," he admitted then said in a rush, "I have a few friends in Los Angeles. I can call them and see what jobs they know about.... You never know."

She could barely breathe at the concern she heard in his voice. Graham might not be in love with her, but he was concerned about her. She abruptly turned in his arms, ignoring his grunt of pain as her elbow rammed into his stomach.

"Why did you send Wyatt over here the other day?" she demanded.

He frowned, confused. "What?"

"Wyatt said you called him after you left here the

other day morning and told him to come do a few repairs because you didn't want me to break my neck—"

"Charlie, we're talking about your future here," he said, irritably. "You need a game plan. If the museum does close, you're going to need a job—"

"Did you really send Wyatt over here because of me?" she pressed.

He groaned and raked a hand down his face. Finally, he held her gaze and muttered, "Of course. I don't see Kendra or Quinn getting on any ladders trying to fix up this place. You looked like hell the other morning. I bet you were cleaning this place all morning, and if I didn't do something I could picture you on the roof with a hammer and nails trying to fix shingles and giving me another damn heart attack."

That part of her that always melted when he was around, turned to mush. "Thank you, Graham," she whispered.

He looked confused then said, "I'm completely lost. What are we talking about?"

"You," she said simply then claimed his mouth with her own.

He definitely was not confused now, as he took control of the kiss. She sighed into the sweet invasion of his tongue. This kiss was different than the others. More demanding, more desperate. Maybe because she was no longer depriving herself.

His hands tangled in her hair and the swing creaked as he twisted their bodies until she was underneath him and he was on top. The weight of his erection rested between her thighs as if the two were joined. The pressure felt foreign and comfortable at the same time, as if Graham had the right to be in that exact spot.

He nipped her bottom lip then drew back to stare at her, his eyes bottomless pools. His voice was deep and thick, as he whispered, "Am I crushing you?"

Charlie shook her head then pulled his face towards hers. She memorized his mouth with hers, circled her tongue through his depths, enjoyed the feel of his slick tongue bathing hers. She clung to his neck, trying hard to give him everything that he asked for, but not sure if it would be enough. It would never be enough.

He groaned and his hands moved from her hair to her breasts. Charlie squirmed underneath him as white-hot fire followed his touch and pooled in her breasts, they felt like heavy weights under his touch.

His hands were gentle and firm as he massaged her breasts and learned the feel of them, even as his mouth never left hers. Charlie could have drowned in his kisses. Each kiss seemed to melt into the next one, until there wasn't a moment when she felt that didn't exist without Graham's mouth and his hands that moved lower and lower on her body, lighting every inch on fire.

"Please say yes, baby," he murmured against her mouth before his tongue plunged into her mouth again.

"Yes," she whispered, not knowing what she was saying yes to, but it didn't matter as long as it involved him.

Graham smiled against her mouth and she felt his sure hands unbuttoning her shorts. The sound of the zipper was like music in the quiet country air. One of his hands slipped into her shorts and palmed her heat that had now become wet and slick. Even over her serviceable cotton underwear, Charlie felt every ridge on his hand, the heat of his hand.

She gasped and her hips reared off the swing of their own volition. His teeth flashed at her in the dark, before he placed a kiss on one eyelid then the other.

"You're beautiful," he whispered, staring at her again. "I don't know why I didn't see it before."

"I get lost in the crowd," she said, with a slight smile, as she stroked the side of his face.

"Never again," he vowed, then moved aside the panel of her panties and slowly and carefully submerged one finger into her depths.

Charlie's eyes slid closed of their own accord as her body gripped him. She bit her bottom lip to keep in the guttural moan that threatened to escape. She had never felt like this. Free. Beautiful. Sensuous. She felt every bit the beautiful woman that Graham believed her to be.

"You feel… Don't move, Charlie. Not yet." He sounded in pain even though she was the one who was writhing for completion and grasping his arm for support. His breath was ragged as he whispered, "You are so hot. So tight."

His words alone caused a shiver of delight and decadent pleasure to race through her body. Then his finger moved and she thought she'd found heaven. She gasped his name. He shoved her shirt up, catching her bra with his other hand and his hot mouth latched onto one nipple and he sucked.

As the night air fell against her breasts, tingling already alive nerve endings and he worked inside and on top of her, Charlie could no longer be silent. His finger was pumping in and out, his hot mouth was working over one breast and she had never felt so alive and vibrant in all of her years. Now, she knew what the whole hoopla was about.

She gripped his shoulders, digging her fingernails into his shirt, through his shirt. He licked a trail across her chest to the other breast. He teased her already erect nipple with a few tongue swipes. She gripped him tighter and threw back her head at the sheer ecstasy washing over her. She couldn't handle much more. The feelings were overwhelming her, taking over, causing her body to move and twist and turn under his skillful and wicked hands and tongue.

Graham's finger continued to slowly torture her at the same time that his thumb pressed her nerve-filled, sensitive clitoris. Completion slammed into her and she opened her mouth to scream, but Charlie enveloped her scream with his mouth, kissing her as she rode the wave, bathing her mouth with his sweetness.

She slowly fell back against the swing, every muscle in her body unwinding until she felt like a limp rag doll. Graham's smile was more than smug as he zipped up her shorts and pulled down her shirt. She told herself to fix her own clothes, but she couldn't move. She could only watch him.

For the first time, she noticed the gentle sway and creak of the swing. Quinn might have heard everything, but Charlie could not bring herself to care.

"I'm not trying to come on too strong or anything, but I just wanted you to know that my parents are very heavy sleepers," he whispered in her ear, causing her to laugh.

"Not on your life, Forbes," she growled then wrapped her arms around him. His erection still pressed against her. She shifted to allow him better access, and he groaned.

"You have a sadistic streak," he muttered then reluctantly pulled away from her to stand. He stared down at her and smiled at whatever he saw. "You are a hard woman to walk away from."

"Good," she responded, grinning. No one had ever told her that before, and he so obviously meant it.

He laughed then placed a gentle, chaste kiss on her forehead. "I'll see you tomorrow."

Her good mood dissipated and she sat up, feeling slightly lightheaded. "I don't know—"

"There's nothing you can say to keep me away, Charlie, so don't even try."

"You're awfully sure of yourself."

He leaned over, his nose almost touching hers. "That's because I was the man whose name you were screaming."

Charlie tried to feel self-righteous and indignant, but she could only shake her head and laugh. Graham caressed her cheek and murmured, "Dream about me."

Charlie watched him walk across the field towards his house. She sighed in contentment and wrapped her arms around her chest. For however long it lasted, Graham was hers. And that was all that mattered at that moment.

Chapter 14

It had to be done. Graham begrudgingly admitted as he turned his truck onto Main street. He had put it off as long as he could, but he had to talk to Boyd. People all over town, including several of the workers at the ranch, had passed along Boyd's message that he wanted to see Graham. Now. Graham could have played the whole drama out for another few days—mostly to amuse himself—but he had other things to think about now. Mainly one thing to think about now—Charlie.

Last night… Even now, twelve hours later, after a half day of working in the fields and then a couple of hours of handling business calls and then dealing with Theo, who had finally discovered that Graham had lied and there was Internet access in the house, just thinking about Charlie in his arms last night was enough to make

him horny as hell. He was long past the age of sprout-
ing unwanted hard-ons in public, but just thinking about
her beautiful breasts gleaming with his thorough
bathing and her soft groans of pleasure as he had
pumped in and out of her sweet warmth was enough to
give him one.

The only thing he wanted to do after a full day was
to ride to the Sibley house, throw Charlie in his truck
and drive to where no one would be able to hear her
screams of ecstasy. Last night had not been nearly
enough to whet his appetite for her. In fact, it had done
the opposite. Graham wanted her even more now.

But, he had to contend with Boyd. If Graham didn't
heed the urgent messages, he could look forward to a
visit from Boyd later in the evening when Graham
would have absolutely no patience.

Graham parked his truck in front of the picturesque
town hall that housed the few public works in Sibleyville, the town council meeting rooms and the mayor's
office, which unfortunately had belonged to Boyd for
too long. Graham stood down from the truck and stared
at the town hall. He had to hand it to Boyd—the building
was nice, a testament to Boyd's ability to cajole,
threaten and bully whoever he wanted, for whatever he
wanted and ten years ago, Boyd had decided that he
wanted a town hall that would epitomize the small-town
life that he wanted for Sibleyville.

As Graham climbed the broad, ornate staircase that led
to two oversized wooden doors, left open during office
hours, he was once more surprised by the animosity that
raced through his body as he entered the building.

"Hi, Graham," Gracie Lou Latham greeted when he walked into the reception area of the mayor's office.

He and Gracie Lou had attended high school together and had dated a few times. When Graham left for college, Gracie Lou had married her high school beau and popped out a few kids. The same pattern as most every other person in Graham's high-school graduating class. Graham hadn't felt like a hopeless old bachelor until he'd come back to Sibleyville. Being a bachelor in Tokyo had been a sign of honor and respect, worth at least a few cups of sake. Here, it made him the town pariah. He had to remind himself every day that not everyone in the world had their first baby at nineteen years old and their ten-year wedding anniversary at twenty-eight.

"Looking beautiful as ever, Gracie Lou. Where's His Honorable Pain-in-My-Ass?"

Gracie Lou laughed then whispered, "He told me to make you wait twenty minutes and then show you in."

Graham winked at her then walked to the closed double doors that led into the mayor's office and swung one open. As he walked into the office, he heard Gracie Lou's mock protest, "No, Graham, don't go in there."

He rolled his eyes because Gracie Lou was as bad an actress as she had been in high school.

Boyd sat behind a gleaming oak desk and looked up surprised when Graham barged into the room. The office was like Boyd—efficient, sturdy and boring. All of the dark, heavy furniture made Graham think of hunting lodges. And then there were the multitude of framed photographs of Boyd with various military bigwigs, which Graham had to admit some grudging respect for.

"It took you long enough," Boyd greeted.

"What couldn't wait until council meeting?" Graham asked, without pretense, while plopping into one of the leather wingback chairs across from Boyd that Boyd had not—and no doubt would not have—invited Graham to sit in.

"You were busy last night, from what I hear," Boyd said, getting right to the point.

Graham refused to believe that even the Sibleyville gossips could have known what he and Charlie had done on the back porch last night. And if Boyd even hinted that he did know, Graham promised to slam his fist straight into the older man's face.

"What are you talking about, Boyd?"

"You were at the Sibley house until all hours of the night," Boyd accused.

Graham marginally relaxed and tried to work up a good yawn. None was forthcoming. "So," he finally said.

"So," Boyd repeated, his eyebrows raised in outrage. He rose from his chair to pace the length of his office. "You are a town council member, Forbes—although, how that happened, I'm still not certain—and, therefore, when you are out in public, you represent this town. You must conduct yourself accordingly. And spending all hours of the night at the home of those women is not conducting yourself accordingly. If you continue to smear this town council, I will do everything in my power to remove you from the position you obviously have no respect for."

Graham laughed, which caused Boyd's frown to deepen until Graham worried the lines would permanently mar the older man's face. "Is that a threat or a promise?" he asked hopefully.

Boyd stared at him for a moment then shook his head, disgusted. "You're a disgrace."

Graham could no longer control his anger and rose to his feet. "I don't appreciate being called in here like a damn schoolboy. How I act is my own business. If the people of this town have a problem with it, they know how to write-in enough votes to elect a new town council member."

Boyd studied him for a moment before he said, coolly, "Have you at least found out how the sisters are leaning towards the town?"

"No. And, even if I had, I wouldn't tell you."

Boyd's expression softened as he said, gently, "When are you going to realize that we're on the same team, son?"

"We're not on the same team."

Boyd walked across the office and closed the doors. He turned to Graham and Graham wondered if he had finally pushed the old man too far.

Boyd moved back behind his desk and sat in the chair. He steepled his hands under his chin then said, softly, "You may not give two hoots about this town, but I know you care about your parents. Your parents love Sibleyville and so do I. That means you and I are on the same team."

Graham slowly returned to his seat, still suspicious of Boyd's sudden thoughtfulness. Boyd handled most circumstances in one of two ways—screaming and bellowing.

"Did the girls tell you why they're here?"

"They're here to see their grandfather's roots, to spend time with each other."

"That's the nursery-school version," Robbins said, worriedly. "The real reason is money."

"What are you talking about, Boyd?"

Boyd continued, for once taking no obvious pleasure in schooling Graham. "When Max died, he was worth at least fifty million dollars. In order for his grand-daughters to see one penny, his will requires them to live together for two weeks in that old house. Two weeks and the girls split their inheritance three ways, which potentially includes all of Max's holdings…including this town. We can't live our lives based on contingencies, Graham. If the women have the money, at least we know that we can convince them of the goodness of Sibleyville. A soulless corporation—we have no chance."

"How do you know this?" Graham asked, suspiciously.

"Mandy Spektor's husband's cousin's sister-in-law works in the offices of Max's lawyers. She's a secretary and saw the will. She didn't see all of the terms, just the part about the sisters living here for two weeks."

"So, let me get this straight. Now, you want the Sibley sisters to inherit this town? I thought you didn't want Sibleyville being under the reins of a bunch of women."

The old temper flared in Boyd's eyes as he said, tightly, "Does it matter anymore? All that matters is who gets their hands on the notes to this town's future, including your parents' farm."

"You've gone too far now, Boyd. Leave my parents out of this."

"They're farmers in America, Graham. Do you really think they don't have the same financial pressures as the rest of us?"

Graham had been running the farm for the last six months. Of course, he knew the finances. It was a struggle. But, since Graham had more money than he had ever dreamed of, he could buy the damn farm five times over if he wanted to. Except he knew that his parents would never let him.

"My parents' farm is fine," Graham said finally, silently daring Boyd to contradict him.

"And how would your parents like living in this town with no one else here? Because that's what will happen, Graham. Large corporations are buying small farms— like the farms in this community—across America, swallowing them whole. This town might not exist in another ten years, whether the Sibley sisters or some corporation takes over, but wouldn't it be better if we all could decide our own fates?"

Graham liked to think he viewed Sibleyville through an impartial prism, but it was a lie. This was his home, if for no other reason than his parents were here and would never leave. If Sibleyville didn't exist any-more…Graham quickly discarded the thought. The town had to exist. As much as he complained about it, he couldn't imagine a world where there was no Sibleyville.

"What am I supposed to do?" Graham finally asked. "The Sibley sisters haven't told me any of this. They ob-viously don't want me to know."

Now, everything made sense at the Sibley house. Their arguments, their awkwardness around each other. They were in the house because they had to be.

"You're a salesman, right? Sell this town," Boyd said, simply.

Graham hesitated as he actually found himself agreeing with Boyd. Something had to be wrong with the side he was on, if he found himself on the same side as Boyd Robbins.

"I'll see what I can do," he said finally.

Boyd's jaw tightened for a moment, but then he stiffly nodded. "I hadn't even expected that much out of you."

"Sorry to disappoint," Graham responded, dryly.

He ignored the older man's glare and walked out of the office, making certain to leave the door open just because he knew it would irritate Boyd.

"Do you think if I click my heels together three times and say, There's no place like home, I'll be back in Los Angeles?" Quinn said, as she sauntered into the kitchen the next afternoon.

Charlie forced a smile then discreetly studied Quinn as she poured herself a cup of coffee. After Graham had left last night, Charlie had fallen into a restful sleep. It wasn't until her shower this morning that she remembered the awful scene between her sisters. Quinn, however, showed no signs of the distress she had felt last night. She looked radiant as ever.

"What are you reading?" Quinn asked, while sitting across the table from Charlie.

"The *Sibleyville Crier.*"

Quinn wrinkled her nose in distaste. "I was hoping you had smuggled in a copy of the *New York Times*."

Charlie forced another smile at Quinn's obvious attempt to keep the conversation light. "No such luck. But, the *Crier* is filled with interesting tidbits."

"Like what?"

"Melvin Parker just came back from visiting his daughter in Los Angeles. She's doing well. Just had twins," Charlie said, with dramatic enthusiasm.

Quinn laughed, but it was forced. Silence fell between the two women, and Quinn stared into her cup of coffee, while Charlie stared at her.

"Are you all right?" Charlie asked, concerned.

Quinn looked up from her coffee with a pasted-on bright smile. "Of course I am. Well, except for the three chili-cheese-dogs and two beers I drank last night. I can't remember the last time I drank domestic beer."

"Quinn—"

Quinn interrupted Charlie's serious tone with a bright smile. "And Wilson didn't even bother me last night."

"Wilson," Charlie said, confused. "Who's Wilson?"

"Graham's friend."

Charlie ground her teeth in annoyance. Quinn rarely remembered the names of people who didn't fawn over her, or who she didn't want to fawn over. "His name is Wyatt."

Quinn waved her hand in dismissal, her favorite move, and said, "Of course. Wyatt. I knew it was something very cowboy. Anyway, he didn't even bother me last night. Usually, he does. He's always watching me. Waiting for me to do something. It's tiresome."

"I never noticed that."

"Last night, he actually acted normal. I heard that he's the town's mortician. Isn't that ghastly? He's touched dead people—"

"Quinn," Charlie interrupted firmly. Quinn stared wide-eyed at her, the picture of innocence. "Is what Kendra said true? Is the show not renewing your contract next year?"

Quinn hesitated then sent Charlie another beauty pageant smile. "There are always these rumors floating around the business—"

"Is it true? Yes or no?"

Her shoulders slumped and her smile disappeared. She stared into her coffee as she murmured, "Yes."

Charlie sucked in a breath of shock. "Why didn't you tell me?"

Quinn abruptly stood to her feet, dumping the contents of her cup into the kitchen sink. She busily washed the cup, scrubbing it an inordinate amount of time. "I didn't want your pity," she finally answered.

"What are you going to do?"

Quinn slowly turned off the water then dried her hands on a nearby dish towel. She turned to face Charlie, and Charlie instantly felt sympathy for her beautiful sister as she saw the misery swimming in her eyes.

"I don't know," Quinn answered in a soft whisper. "I didn't save like I should have."

"What do you mean?"

"I mean that I have no money," Quinn said, a little too loudly. At Charlie's wide eyes, Quinn lifted her chin. "I made some mistakes, I will admit that."

"When you say *no money,* what exactly do you mean?" Charlie asked, hesitantly.

"I mean that I have twenty-three dollars and four cents in my bank account as we speak."

Charlie rubbed her face, feeling an onset of fatigue. "Oh, Quinn," she said, shaking her head in disbelief. "You made so much money from the show. How is it all gone?"

Quinn visibly hesitated then said, "His name was Simon Collinsworth."

Charlie groaned in disbelief. "A man, Quinn? A man stole all of your money?"

"I was trying to be like Kendra and Grandpa Max. It sounded like a good deal. And he was very handsome and smooth. He took my money and that of some other people on the show, whom I referred to him."

"Quinn—"

Quinn slid into her seat again and took Charlie's hands, forcing Charlie to look at her. "I'm not concerned, Charlie. You shouldn't be either. In two weeks, I'm going to be a multi-millionaire."

"Anything can happen," Charlie said, patiently, as if she was speaking to a four-year-old. "You can't count on that money to solve your problems."

"Of course, I can," Quinn insisted cheerfully.

Charlie shook her head again then studied her sister. Sometimes she forgot that Quinn was only twenty-six years old. Quinn had moved out of the house at seventeen and had gone to New York to "make it" as a serious stage actress. She had turned up her nose at the Hollywood scene for the Big Apple. A lot had changed. Charlie felt the familiar guilt that she felt whenever Quinn gave another example of how Charlie had let her down in the big-sister department.

"What if we don't get the money, Quinn? Have you thought about that? What are you going to do then?" she demanded.

"I'll deal with that if and when it occurs," Quinn said, lightly, then stood up. "Now, where is She-Devil? She and I need to have a little talk. She had no right telling Wyatt… That is his name right?… Anyway, she had no right telling Graham and his friends my business."

"If you need anything, Quinn, you know that you can always count on me," Charlie said, quietly, hoping that it wasn't too late for her sister to at least know that much.

Quinn sent Charlie the first genuine smile of that morning. "I know, Charlie. Even though I don't deserve it."

Charlie smiled then stood. "Kendra went on a run."

"Didn't she have a hangover?" Quinn asked, hopefully.

"Yes, but she said that the only way to work off a hangover is to run it off."

Quinn gave a delicate snort of disgust. "How can she be related to us?"

Charlie smiled in response then glanced at her watch. "I'm going to the Forbes's house."

Quinn's entire body became alert as she asked eagerly, "To see Graham?"

Charlie's heart skipped a beat at the mention of his name. She would be old and gray and never forget that porch swing or Graham.

"No. To see his father. Lance is a painter and has some wonderful paintings that I want to display in the center—"

"If Graham is around give me a call. It'll be nice to

score some points without Kendra around." Without another word, Quinn sashayed out the kitchen.

Charlie gritted her teeth and tried to remember why she had felt a rush of affection for a woman who was so spoiled.

Chapter 15

Charlie surveyed the ten paintings on the easels before her, as she and Lance stood in the cramped attic of the Forbes's house. The sloped ceiling made it impossible for Lance to stand upright, but for the last hour he had guided Charlie through the covered paintings in the attic and tried to pretend that he was not nervous.

"So, which ones?" Lance finally demanded, obviously no longer able to hold his silence.

"I can't decide," she murmured then shrugged in defeat. "We'll just have to show them all."

"Really?" Lance asked, excitement bubbling in his eyes like a child on Christmas Day.

Charlie grinned. "Really."

He laughed then shook his head. "I personally think you'll be laughed out of L.A. for putting these on the wall and calling it art, but…who am I to argue? I'm just a simple farmer."

"There is nothing simple about you," she said, with a smile. She was now in familiar territory, with an insecure artist, on pins and needles at the prospect of the public judging his work. Over the last few years, Charlie had held many hands and had dried many eyes.

Lance grunted unintelligibly in return then motioned for her to follow him down the stairs to the office on the second floor.

A large oak desk sat near the row of windows on one wall. The desk was immaculately organized with rows of papers stacked on top of each other. A modern computer sat on one corner of the desk, along with a phone that had enough buttons to launch a space ship. Charlie smiled to herself because she knew that the state of the desk, as well as the other masculine and expensive furniture in the room was due to Graham's influence.

Lance settled behind the desk, while Charlie sank into one of the plush dark leather chairs arranged on the other side of the desk. A thick Oriental rug was underfoot, drawing her attention to its intricate, beautiful design.

"Graham brought that back for us when he worked in India," Lance said, proudly, noticing the direction of her gaze.

Charlie's face flushed hot at having been caught daydreaming about Graham. "It's beautiful," she murmured. Before Lance could say something else to embarrass her, she said, "We need to talk about your press kit. Usually, most museums have a public relations department that handles these details, but…I've mentioned our…financial difficulties and, basically, Lance, you're looking at the African-American Art Center's public relations department."

Lance smiled. "We'll just say that you like to give every artist the personal touch."

"You're already better at spinning than I am," she said, truthfully. "We'll need to write press releases for the show, your biography, information on the paintings. We'll have plaques made for each painting to put next to it on the wall. We'll arrange a huge opening, something to draw the public's attention to you and your work. Since I can't do any of the work here for, uh, various reasons, we won't get into the heart of the preparation until I return to Los Angeles. But you have a great story, Lance. Who better to represent African-Americans in the Wild West than you?"

"Four generations of Forbeses have owned this land," Lance said, proudly. At her surprised expression, he nodded. "My grandfather's grandfather, Red, was a slave in Louisiana. Before the end of the Civil War, his owner, some bigwig in the Confederacy, took him to Texas as a porter. One day his owner left him alone at the hotel, as if Red was happy as a clam living as a slave and had no desire to fight as thousands of other ex-slaves were doing.

"Red stole a horse, which was a hanging offense in and of itself, and rode all night and all day north. His plan was to find a Union army battalion and join with them, doing whatever he could until he could join a colored regiment. That's what they called them back then—colored regiments."

"After the war, he settled here?" Charlie asked.

Lance laughed quietly for a moment then said, "We Forbeses, have never had a great sense of direction. Instead of heading north, Red headed west." Charlie laughed in disbelief as Lance shook his head. "Thankfully, some Indians found Red before the whites did. He remained with the tribe while they spent one winter on this land. When they left, Red stayed. My grandfather said Red told him that he had never seen anything more beautiful in his life and that's how he knew he was home. And that is how the Forbeses came to be farmers in Sibleyville."

"That is exactly the type of story I'm looking for," she said, excitedly, then rested her elbows on her knees and leaned forward. "How did Red meet your great-great-grandmother? There couldn't have been many Black people around here, besides Red."

"After the war, when Red had made some money, he sent for his family, who had remained in Louisiana after the war. While he had been gone, his mother had taken in an orphan. A little Creole girl named Simone. When his mother came to Sibleyville, she brought Simone with her."

"Love at first sight?" Charlie asked, smiling.

"That's the only way we Forbes men know how to do," Lance said, with a resigned shrug. "Love at first sight. Most people don't believe it, but for the last four or five generations in my family, a Forbes man has looked at a woman and just known she was going to be the one. Since Red, we've all met and married our wives within a span of a few weeks. Not a divorce among the lot of us. If it wasn't for love at first sight, we would have died out a long time ago. Take Eliza and me. I was in New York on business, hoping to leave a day early and then— bam—I saw Eliza walking down the street. I could barely speak the first time I saw her."

Charlie forced a smile even as her heart sank. It's not that she had been thinking of marrying Graham. Of course, she hadn't. She barely knew the man. He had only decided to like her less than one day ago, and she wasn't sure if she really liked him, come to think of it.

So, maybe she *had* been thinking about him as The One, not that a woman raised by Max Sibley would believe in anything as romantic as that. But, she had to admit that a small part of her had maybe, in the deepest, darkest part of her heart dreamed about standing in front of Graham in a poofy white wedding dress that her sisters would scoff at and then having a bunch of little brown babies with Graham's smile.

But now, besides the fact that it never would have happened anyway, Charlie knew for certain that it would never happen—not if Lance was right about Forbes men. Graham had not fallen in love with her at first sight. Even Graham had admitted as much last night. Maybe dislike at first sight meant something, too.

Lance apparently didn't notice her sudden dark mood because he was saying, "All in all, this exhibit thing sounds like it will be a lot of work."

"If we had a real public relations department, it wouldn't be," she said, apologetically. "I'll do most of the work—"

"No, Charlie, I want to help in whatever way I can. You have enough on your mind."

Charlie tried not to leap against the desk and hug him. "Thank you, Lance, because we will need your help to make this a success. And I know I've mentioned this before, but I should warn you that we may do all of this work and none of it will matter because the museum may close down before the exhibit can take place."

Lance smiled, unconcerned. "I have a feeling that everything is going to be fine, Charlie. Don't worry about your museum."

Charlie forced a smile and murmured, "I wish I had your confidence."

He shrugged, then leaned back in the chair and stared out the window at the fields in the distance. "Ever since you told me about this exhibit, I've been feeling that old excitement I used to get at harvest time. Don't get me wrong. Farming is in my blood, and I'll do it 'til the day I die, but the chance of having my doodles on display somewhere is… It's more than I ever thought possible. And that made me think of Graham."

She noticed his eyes were focusing a little too intensely on her. "Graham?" she croaked.

"I've kept him here too long," Lance said quietly, as if he was admitting the truth to himself for the first time. "This is not the life Graham wanted, but because I thought he would come to love it—or, at least, accept it, as I did—I've been pretending that I'm not well enough to take over all the things he's been doing around here. And because he's a good son, he's done it. But, the prospect of seeing my paintings in a museum… It made me remember that I once wanted more for myself. I can't stop my son from wishing for the same thing."

"Lance, I'm sure Graham loves being here—" The look he shot her made her instantly clamp her mouth closed. She tried for a little more truth. "Maybe Graham is itching to get back to his job, but I know that a part of him loves being here with you and Eliza."

Lance shrugged in response, then took off his baseball cap to squeeze and bend it in his hands. "Tonight, I'm going to tell him that he's free to leave. He's done his time in the Sibleyville jail."

Charlie didn't know whether to smile or cry. She knew it was what Graham wanted, but she wasn't ready to see him go, which she knew he would as soon as Lance told him. Theo probably had a charter plane on standby for that exact moment.

What would Charlie do once Graham left? She didn't know what she had done with herself before she knew him. It seemed like there was no time without him. Maybe Graham hadn't fallen in love at first sight, but she had.

"I've loved having him home again," Lance murmured wistfully, staring out the window again.

Since he wasn't looking at her, he never saw her wipe the silent tear that escaped her control and tracked down her cheek.

Graham groaned in fatigue as he walked into the Forbes's house. It had been another long day. He had forgotten how punishing working a farm could be. One more day and their planting season would be over then he could leave the farm to his father and return to Tokyo with a clear conscience. He didn't understand how his parents handled all of the physical and emotional fatigue from running a working farm. Even with the seasoned help they had, Graham found himself trying to do three different things at once, while thinking of another three things he should have been doing. And it wasn't like the money was worth it. They made just enough to cover bare necessities, plus an occasional splurge.

The thought of money made Graham frown and think of his talk with Boyd that afternoon and the Sibley sisters. Eliza and Lance complained about the farm, but Boyd had been right about his parents; they loved their farm. They would never leave. And Boyd had been right once more when he had said that it wasn't just the farm that they loved, it was the town. The boring, stupid little town in the middle of nowhere that no one came to unless they were lost.

Loving their town, their friends and each other made the whole thing work for Eliza and Lance. If they didn't have the farm or the town, Graham shuddered to think what would happen to his parents. With the money Graham had made from his job, his parents would always be well taken care of, but Graham could no more picture his parents living in some sterile, paved subdivision than he could picture Sibleyville no longer existing.

And apparently the fate of the town, and therefore, his parents, rested in the hands of the Sibley sisters. It was almost ironic. Graham had come here thinking he would have a little peace and quiet, and instead he had stumbled upon three of the soon-to-be wealthiest Black women in America. His fatigue grew deeper as he thought of all the fame and attention that wealth brought. Men were already beating down Kendra's and

Quinn's doors. Once word got out about their inheritance, there would be no stopping the level of scum who would attach themselves to the women.

Graham paused in the foyer to tug off his boots. And, of course, Charlie drifted into his mind. Any time he did not occupy his thoughts with other matters, she was there. Her soft gasps from the night before, her luscious lips, all of those hips and that ass… Now, he wasn't just tired, but he was horny. And angry. Because Charlie would also be on some scum's radar. The idea of some man hurting her or cheating her or doing anything short of shaking her hand and nodding in greeting made Charlie want to hit something or someone.

"You look mad enough to spit nails," came Theo's voice from the bottom of the stairs. Graham turned and his bad mood slightly abated when he saw the look of horror on Theo's face. "Did I just say what I think I just said?"

"You sure did. You used a country expression," Graham said, exaggerating his own drawl just to rub it in.

Theo shook his head in disbelief then held up four fingers. "I've been here four days. Four measly days, Graham, and this town has already taken the Tokyo out of me."

"I thought you were from Compton."

"You know what I mean," Theo grumbled, annoyed.

For the first time, Graham noticed that Theo wore a dark, tailored suit and tie. "Where are you going?"

"I need a meal that does not involve beef or cholesterol," Theo said as he straightened his tie in the oval mirror on the wall in the foyer. "I have an ex-girlfriend who lives in San Francisco. I convinced her to let me take her to dinner."

"At this hour? San Francisco is a four-hour drive from here."

"At this hour?" Theo repeated, while shaking his head in disbelief. "It's barely six-thirty, Graham. The sun is still up. Besides, I chartered a plane. We'll be there in less than an hour, which should coincide nicely with our eight-thirty reservation at Le Cirque."

Graham felt sufficiently chagrined. In the old days, at six-thirty he would just be catching his second wind and getting ready to head out to bars and clubs. But in Tokyo, he also didn't wake up at five in the morning and put in ten hours of back-breaking work in the fields, hassle with Boyd Robbins and spend half of the day hard as a rod because he couldn't stop thinking about a woman, either.

"We only have a few more days left in Sibleyville," Theo said, oblivious to Graham's thoughts. "Have you spoken to Lance yet?"

"Tomorrow," Graham promised.

"Where have I heard that one before?" Theo muttered dryly. Finished admiring his reflection in the mirror, he turned to Graham, with a serious expression. "I'm not going to pressure you anymore, Graham, but I will give you some advice. If you pass up this opportunity, you will regret it every day for the rest of your life."

"No pressure, right, Theo?"

Theo shrugged innocently then said, "What can I say? I'm honest to a fault. I'll be back tomorrow. Oh, and your parents headed to Bentonville to catch a movie. The fact that you people have to drive an hour each-way to see a movie should be a big enough sign that it's time to move."

Graham shook his head then said, "Have fun, Theo."

"I will." Theo headed for the door then stopped and studied Graham for a moment before he said, "By the way, Charlie has been here all day talking to your father about his paintings."

Graham's heart tripped a beat at the mention of her name. He realized that he had more than just his early bedtime to be embarrassed about. His reaction to this woman was out of proportion to anything he had ever known. She was just a woman. Not some magic, ethereal being. Maybe if he saw her again, and kissed her again, and of course had wild, uninhibited sex with her, he could convince himself of that fact.

"Lance told me that she's planning to display his paintings at her museum in Los Angeles," Theo continued in that same calculating tone.

"Really?" he asked, with just the right amount of nonchalance to make Theo smile in disbelief.

"Yes, really… And I think she's still in the attic, cowboy. Go get her."

Theo winked and walked out of the house, closing the door on Graham's prepared protests about his interest in Charlie. Graham told himself to play it cool. He hadn't eaten dinner. He was sweaty, probably didn't smell like a bed of roses either. He should take a shower then find Charlie and politely ask her if she wanted to join him for dinner.

"Oh, hell," Graham muttered to himself then turned on his heel and ran up the stairs.

Chapter 16

Graham reached the door to the attic and forced himself to slow down and to catch his breath. He had never run over a woman before and he definitely didn't want this particular woman getting any wrong ideas that he had been running to her like his life depended on it…even if he had.

Graham inhaled then slowly released the trapped air, remembering the calm teachings of a yoga instructor who had come to Shoeford Industries once. He nodded to himself then reached for the doorknob just as the door swung outward and straight into him. The door slammed into his face, causing a flash of pain to ricochet through his entire body.

Graham screamed a vicious curse and placed both hands over his nose as he stumbled back several steps into the wall. He glared at Charlie as she peeked around the now-open door. Of course, it was her.

"I'm so sorry," she said, breathlessly, rushing to his side. Her warm hands moved on top of his and she moved close enough to kiss, her gaze focused on his hands. "Is it bleeding? Move your hands, so I can see."

Graham dropped his hands then held his head back for a moment to hold back any unwanted bodily fluids. "Thank God, my nose stopped the door before it could do any real harm," he managed to growl.

"I didn't know anyone else was home," she said.

He saw the amusement glittering in her eyes and that made his own smile harder to fight. "Lady, you are going to be the death of me."

"I am sorry," she said, but then she laughed. "You have to admit that it's kind of funny. I mean, I'm not that clumsy…" At his look, she cleared her throat and said quickly, "Maybe I'm a little clumsy, but around you, I become a full-blown klutz. Although, what were you doing lurking at the door?"

Graham shook his head to shake away the pain. "I wasn't lurking. This is my house."

"I'm sorry," she said again then added, "I'll get some ice. We don't want it to swell."

It was something about the way she said *we,* as if she and Graham were a team. As if they faced things head-on together. That's what made him forget the pain that still throbbed in his nose and grab her arm and pull her flush against his body.

He also realized that she looked damn adorable in the jeans and tank top she wore. He used to need women in cocktail dresses and stilettos and now it was a pair of faded jeans covered with streaks of dust and a purple tank top that emphasized the plumpness of her breasts, and he was a goner. Her hair was mussed from the sloping attic roofs and sported a few strands of cobweb.

Her eyes momentarily widened until she smiled and asked in a tone that told him she knew exactly what he was doing, "What are you doing, Graham?"

"Maybe I'm a glutton for punishment, but I can't stay away from you," he admitted in a low whisper.

She laughed and shook her head, even as desire instantly sparked in her eyes. "I'm sweaty and dirty from crawling around the attic all day—"

"Sweaty and dirty... Are you trying to turn me on even more?" he murmured, nudging her ear. His body tightened and hardened everywhere. His arms that she clung to, his jaw, his groin. He wanted this woman and, even if it cost him a few limbs, he was going to have her. "Should I even ask why you've been crawling around my parents' attic all day?"

"Your father has agreed to display some of his paintings in my museum. I'm planning an exhibit for later this year."

"My father?" Graham asked in disbelief. "Lance Forbes? The tall guy with the Chicago Cubs cap?"

Charlie laughed and nodded enthusiastically. "His work is amazing. He brings an entirely new perspective to the African-American art scene. Have you seen his work?"

"Of course. You really think he's that good?"

She squeezed his arm, as if sensing his concern for his father. "He's that good, Graham."

Graham smiled and murmured, "The old man must be floating on thin air right about now."

"And he told me that he's going to send you back to Tokyo," she said, excitedly.

"I'll believe it when I hear it," he said, dryly.

"No, Graham. He really means it. I don't think he had a choice in taking over the farm, and he feels guilty that he's put you in that same position. Looking at his paintings, remembering how he used to feel about painting, has reminded him of all that."

Graham stared at her excited smile for a moment, uncertain why the thought of returning to Tokyo didn't fill him with the usual longing. Maybe because it was replaced with a new longing for her.

His gaze dropped to her mouth and he said, "You seem to make everything around here better, Charlie."

He lowered his mouth to hers, prepared to coax and cajole, but she instantly opened for him. Their kisses were long and erotic. Carnal. Graham liked kissing just as much as the next guy, but he had always viewed it as a precursor to bigger and better events. With Charlie, kissing was the main event. He could kiss her all night and never tire of it. His hand on her arm slipped to entwine with hers, while his other hand grabbed the back of her head, not allowing her to go anywhere, if she even had the thought.

Their tongues locked and mated, until he couldn't stand the slowness of it all. He trapped her against the wall and took control, plunging his tongue into her open and sweet mouth until they both were breathing hard. Her hands traveled up his arms, down his chest and to the hem of his T-shirt. He felt one of her knuckles against the skin above his jeans waistband. He groaned into her mouth. With her, everything was different. He had never become so hard so fast or so close to being out of control for any other woman.

He abruptly tore his lips from hers, forcing himself to slow down, to calm the cry for fulfillment that resonated in the very depths of his soul. He quickly calculated how long it would take his parents to return to town. He had more than enough time. There was no need to rush anything with Charlie. Ever.

He leaned his forehead against hers and stared into her dark eyes. "I'm sweaty and dirty, too, and my sweat and dirt is distinctly less appealing than yours. Let's continue this in the shower."

His building anticipation crashed to the ground like a rocket as her expression froze at the mention of the word *shower.* She stepped from his arms and folded her arms across her chest in the most subconsciously self-protective gesture that Graham had ever seen. The part that hurt was that she was obviously protecting herself from him.

"You take your shower first, and I'll rustle us up something to eat since I know you must be hungry, and then I'll shower—"

Graham knew he was being a Neanderthal, but he didn't like not having her in his arms and he didn't like her protecting herself from him. She was stiff in his arms, but he refused to let that detour him as he nipped her right earlobe then nuzzled his way down her neck.

"Food can wait. I can't," he growled then planted a kiss on the side of her luscious neck.

She pushed against him and Graham reluctantly released her, because whatever he was saying or doing was not working.

"I'm not taking a shower with you, Graham," she said, flatly.

"Why not?" he demanded, his hurt at her blunt statement making him slightly obnoxious. When she refused to answer and only looked at him, Graham berated himself again. He kept pushing her and pressuring her. He didn't mean to. All right, he meant to, but he had never wanted a woman so damn much. It was obvious that this night was going to turn out much differently than he had hoped, but if walking around with a hard-on was what he had to do to spend a little private time around Charlie then he would. He conceded, with a forced smile, "All right, separate showers, but you go first."

"I'm not like Kendra or Quinn," she blurted out. His confusion must have been apparent because she sighed in frustration then said, "You've seen them…Kendra has zero body fat, and Quinn—she has her own swimsuit calendar, for God's sake. I have cellulite and jiggly spots and other areas that I'd rather not showcase."

Graham shook his head in disbelief. He would never understand women, especially this one.

"And how exactly are you planning to deal with that issue when I have you naked in my bed?" he asked, confused.

She smiled for the first time since he'd mentioned the dreaded *s*-word. "You're awfully presumptuous."

He traced her plump, glistening lower lip, swollen from his kisses, with his thumb. "It's called hope. It keeps many a man warm at night." She smiled, which made him smile. Her body began to relax one tense inch at a time. His hand moved to trace the silky length of each arched eyebrow. "Believe me, baby, you're perfect to me." He ignored her snort of disbelief.

She stared at him for a moment until she whispered half in awe, "You're deluded enough to believe that, aren't you?"

He couldn't take it anymore. Graham kissed her until she was breathless and clinging to his shirt, her mouth receiving whatever punishment and pleasure he gave her.

He pulled from her mouth, smiling as she followed him, dragging him into another endless kiss.

"Give me one chance to show you how much I believe it," he whispered, against her mouth, their hot breaths mingling. He had never worked this hard for a shower before. When she still didn't answer him, he asked, quietly, "You've never showered with a man before?"

She didn't meet his eyes, but shook her head in response. Graham wanted to ask her what else she hadn't done with a man before, but he had a few guesses and, frankly, it didn't matter. He planned to love Charlie so hard this night that she would forget who came before or after.

She ducked her head as she murmured, "If you promise not to peek, we can take the shower together."

Graham laughed and said, truthfully, "Darling, I plan to peek."

She laughed in response and pouted. "You could at least have lied about it."

Charlie was actually flirting with him. It made him

even harder, if that was possible. He took her hands and turned them over to press kisses in her palms.

"Are you sure, Charlie? I don't want to pressure you, even though I've done nothing but pressure you for the last—"

Her fingers against his mouth instantly shut him up. The look in her eyes as she stood on her tiptoes to almost meet him at eye level made him groan. "I'm sure, Graham. Besides art and chocolate, the only thing in the world I know for sure is that I want you."

Graham was rocked to the core of his feet. An inexplicable shiver raced through him. He ignored it and whatever feelings it conjured and led Charlie to his bedroom and its connected bathroom.

Graham definitely peeked. In fact, he openly gawked at her as she stepped into the steam and warm needle spray of the shower. Charlie ignored the butterflies in her stomach, and the fact that her stomach was probably bigger than his, and decided to look her fill, too. She instantly forgot about her cellulite and thighs. She sucked in a breath. The man was beautiful.

He stood directly under the spray of the water and water sluiced down his rock-hard body. Her eyes focused on one particular bead of water that went from the corner of his wicked mouth and dropped to his chest and then slid lower and lower until it hung on the tip of his engorged penis that was nearly standing upright. She gulped and continued to stare at it. Her body clenched in response as if somehow it knew where she looked and where it should go.

She was suddenly glad that she had waited for Graham. She was probably the last remaining twenty-eight-year-old virgin on the planet, but she had waited for this exact moment, waited to be standing in the shower with Graham. And even if she never saw him again, she knew that this was the exact moment that it should have happened. Her nipples beaded at the thought of what they would do and how they would do it.

Graham studied her with heavy-lidded eyes, his gaze as always going back to her breasts. For some reason, Charlie smiled. Graham wanted her. It was obvious. That his desire should instantly make her feel secure shook her to the core of her twenty-first-century mind, but maybe when it came to things like men and women, some things were primal.

Graham reached for her at the same time that she stepped towards him. Their foreheads collided with a loud smack. Graham cursed as Charlie laughed, while massaging her head.

He massaged her forehead in deep, gentle circles and stared down at her with such gentleness that tears filled her eyes. She hoped that Graham thought it was just the shower.

"We're going to kill each other someday," he murmured, then pressed a kiss on the center of her forehead.

"There are worse ways to go," she whispered, touching one of his rock-hard nipples.

He gasped and sucked his stomach in, which made his penis bobble. Charlie gave in to an impulse and ran her tongue along one of his nipples. Graham cursed again then grabbed her neck and pulled her away from him to ram his mouth against hers. Whatever had been holding him back was now gone. It was as if a torrent of desire and lust had been set free, and Graham was like a crazy man.

His hands ran across her body, massaging, rubbing, inserting and generally branding her like no man had. His kiss was carnal, too, sensuous. Charlie couldn't believe that men and women did this and actually left the bed. She could be like this with Graham for the rest of her life.

He gently moved her against the shower wall then slowly nipped her bottom lip as he pulled back. He stared at her for a moment, as if on the verge of asking her a question, then he stared down at her breasts. He placed his hands on both her breasts. He tugged her nipples and gently squeezed the globes until she was gasping his name. Then he took one nipple in his mouth and swirled his tongue around the over-sensitized point.

The tingling made her close her eyes and drop back her head against the shower tile. Her hair was getting wet and there would be hell to pay tomorrow, but she couldn't do anything else. The sensations were too much: the heat from Graham's body surrounding her, the warm water cascading down her face and his hot tongue moving across her breasts in an almost obscene pattern.

He lifted his head and his eyes were positively midnight. "Turn around," he said, in the deepest voice she had ever heard.

Charlie stared at him questioningly, but obeyed. She felt his hot breath on her neck and then his hands were on her, filled with bubbles from the bar of soap. Her eyes slid closed and she bit her bottom lip as his large, hot hands slowly moved over every inch of her body, as if they had all the time in the world. Her face, her neck, her breasts— her breasts again—her butt, in between her legs, cupping her enough to make her eyes fly open on a gasp.

"It's okay," he whispered, his lips against her ear, calming her.

Charlie swallowed the lump of desire and arousal in her throat, as his hands returned to soap her body. The sensations of his hands and the slickness of the soap on her body was a deadly combination that alerted and fired every nerve in her body. They made her rock on her feet like a spineless jellyfish. They made her writhe. He was moving too slowly and she was on the edge. If she had any reservations about Graham seeing her body, it was too late. He was studying her, dropping kisses where he needed to and getting to know every inch.

She groggily opened her eyes as he used a sponge to cascade warm water down her body. His gaze was intense on her body, gently moving the sponge across places where soap remained. Graham dropped the sponge then gently turned her to face him. Her cheeks heated as she saw where his gaze was directed. Her dark curls between her legs.

He met her gaze and kissed her once, languidly, not rushing. His tongue swept through her mouth in slow, purposeful jabs that made her core clench as if he was inside her, not just inside her mouth. He placed a soft kiss on her forehead then a kiss on her left breast, the dip of his tongue in her belly button and then he was on his knees in front of her. Too close.

"Graham, what…" Her voice trailed off as his hands ran down her back and covered her behind, massaging and kneading, and then dipped in between her legs.

"Come here for me, baby." His voice was a sensual whisper in the steam of the shower, as he caught her right leg at the knee and lifted it for her foot to rest on the wide ledge of the bath tub. She was completely opened to him, exposed, and along with a brief flash of embarrassment, came a heat like nothing like she had ever felt. She placed both hands on the shower tile to steady herself, even as she told herself to close her legs and pretend to be somewhat decent.

She looked down at him, still on his knees before her, his gaze on her curls.

"Graham," she tried again, not certain if she would beg him to touch her, or if she would beg him to stop.

He looked at her and she was lost. "You are beautiful," he said.

She opened her mouth to respond, but no sound came out. Graham smiled at her then redirected his gaze to her curls. He leaned forward and she barely restrained a scream when she felt his tongue probe through her curls to her pulsating, filled knob of nerves. His tongue pleasured her, in low, languid strokes.

Her body undulated before him, even as she found herself falling against the shower tile, unable to support her weight anymore. Graham caught her around the behind, holding her in place as his tongue grew more insistent. One of his hands moved to her center and one of his long, blunt-tipped fingers moved inside her. Slowly.

She could no longer be quiet. She screamed his

name, which seemed to edge him on. His finger inside her moved faster, as his tongue became more insistent against her knob. She wanted the torture to end. She wanted it to continue forever. Her deep breaths were punctuated by gasps and squeals that she'd never thought herself capable of. She closed her eyes as the pleasure and pain of hovering on the edge of release became unbearable.

He removed his finger which was quickly replaced by his tongue. He lapped her like his favorite treat. She lost all sense of where she was, who she was or even who Graham was. Nothing mattered but the intense feelings rolling through her like waves.

Then his fingers began to roughly caress her knob. And it became unbearable. She shrank from his touch and screamed as something close to perfection ripped through her body.

Chapter 17

Graham should have felt some sense of pride as he noted Charlie's unsteady legs, as she sagged against the shower tile, her wet hair pasted against the wall, framing around her. Instead, he was too busy controlling the caveman need to turn her around, and plunge into any open hole that he could find. He was losing all sense of humanity. He was harder than he had ever been in his life and her taste on his tongue was enough to drive a man insane.

Instead, Graham slowly stood, coming back to his senses. He once more became aware of the gentle rain of the shower spray, which had disappeared into a fog of desire. The steam. The blinding-white shower tiles. The clear shower curtain. His gaze once more flew to Charlie, who was still trembling, staring at him.

"The things I want to do to you…" he rumbled from somewhere deep in his chest.

His abrupt confession caused her to blink. Graham laughed, for some reason, then quickly washed himself with the sponge and soap, while Charlie watched. He rinsed off then stepped from the shower and grabbed a plush navy-blue towel off the sink. He held it open for Charlie and she unhesitatingly came to him.

Graham wrapped the towel around her, trapping her arms inside, pulling her close to his chest. He couldn't resist and kissed her. Long. Hard. And deep. Exactly how he wanted to bury himself in her, but, as he had discovered a few minutes ago, tonight he would have to be gentle because, dammit all to hell, Charlie Sibley was a damn-near virgin.

Graham had suspected since their first kiss that she didn't have much experience with men, but he hadn't known exactly how much until that moment. She was too tight, too hot. The discovery made Graham want to bury himself deeply inside of her as soon as possible, or to run from the room screaming.

Graham broke the kiss that left them both breathless. He forced himself to concentrate on more mundane tasks in order to give his raging body time to cool down. He turned off the shower, grabbed a towel for himself then led her into the bedroom. Her eyes darted to the bed then back to him. The obvious eagerness on her face made him smile.

"Are you sure about this, Charlie?" he asked, dropping his towel.

Her gaze went directly to his still-raging erection. She bit her bottom lip and he almost dropped to his knees.

She met his gaze then dropped her own towel in response. She held his gaze as she walked backwards and then climbed onto the bed, never breaking his gaze. She was flaunting her body for him. A body that held more curves and smooth skin than a man had a right to wish for. Her breasts softly bobbed for him, her nipples still beaded from their shower. Even her waist, sitting above flared hips, seemed to be calling to him. She moved more gracefully than he had ever seen.

Whatever little control he had managed to salvage to that point snapped. He was on top of her in two steps, kissing her, becoming reacquainted with all of the places he had visited in the shower. Charlie's response matched his own. Her hands were everywhere on his body: moving over his back, squeezing his behind, massaging his neck. She smelled clean and fresh, like his soap and, for some reason, that made him harder.

Graham tore his mouth from hers and levered above her, balancing himself on his arms. He stared into her dark eyes. He had never believed a man could be lost in a woman's eyes, as many poets had waxed about for centuries, but here he was, lost in a woman's eyes.

"I'll try to go slow, but…" His voice trailed off.

"Don't go slow," she whispered then pulled him down for a kiss that seared the hair on his chest.

He cursed and pulled away from her, ignoring and reveling in her disappointed moan. "Hold that thought," he murmured, then jumped off the bed.

He pulled his suitcase from the closet and rummaged around until he found a condom. He had not anticipated needing condoms in Sibleyville, but they were left over from an earlier trip and he had simply forgotten to unpack them before he came home. Graham for once was glad that he abhorred unpacking.

He tore open the package, cursing that his hands were trembling. He felt like an addict. He needed another shot of Charlie. His body needed to be inside her, around her, just near her. He cursed again, then rolled on the condom, his movements jerky and uncertain, which he hadn't experienced in the bedroom since college.

Graham moved back to the bed and hesitated when he saw her watching him with the fascination usually reserved for predators in the jungle. Her gaze moved across his body and Graham could feel the places where her gaze had landed.

"You're gorgeous, Graham," she whispered. Something like hesitation entered her eyes and her long, brown legs fell against each other as she said, softly, "I never imagined doing…this…with you."

Graham climbed onto the bed, covering her. He allowed her legs to remain closed for now and instead settled around her.

"I've imagined doing this with you many times over the last few days," he said, with a slight smile, while smoothing damp, thick hair from her forehead.

"My hair is wet," she muttered, out of nowhere. "I must look a mess."

He looked from her thick, wet hair to her swollen lips, flushed cheeks and gleaming eyes. He smiled because he couldn't help it. She laughed and swatted at his chest.

"This is the part where you're supposed to protest and tell me I look beautiful," she informed him.

He nudged her stomach and her smile softened. "You can tell how I feel." He planted kisses across her forehead then whispered, "Open for me, Charlie. Please."

She bit her bottom lip again then moved her legs apart a small fraction of space. He smiled and stared at her. He was going to die tonight. It was that simple. Charlie was going to kill him.

"This is your first time, isn't it?" he asked, gently, framing her face with his hands.

"With another person, yes," she answered.

Graham's erection grew another painful inch as he pondered the hidden meaning behind her statement. He forced out a laugh. "You really are going to be the death of me, Charlie Sibley."

She smiled and her body softened underneath him even more. Graham gritted his teeth and slid one glorious inch into her wet, luscious channel. It was the most unimaginable pleasure he had experienced in his life, to be encased in her, even that small bit. He wanted to move forward. He had to move forward. He felt sweat bead on his forehead as he tried to control himself.

He pushed forward more and she shifted underneath him, discomfort flashing across her face. Her hands went to his shoulders.

"Graham," she said, sounding uncertain.

"I'm trying…I've never been with a virgin before," he admitted, shaking his head. "I don't want to hurt you."

"Go slow," she ordered, in direct contradiction of her earlier order.

His body betrayed him and he fought his way in farther. She gasped and her hands squeezed his shoulders. Graham cursed because he couldn't stop. He wanted to ease her pain, soothe her, maybe joke a little, but it was all he could do not to howl at the damn moon. And he had the sinking feeling that he was on the verge of ending everything before it started. And that would be really embarrassing.

"Try to relax, Charlie," he said through clenched teeth. "I promise that it will get better."

He tried to wait while she grew accustomed to him. Her eyes were wide as she said, "This is *not* what I expected."

Only Charlie could make him laugh while he was on the verge of imploding. "That disappointing, huh?"

"No, just…so much *more*," she whispered, then placed a chaste kiss on his lips. He saw her make a concerted effort to relax. He felt her body under him go even softer. Her internal muscles gripped him, and he almost reared off the bed at the intense white heat of desire that made his feet flex. "Don't go slow, Graham."

Graham knew that he should have been valiant and made certain she was all right to continue, but instead he began moving. Plunging into her. He tried to slow down, but he was beyond that. Tasting her in the shower had driven him to a near fever pitch and now being inside of her drugging depths had pushed him to the point of no return.

Soon, her gasps of discomfort turned deeper, richer. She was clinging to his shoulders now, holding him to her, not on the verge of pushing him away. Graham's entire body tensed. He searched through her curls for her button and caressed it hard. She bucked underneath him and screamed his name. It didn't take long for

Graham to follow with a roar that would have made his cowboy ancestors proud.

A few moments later, Graham returned from the bathroom, after disposing of the condom. The calm he had fought for in the bathroom disappeared at the sight of Charlie in his bed, her brown body covered up to her armpits by the sheet. Graham grinned and accepted the double beat of his heart as he crawled under the sheet. He pulled her into his arms. Her willingness to come into his arms was what made him want to start the whole process over again.

Instead, he forced himself to wait. She was quiet as she traced a pattern on his chest with her hand. It was soothing and arousing as hell all at once.

"Are you okay?" he asked, breaking their comfortable silence. She nodded against his chest. His arm tightened around her as he asked, "How in the world did a woman like you manage to remain a virgin for so long?"

She pulled from his arms as she laughed. "You sound like it was my choice."

"A woman can have sex any time she wants."

"That is not true."

"Of course, it is. A woman can control any man she wants," he said, confidently.

She shot him an amused look as she said, "I can't picture any woman controlling you."

"I'm the rare exception," he said, with a casual shrug. When she only laughed, he pressed, "You really want me to believe that I'm the first guy to come along?"

"There have been others," she admitted, begrudgingly. "But, the type of men attracted to me are either too old or too ambitious." At his questioning look, she explained, "My grandfather. Men often thought if they got close to me, they could somehow benefit from my grandfather's money or his contacts. Of course, Grandpa Max could spot a fake from a mile away. Then there are my sisters. As soon as a man would take one look at them, he would do something stupid—like try to slip them his number when he thought I wasn't looking. After a while, I just gave up," she said, with a smile that didn't reach her eyes.

Graham wracked his brain for the right words, but he sensed that her hurt was too deep for him to reach. Instead, he moved thick strands of hair from her face and murmured, "Then the men you've met are stupid and blind."

She smiled, as he wanted her to, then she snuggled into his arms again. "Not all of them," she mused. "There is a vice president at one of Grandpa Max's companies—Bradley Anderson. He has wonderful manners. Before I left to take over the museum, I worked in the marketing department there. Brad would always find a reason to stop by my office. We went to lunch a couple of times. He even has stopped by the museum a few times. At the funeral, he was very kind. Maybe when I get back to L.A., I'll call him. Grandpa Max thought he was a decent man."

Graham grimaced. She obviously had no sense of a male ego. Like he really wanted to hear about another man while she was in his bed and he was still half-hard from wanting her.

"He sounds like a great guy. Wonderful manners and decent. I'd love for a woman to describe me that way," he muttered dryly.

She laughed. "Maybe he's not the most exciting man, but growing up with Kendra and Quinn I've had enough excitement to last me a lifetime." She abruptly turned in his arms and glanced at the alarm clock on the nightstand next to the bed. She groaned and tried to move from his arms, but Graham held tight. She stared at him. "I have to go. I didn't realize the time. Kendra and Quinn will be worried."

Graham highly doubted that either one of her self-absorbed sisters would think about her absence, but he kept his thoughts to himself. For the first time since he had kissed Charlie earlier, he thought back to his conversation with Boyd. Graham would bet that the conditions of the will required the sisters to spend each night in the house. Otherwise, he figured that Kendra and Quinn would have called a truce to stay at the Ritz in San Francisco and driven down every morning, rather than stay in the shack.

"Graham, let me go," she said, sounding near panicked. He instantly released her and she sat up in the bed, clinging to the sheet. She scanned the room for her clothes, looking frazzled and harried and as though Graham should grab her again and kiss her senseless.

"At least, let me feed you. It's barely eight o'clock." She paused at the mention of food. Graham had the good sense to hide his smile as added, "We still have left-overs from the party. Fudge brownies with chocolate icing."

She was torn. "Fudge brownies," she whispered.

He had her. "With chocolate icing," he repeated.

Charlie sighed in frustration then fell back against the bed. "I'll stay."

"You drive a hard bargain," he murmured before pressing a kiss against her soft lips. "Stay here. I'll be back."

He couldn't resist and kissed her again. She glared at him and crossed her arms over the sheet. "As you're well aware, I'm not going anywhere."

Graham once more wisely chose not to comment. He pulled a robe from his closet and slipped it on as he ran out the room. He even found himself whistling.

Chapter 18

Fifteen minutes later, Graham returned with a tray laden with food. He thought he might have gone overboard, but he hadn't known what Charlie would like so he had brought everything in the refrigerator. And, of course, the fudge brownies.

Charlie sat up in the bed, still clinging to the sheet. Graham smiled to himself as he set the tray on the bed. He would make Charlie get rid of that sheet if it was the last thing he did. Charlie gasped in shock when she saw the food and then her stomach's growls sounded through the room.

"Hungry?" he teased.

Her gaze flitted from the fried chicken to the corn on the cob to the potato salad. She tied the sheet around her chest as she murmured in awe, "All of this was left over from the party?"

"Don't be shy. There's plenty more where that came from."

Charlie eagerly dug in, and Graham had a feeling that the entire sheet could have disappeared and she wouldn't have cared. Graham laughed, then grabbed a chicken leg. He sat on the bed, careful not to disturb the tray.

"I really can't stay that long," she murmured through a mouthful of unrecognizable glob.

In response, Graham lifted the silver cover off the plate of brownies. Her eyes grew wide and her gulp was audible. "You have to eat," he said, trying to sound concerned about her hungry state.

Charlie nodded wordlessly, and this time Graham was unable to hide his smile. He pulled two cans of soda from the pocket of his robe and handed her one, then he sat back against the headboard and studied her. She ate with the same enthusiasm she used to respond to his kisses. The thought made him hard. And it made him recall the strong feelings she aroused, which made him uncomfortable because he didn't know how to identify them or what to do with them.

"You're staring at me," she accused. "You've probably never seen a woman eat this much at one time."

Graham smiled and said, with a shrug, "You won't get an argument from me."

She laughed, and Graham was reminded how much he liked that sound. "I don't eat that much."

"You do have an unhealthy obsession with chocolate," he teased.

She licked her fingers clean then said, defensively, "I like to eat."

"I like watching you eat," he murmured in a deep voice, imagining her mouth licking something else clean.

Her face flushed as she averted her gaze. Even after everything they had done, she was still shy around him. Graham resisted the urge to pull her into his arms and make her blush all over.

Graham smiled to lighten the sudden tension in the air, then said, "I haven't even taken you on a real date."

"That is a problem," she said, soberly. "In some circles, I might be considered a tramp."

Graham laughed. "No one thinks you're a tramp, Charlie. Trust me."

Her smile faded as she said, "Grandpa Max said never to trust a man who told you to trust him."

"He sounds like a smart man."

"He was. He was also driven and obsessive and mean."

Graham studied her for a moment as she focused on the plate, her appetite apparently gone, as she moved the food around the plate with a fork. "And you loved him."

She met his eyes then nodded. "He was the only man who ever loved me and accepted me. He was such a walking contradiction. He wanted Kendra, Quinn and I to be so tough, but he would have given his left arm to make certain we never had to shed a tear. He had a lot of money, but he was one of the loneliest men I've ever known. He told me right before he died that he didn't want Kendra, Quinn or I to live that way, and that's where he thought we were all headed."

Graham hated himself for asking, but he did. "Is that

why you three are here?" She stared at him, surprised, before she averted her gaze. He quickly covered his tracks. "I just meant that I would have thought you three would have been sorting out your inheritance, not living in Sibleyville and at each other's throats."

"What makes you think we inherited anything?"

"As you said, Max was a rich man. I assumed that he passed it all to you three, as his only living heirs."

"You would think," she muttered, more to herself than to him.

Graham knew he could have pushed her. He could have found out whatever he wanted from her at that moment. She was dying to tell him. But Graham pulled back. He should have helped his parents, helped Sibleyville, but he couldn't do that to Charlie. Never to her.

Her eyes narrowed as she studied. "You remind me of him."

"Of Max?" he asked, surprised. "I'm not certain that's a compliment."

She laughed, as she said, "I meant it as one. You see the world the way he did. You see my sisters and me the way he did."

"What do you mean?"

"When you first met the three of us, you were blinded by Kendra and Quinn. I was an afterthought—"

"Are you going to throw that in my face…?" His voice trailed off as he prevented himself finishing. He had been on the verge of saying, *for the rest of our lives.* But, that wasn't right. Graham didn't want to be with Charlie for the rest of his life. He wasn't ready to commit to any one woman, and if a man said anything about forever to Charlie, he could guarantee that he would be walking down the aisle of a church soon. Or maybe that honor was only reserved for the solid, dependable and thoroughly boring Bradley Anderson, Graham thought darkly.

"It's true, though," Charlie shot back, oblivious to his conflicting thoughts. "You've admitted it, but let me finish." Suddenly, she was crawling across the bed towards him, causing the tray of food to sway precariously back and forth on his white sheets. She swung one leg over his hips until she straddled him.

All parts of Graham's body perked up and he placed his hands on her sheet-encased hips.

She held his gaze as she said carefully, "I love my sisters, Graham. And part of the reason that I love them is that they're so confident and so beautiful. They can walk into a room and the room stops. But, I'm not like them, and I don't want to be. All of my life everyone expected that I *should* want to be like them, except Grandpa Max. And now you…even though it took you a while. You see that I'm more than just the other Sibley sister. You see me for me. Clumsy and all. And, no matter what happens after tonight, I want you to know that I'm glad I waited for you."

Graham's thoughts of lust quickly dissipated as he stared at the woman he slowly suspected that he was beginning to love.

"I'm sorry, Charlie," he whispered.

"For what?"

"I don't know," he said, shaking his head. "For making you defend yourself to me, for prying, for—"

She leaned down and kissed him, effectively cutting off his apology. It was a kiss of comfort. She was comforting him. He opened his mouth, and her tongue soothed his, seeking all the secret places and claiming them as her own. She opened the robe and her hands moved across his chest, through his chest hair, palming his nipples. Graham groaned and his fingers reflexively dug into her soft hips.

He tried to control his desire, but she was subtly moving against his hips and her kisses were soft and gentle and too soft and too gentle. He flipped her over until she lay on her back, breathless and laughing. He kissed her then, claiming her with all of the feelings that he had running through him that he didn't want to claim, so instead he claimed her mouth.

"The food—" she said in between his hungry kisses.

He stopped kissing her, staring at her amazed. "You want to stop *this* to eat?"

She laughed and caressed his face. "Graham, I choose you over chocolate, but I also don't want to roll around in fried chicken and potato salad."

Graham followed her amused gaze to the tray dangerously close to their heads. He quickly moved it to the dresser across the room then pulled off his robe as he crossed the room. He tore off the sheet, causing her to laugh and exposing her gorgeous body. He looked at her breasts and her rounded stomach and her hips. His gaze stuck on her curls and he inhaled.

She grabbed his arms, drawing his attention back to her face. "Don't go slow, Graham," she ordered, with a slight smile.

He didn't.

* * *

Charlie opened her eyes and stretched her arms over her head, feeling as if she had been sleeping for years. She felt refreshed and relaxed and… She suddenly realized that she was staring at a white ceiling with no water stains and that a large, hairy arm was wrapped around her waist. She suddenly realized that she was in Graham's bed with Graham.

She gasped when she saw the dark night sky out the bedroom window. She gasped even louder when she saw Graham sprawled next to her on the bed. Her cheeks flushed at what she had done to him and what she had allowed him to do to her. She had never planned to remain a virgin until marriage, but the older she got, the more it had seemed more practical considering she was almost thirty years old and hadn't slept with anyone. But, now, she had slept with a man who lived in another country and had made no promises about even seeing her again after he left Sibleyville.

Charlie ignored the tug on her heart that the sight of his completely relaxed face did to her. She glanced at the clock. It was almost eleven at night. She had to get home. Panic and fear raced through her, and she wasn't sure if she was more scared of her sisters' reaction, or if she was scared of abandoning Graham.

She tried to move from his arm, but his arm only tightened around her. She groaned and his eyes fluttered open. Whatever berating she had just given herself was lost as she stared into his dark eyes. What woman could resist him? She would never regret being with him. Never.

He smiled then slightly rose to plant a kiss against her lips. "Where are you going?" he murmured, as he fell back on the pillow. He closed his eyes, as if he was prepared to go back to sleep.

"Home."

"Stay the night," he growled, tightening his arm even more, until she was pulled flush against his side.

Charlie ignored the temptation to give in, no matter how much she wanted to. Not just because of the will, either. She had to keep some distance from Graham to protect her heart when he left. "I can't, Graham. My sisters will worry."

"We'll call them and let them know that you're here," he responded, simply, his eyes still closed.

"Your parents," she said, flatly.

His eyes opened and he smiled. "They like you. They'll be cool with it."

"Graham," she warned.

He groaned and released her. "I'll drive you home."

She sighed in relief and jumped from the bed, using a sheet to cover her nudity. Graham walked, tall and proud, to the closet to retrieve a pair of jeans. He glanced at her and smiled. "You know, when you cover yourself up like that, it makes me want to go caveman even more."

Charlie frowned at him as she pulled on her wrinkled clothes that had been on the floor. She tried to smooth out the wrinkles, but it was no use. She looked at her reflection in the mirror over the dresser and groaned. Anyone who took one look at her would know what she had been doing.

Her normally straightened hair was now wavy and

thick from the shower and in no presentable shape. She hesitantly touched her face, wondering if she was glowing or if it was the moonlight. She looked different, and she felt different.

"Ready?" Graham asked, coming to stand next to her.

Charlie ignored his gaze and walked from the room, careful not to make a sound. Graham, of course, stomped down the hallway in his boots, as usual. She shot him a silencing glare, but he just shrugged his shoulders innocently. His parents had to be back in the house by now. Charlie would prefer not to run into them.

She carefully picked her way down the stairs and sighed in relief when she saw the front door. She was almost home free. Just as she stepped into the foyer, Eliza walked out of the darkened kitchen, holding a bowl of ice cream in her hands.

Charlie abruptly stopped in her tracks and Graham, who obviously hadn't been paying attention, ran into her. She grunted and Eliza looked up.

Charlie wanted to sink into the floor when she met Graham's mother's gaze. The older woman looked surprised then quickly recovered as she smiled.

"Good evening, Charlie," she said, as if it wasn't the dead of the night and Charlie had not been sneaking from her son's room.

"Eliza," Charlie greeted in a strained voice.

"Mom, I'm going to drive Charlie home," Graham said, as if he didn't have a care in the world. Charlie wanted to hit him.

"See you in the morning," Eliza said then continued past the couple with a glance at Graham.

"So, now can you stay?" Graham asked Charlie, amusement lacing in his supposedly innocent question.

Charlie jabbed him in the stomach and walked out of the house, ignoring his soft laughter.

Chapter 19

"A penny for your thoughts?"

Graham smiled at the familiar question, as Lance walked onto the porch and sat in the wicker chair across from Graham the next morning.

Since Graham had been thinking of Charlie and all the things he had done to her last night and that he still wanted to do, he didn't think his father would want to know. In fact, Graham *knew* that Lance would not want to know.

"Just daydreaming," Graham murmured then stared towards the expansive fields behind the house. "We'll finish the last of the rows tomorrow and then planting season for Forbes Farms will be officially over."

Graham didn't bother to hide the thrill of satisfaction he felt at the words. He had helped his father many times with planting, but had never been in complete and total charge himself. He had to admit that there was something nice about finishing a job as large as this one had been.

"Good," Lance said, nodding.

The two sat in a comfortable silence for a moment before Lance said, casually, "Your mother told me about the sight that greeted her when she went to get a snack last night."

Graham smiled when he remembered how embarrassed Charlie had been.

"Sorry about that," Graham said, unable to wipe the smile off his face.

Lance shot him an amused glance and asked, "Sorry you got caught or sorry it happened?" At Graham's look in his direction, Lance laughed and said, "I was living in this house with your grandparents when Eliza came to visit before we got married. At least, I had the sense to know which floorboards creak."

Graham decided it was best to change the subject before his father mentioned something else about his parents' sex life he'd rather not know. "Charlie told me about the exhibit. I didn't know you had it in you."

"Neither did I." Lance visibly hesitated, which made Graham instantly interested. Lance didn't hesitate about anything. "Charlie said there's going to be a lot of work that needs to be done for this exhibit, and I told her I'd help. In fact, I can't wait to do something different. Don't get me wrong, Graham. You know how much I love this farm. It's been in our family for generations and I hope when it's passed on to you, it'll stay that way, but…planting season is over.

I can handle the rest myself. Go back to Tokyo. Go back to your life."

The words that Graham had been waiting for six months to hear sliced through the air. And instead of feeling the joy and elation that he'd thought he would feel, he felt strangely uncertain, just as he had last night when Charlie had told him.

As if picking up on his thoughts, Lance said, dryly, "I thought you'd be doing cartwheels right about now."

"I… Thanks, Dad," Graham said, belatedly. "I'm just surprised."

"It's time, don't you think?"

"It was time six weeks ago when I caught you dancing with Mom on the back porch."

Lance laughed, clearly unashamed of his behavior. "I liked having my son around. Sue me."

"I should," Graham muttered. "You manipulated me."

"You've had a good time these last six months, Graham. Admit it."

"You're joking, right?"

"You got to hang out with Wyatt again, join town council, make Boyd's life miserable. City folk pay for the opportunity to spend a few weeks working on a ranch or a farm or to ride a horse. You got all that, plus clean, country air, blue skies, Main Street and your mom's cooking. And then there's Charlie."

Graham stared down at his hands, his sarcastic reply cut off at the mention of Charlie. He knew his father was watching him for any sign. Lance would never mention grandchildren, but Graham suspected that Lance probably pressured Eliza to mention it to him.

Graham finally met his father's gaze and said, quietly, "Charlie is a... Once I leave Sibleyville, I'll never see her again."

"Of course you will."

"No, Dad, I won't." He spent a little too much time studying the stitching on the work gloves next to him. He murmured, "I guess I'll tell Theo to make our flight plans."

Lance once again sounded hesitant, as he said, "Son, if you don't want to go back, you can stay here—"

"Of course, I want to go back," Graham said, although his response was not as quick or as convincing as it would have been just a few weeks ago. He stood and said, "I've got to get ready for council meeting. I'll talk to you later."

Lance just stared at him, and Graham quickly walked into the house because the one person who could read whatever was on Graham's mind was Lance. And, frankly, Graham didn't want to hear questions about Charlie that he couldn't answer in his own mind.

Charlie heard the back screen door to the shack slam closed and looked up from the book she had been reading on the porch swing. Kendra frowned at her and sat on the swing next to her, causing it to ricochet wildly. Charlie ignored Kendra and went back to her book.

She had spent all day walking around in a daze, wanting to talk to her sisters, wanting to talk to anyone. Something amazing had happened to her last night, and even though she was living with the two women in the world who she was supposed to be the closest to, she couldn't talk to them. And it wasn't because of their bet about Graham. It was because she feared their reaction. They would make fun of her naiveté for falling for Graham in the first place, and for sleeping with a man she had only known a week. And they would have been right.

"You cut it close last night," Kendra bit out. "Where were you?"

"I told you, I was at the Forbes's house," Charlie answered, without looking up from her book.

"Working," Kendra accused, angrily. "Something that none of us are supposed to do while we're here. We're supposed to be spending time together."

Charlie finally looked up from her book, surprised by the anger in Kendra's voice and more surprised by her own anger. "We don't spend any time together even when we're all in the house. What does it matter if I want to crawl around the Forbes's attic and look at a bunch of paintings? I didn't call anyone at work. I haven't even drafted contracts, even though that's what I should be doing now. Unlike you, Kendra, I don't have a staff of twenty at my disposal. The more time I spend here, the more likely it is that I will lose the museum. Don't begrudge me for trying to save it while I'm here."

Kendra jumped to her feet and stalked to the railing. She whirled around to face Charlie. Charlie grew concerned when she saw the tears in Kendra's eyes.

"So, now you hate me, too?" Kendra asked, a sniffle muting her harsh tone.

"What—"

"You haven't spoken to me since the night Graham and his friends came over. You hate me, too, just because I picked on Little Miss Perfect."

"Kendra, I don't hate you," Charlie said, surprised by the hurt hidden under the anger in Kendra's tone. "I could never hate you. You're my sister."

"Fine. You don't like me then. Right? All because of Quinn. She's turned you against me, too," Kendra screeched, sounding on the verge of massive tears.

"No, she hasn't. I thought what you did to her was mean, but—"

"Mean? Mean!" Kendra repeated, her anger and tears making her voice raise several octaves. "So, you're defending her now, too? Just like Theo. No one messes with perfect Quinn. No one says a word about beautiful Quinn. She must be protected and defended, especially against the horrible Kendra. No one ever thinks to defend me. No one ever stands up for me. Everyone just thinks that I'll roll with the punches, that I can figure it out on my own, but maybe I want someone to protect me. Did you ever think of that, Charlie—" Kendra's rant ended on a sob and she buried her face in her hands.

Charlie had never seen her sister so emotional, so anything but perfect, take-no-crap-and-no-prisoners Kendra. Charlie was frozen with indecision as she watched Kendra struggle to breathe through her tears. Charlie berated herself for even hesitating, then crossed the porch to take Kendra into her arms. Kendra stiffened for a moment, but then slowly lowered her hands and leaned onto Charlie's shoulders, wrapping her arms about Charlie's waist.

Charlie smoothed down Kendra's silky hair. Kendra was trembling. Charlie felt tears fill her own eyes. She had not known how much Kendra had been hurting.

As Kendra's sobs lessened and her trembles receded, Charlie led her to the porch swing. They both sat, still holding hands, both of their eyes red and watery.

"I'm sorry," Kendra said, through a sob-choked laugh.

"I don't think I've ever seen you cry," Charlie murmured, staring at her sister as if seeing a stranger. "Not at Mom and Dad's funeral, or Grandpa Max's funeral."

"You should have seen me three months ago. You would have gotten your fill of my tears," Kendra said, with another strange laugh.

"What happened three months ago?"

Kendra inhaled deeply then slowly let the breath out. She smoothed her hair down and wiped her wet cheeks with the backs of her hands. She finally turned to face Charlie.

"I got fired from the investment house."

Charlie had been expecting many different responses, but not that one. "What? How?"

"How it always happens…I made stupid mistakes and people lost money. A lot of money. And, instead of coming clean when it happened, I tried to fix it. And my attempt to fix the situation only made it worse because it looked like I was trying to cover it up and cheat my clients. But, I swear that was not my intent, Charlie. I wanted to get everyone's money back and save my career, but in the end…I lost everything."

Charlie gripped her sister's hand again. "Kendra," she whispered, shocked and concerned.

"I barely got out of this without having to spend time in jail. Can you imagine me in jail?" Kendra's laughter sounded half-maniacal as she shook her head. "The bottom line is the company fired me and no one in the New York financial world will touch me. In other words, I have no job prospects, no income, I have to sell my condo and none of my former friends will talk to me."

"What are we going to do?"

"We? You're not a part of this."

"Of course I am."

Kendra smiled at her, then her eyes filled with tears as she whispered, "I'm just glad Grandpa Max died before he found out. It would have killed him. He was so proud of me and now…now, I'm a failure."

"Grandpa Max would still be proud of you," Charlie said, firmly. "He was proud of all of us, no matter what."

"You couldn't do anything wrong, Charlie, because he loved you. He only paid attention to me when I won something or got a promotion."

"That's not true."

"Yes, it is. He asked you to work in the company. He never asked Quinn or me. He called you. He talked to you. He trusted you."

"Kendra, I was there," Charlie said. "You and Quinn moved away, and I stayed—"

"Why do you think we moved?" Kendra demanded, fresh tears coating her eyes. "You don't even know…I always thought he would leave you everything."

Kendra abruptly shook her head then pulled her hand from Charlie's grasp. She stood and walked back to the rail, suddenly the picture of suppressed athletic energy. "It doesn't matter anymore, because here we both are trying to jump through one last hoop for him. Sometimes I want to strangle that old bastard for making us go through this."

"Kendra, I think I finally know why Grandpa Max did this—"

"You asked me what we can do," Kendra said suddenly, interrupting her. Her eyes were bright with remaining tears. "We can finish this. Stay in the house until the deadline and get our money. I need this money just as badly as you and Quinn. We have to do it together, Charlie. Do I have your word?"

Charlie held Kendra's gaze then slowly nodded. Kendra sagged against the railing in relief.

Chapter 20

Graham twirled the pen around his finger as Boyd droned on in the middle of the meeting room. It had only been a week since the last meeting, but Graham felt as if he had lived a lifetime. His father had released him, he had made love to Charlie and, for the first time ever, he was questioning his desire to live so far from everything he knew and everyone he loved. Did that include Charlie? Graham wasn't sure. He didn't want to be sure because the question was positively frightening, given the powerful feelings that threatened to engulf him every time he thought of her.

"…and, if there are no other issues, then I believe we can adjourn—"

"I actually have an announcement," Graham interrupted Boyd's closing remarks.

He normally would have been pleased by the surprised looks on every face around him. Graham hadn't spoken more than three words at the meeting in six months, and here he was speaking again for the second time in two weeks.

"What is it?" Boyd asked, suspiciously.

From the front row of the spectator area, Alma, who was the only non-member of the council in attendance, cleared her throat.

"I'm returning to Tokyo. My father will take over my seat until a proper election can be held," Graham said, surprised by the lump in his throat. He ignored Boyd's shout of outrage and focused on Velma and Angus. "I'm leaving tomorrow. It's been an honor working with you two."

"So soon?" Velma's eyes coated with tears behind her thick eyeglasses. "You, too, dear. You're really a lovely boy."

"Lance told me that he would give you your walking papers, but I didn't believe him," Angus drawled, while leaning back in his chair. "Looks like he did it, after all."

"You can't leave," Boyd finally sputtered. "You and I aren't done."

Graham shot Boyd a warning look. "We can talk later, Robbins."

"We talk now, you fool. I told you that I would do whatever I had to do to save this town. I thought you were going to help me, but you're going to turn tail and run. Abandon this town. Just like I thought you would."

"What on earth are you talking about, Boyd?" Velma asked, as she looked from Boyd to Graham.

"Nothing—"

Boyd interrupted Graham's stuttered explanation, "Graham promised to help me keep an eye on the Sibley sisters. To decipher their motives about the future of this town and to promote the virtues of Sibleyville."

"Those girls seem perfectly lovely," Velma said, then wagged a finger in Boyd's direction and said, "You leave them alone."

"Leave them alone?" Boyd's chest huffed in outrage as his face turned an unhealthy shade of red. "Those *lovely* girls hold the future of this town in their hands—"

"Boyd, shut up," Graham ordered, jumping to his feet.

Boyd ignored him and stood in the middle of the floor and addressed the town council members, who, for once, were staring at him with rapt fascination, "Those *lovely* girls have to remain in that uninhabitable shack for two weeks in order to inherit Max's wealth. And do you know what part of their inheritance is? This town—"

"We don't know that for certain, Boyd," Graham interrupted, angrily.

Boyd ignored him and continued, "Every note that Max ever hoarded. The shops, the farms, the houses. Who knows what those nitwits might do with it?"

"You know nothing about them," Graham shot back, anger making his voice tight and controlled.

"Is it true, Graham?" came Angus's worried voice. "Do those girls really own all of our notes?"

Graham couldn't stand the anguish in saw in Augus's eyes, as he no doubt thought about his cattle ranch. Graham admitted softly, "We don't know for certain, but they're Max's only heirs."

Angus inhaled sharply and averted his gaze. "My God," he croaked.

"And if they don't stay in the house together, where will the money go?" Velma asked Boyd in a flat tone that Graham had never heard her use before.

"I don't know. That was Graham's job to find out, but as you all can see, he doesn't feel it's his problem anymore," Boyd muttered, sounding almost dejected. "I don't know what we're going to do now. I guess we have to wait until next week to see if we will still be running our farms."

As an awkward silence fell in the meeting, Graham said, "The Sibley sisters are decent people. They would never do anything to purposely hurt the people in this town. I'm sure if you talk to them—"

"You don't know that, Graham. You've known them one week," Boyd spat out.

"I know them," Graham shot back, clenching his fists. He knew Charlie. And if Boyd said one negative word about her, Graham planned to leap across the table and rip his throat out.

"You're going to leave us now, Graham?" Velma asked, worriedly.

Graham's anger faded as he looked into Velma's worried eyes. He hesitated then said, "Velma—"

Velma interrupted his apology as she slowly stood, collecting her purse and sweater. She didn't meet his gaze as she said, "This isn't fair to you. You have served this town well in the last six months. You owe us nothing. Good luck in Tokyo."

She walked from the room, her quiet footsteps on the

wood floor more damaging than any sort of stomps Boyd could have taken.

Graham stared after Velma then turned to Angus, who wouldn't look at him. "What exactly should I be doing, Angus? It's not my responsibility to save this town."

"You're right. It's not your responsibility. You don't live here. This town has leaned on you long enough," Angus said, quietly. He stood, placing his cowboy hat on his head. "I guess I'll see you next time you're in town."

Angus left, too, leaving Graham with Boyd, Alma and Peter. Graham tiredly turned to Boyd, expecting some more yells and screams and maybe a few more threats.

Instead, Boyd motioned to Alma then stalked out the room. With an apologetic smile at Graham, Alma hurried after him. Peter followed, looking confused, as always.

Graham sank back into his chair. He had wanted for so long to be alone in the meeting room, and now that he was, it just didn't feel right.

"Sorry I'm late. I got caught up at the mortuary," Wyatt announced his presence as he stomped into the diner and fell into the booth next to Graham and across from Theo at Annie's Diner.

"Just for future reference, Wyatt, that's a sentence that should never come out of your mouth when a man is about to eat," Theo announced then shuddered in disgust.

Wyatt ignored Theo and asked Graham, "What was the big emergency that I had to drop everything and meet you guys here?"

Graham hesitated and Theo announced, excitedly, "We're going home!" Wyatt looked shocked as he glanced at Graham for confirmation. Graham only nodded. Theo laughed and said, "This is good news, Dubya. Graham has finally been freed. His dad gave him his parole. Now, we just have to work on getting you to Tokyo and then the real fun can begin."

"I can't leave Mom or the mortuary," Wyatt said, quietly, staring at his hands.

Theo rolled his eyes in frustration then said, "Bring her with you. I dig all women."

Wyatt frowned at Theo then looked at Graham again. "Are you really leaving?"

"Of course I am. I've been praying for this day for six months," Graham said, irritated for some reason.

"I know," Wyatt murmured. He visibly hesitated then added, "I guess I just…I always thought that beneath all your complaining and moaning that you kind of liked being home."

"It was nice," Graham begrudgingly admitted. "But, what am I supposed to do? Stay? There's nothing for me here."

"Your town is here. Your family and friends," Wyatt said, incredulously.

"Graham is coming back to Tokyo," Theo said tightly. "The Board is voting on the new president this weekend, and Graham has to be there. This is it for him. Do you want him to throw away everything he's worked for during the last fifteen years to stay here and play Marlboro cowboy?"

Wyatt ignored Theo and asked Graham, "What about Charlie?"

Graham tensed. "What about her?"

"At the house, I thought…I thought maybe there was something between you two."

"Charlie is…great, but she and I are just passing time."

"Passing time?" Wyatt repeated in disbelief. His eyes hardened as he said, "Charlie doesn't seem like the type of girl to just pass time with a man."

"Charlie is my business, Wyatt. Stay out of it," Graham glared.

Annie walked over with three plates loaded with food. She unceremoniously dumped the plates on the table.

"I ordered a salad," Theo protested, staring at the patty melt.

"Well, you got a patty melt and fries," she responded simply then slapped the bill on the table and moved to the next table of customers.

"Not one for small talk, is she?" Wyatt muttered, while staring in disgust at his plate.

Graham stared at his own hamburger. He wasn't even hungry. This was supposed to be a happy day; he wasn't supposed to feel like he was being led slowly inch by torturous inch to the gallows.

"Charlie is a good woman, Graham," Theo said, pinning Graham with a hard glare. "Don't hurt her."

Graham wanted to protest, but instead he stared down at his plate. He pushed it away.

"Why all the long faces?" Theo suddenly announced, his voice too bright and too loud for the diner. "Graham is about to be crowned vice president of one of the largest corporations in the world. We should be toasting with… Well, with this watered-down beer. Come on, glasses—okay, plastic cups—up in the air."

Wyatt held Graham's gaze for a moment then lifted up the plastic cup of beer that had been waiting for him. Graham quickly lifted up his own cup before Wyatt said anything more.

"Here's to Graham," Theo announced then added, "And to me because I talked some sense into him."

Wyatt mumbled something incomprehensible then stood up from the booth, leaving his cup untouched. "Good luck, Graham. I'm sure you'll get the promotion. You always do."

He nodded at Theo then walked out of the diner. Graham set his cup back down, without having taken a drink. His last day in Sibleyville was not turning out the way he'd expected.

"Why do you look like you just lost your best friend?" Theo demanded, annoyed. "We should be celebrating. No more Sibleyville. Drink up."

Graham decided not to respond and, instead, gulped down the remainder of the beer, hoping it would wash the bitter taste out of his mouth.

Chapter 21

Charlie heard a truck's engine in the distance and looked out the kitchen window over the sink. She sighed when she saw an unfamiliar blue truck drive down the road. She had been listening for a car engine ever since the sun went down. She knew that Graham had town council meeting tonight, but she also knew that he would come for her, just as much as she knew her first name was Charlotte.

It could have just been wistful thinking, but her body told her that it wasn't. Even though she didn't have experience, Charlie knew that what she and Graham had shared last night didn't happen often. She might not have been his love-at-first-sight woman, but she had rocked his world last night, even if she did say so herself.

"You've been jumpy all night, Charlie. What's wrong?" Quinn asked, irritably, from the kitchen table, where she sat delicately eating a peach for dinner.

A peach. Charlie wasn't even satisfied with a peach for a snack.

"Are you waiting for someone?" Kendra asked, on the other side of the kitchen table, with her dinner protein shake. "Pizza delivery? Chinese food? Dry-cleaning? Forget it, honey, it's not here."

Kendra had been her usual brash and combative self since their talk on the porch, but Charlie knew what bubbled under the surface. Kendra obviously did not want Quinn to know the truth.

"I'm not waiting for anyone…" Her voice trailed off as truck headlights turned off the road onto their driveway.

Her heart pounded and she sagged against the sink. The truck stopped in the front yard and the headlights turned off. She would recognize Graham's long, lean silhouette anywhere. Although she couldn't see his face, she felt his eyes on her. He walked to the kitchen door and the soft knock startled Kendra and Quinn.

Before either woman could move, Charlie ran to the door and flung it open. Graham stepped into the house, his eyes only on Charlie.

"Hi," he said, quietly.

Charlie grinned. She felt calm now. Settled. Able to cope with whatever else the day threw at her, as long as she had Graham on her side. "Hi," she breathed in a whisper.

Graham smiled then drew her into his arms and kissed her. His mouth demanded entry and she opened for him. His tongue swept through her mouth and she sighed, clinging to his shirt.

He tore his mouth from hers and leaned his forehead against hers. "Come with me."

Charlie bit back the urge to respond *anywhere* and, instead, nodded. He grabbed her hand and she left. Only when she was in the truck did she remember her sisters sitting at the kitchen table with their mouths wide open.

Graham started the engine and sped down the road towards his house. Charlie smiled and just enjoyed the night air blowing through the truck and the soft country music on the radio. The stars blinked in the sky, the only lights on the dark road were the truck's headlights. They could have been the only two people left in the world.

"Now I get it," she said softly.

"What?" he asked, darting a glance at her.

"Your father's paintings. This town. It's small and it doesn't have a Starbucks, but it's beautiful." She looked at him and was surprised to find him staring at her, a strange expression on his face. He looked stunned or disoriented. Either way, Charlie didn't think he should be staring at her like that while they were hurtling down a dark highway at sixty miles an hour. She touched his shoulder and said, hesitantly, "Graham."

He abruptly shook his head, as if breaking out of a trance, and looked back at the road.

The truck sped by his house and she asked, surprised, "Where are we going?"

"The best spot in Sibleyville."

Charlie decided to just sit back and enjoy the ride. She leaned back against the seat and looked across the

cab at him. His side profile was a testimony to everything male and strong. His arms were muscled. And he
handled the steering wheel easily and confidently, the
way he handled everything else in his life, including her.
Charlie's entire body hummed alive.

The road eventually narrowed into one lane. Tree
branches began to encroach on what remained of the
road, as if attempting to claim it again. The ride became
bumpy as the unpaved road gave way to dirt and rocks.
The road appeared to end, but Graham turned left into
a wide clearing. He got out of the truck, grabbing a
blanket and a cooler from the back seat.

"Where are we going?" she asked, looking around in
apprehension at the dark trees.

His smile was her only answer before he held out his
hand. Charlie gritted her teeth then unhooked her seat belt.
She got out of the truck and joined him, taking his hand.

"You won't be disappointed," he promised.

Graham led her into the trees and her concern disappeared as she made out the path gently grooved between
the trunks. With Graham's strong, big hand around hers
and the stars as their guide, Charlie allowed herself to
enjoy the night, to enjoy the scent of nature that couldn't
be reproduced and the sight of Graham's broad back and
taut behind as he walked in front of her on the narrow path.

They entered another clearing and Charlie gasped in
awe at the sight below her. Natural steps in the path led to
a pool of rippling water fed by a small waterfall on the
other side of the clearing that dripped eight feet down the
moss-covered rocks to the pond. The pond was surrounded
by the rock wall on all sides and steam rose from the water.

"Graham, it's beautiful," she whispered. "What is this place?"

He helped her down the path to the grass-covered level ground that encircled the pond as a natural sun-bathing area. "It's the pride and joy of this town. Only the kids use it, while we old folks try to forget it exists."

Charlie laughed and watched him shake out the blanket and spread it on the ground. He opened the cooler and pulled out a bottle of red wine and two plastic wineglasses.

"I do things in style," he told her, while wriggling his eyes like an old-time-movie villain.

Charlie shook her head in amusement and then sat on the blanket. Graham poured the wine and handed her a plastic glass, before settling next to her, his thigh pressed against hers.

"I brought some chocolate, too," he said.

She caught the nerves in his voice and she instantly asked, "What's wrong, Graham?"

"I'm leaving tomorrow, Charlie."

"For Tokyo?" she choked out.

"The board votes on Monday for the vice president, and I have to be there."

"I knew you would leave soon after Lance told you, I just didn't expect it to be this soon."

"Me neither." He seemed unable to sit any longer and stood. "I have to be there. I've been gone for six months, and I hope my past record can carry me, but if I'm not there in person for the vote… I can kiss it goodbye. I have to go."

Charlie stared at the red liquid in her cup, the night no longer feeling as magical as it once had. She had thought she would have a few more days with him. She had wanted more time to feel this wanted and cherished.

"This is what you wanted, Graham," she finally said, forcing herself to sound upbeat. "I'm happy for you."

He stared at her for a moment then sat back next to her again, framing her face with his hands. "I'm sorry—"

"We both knew this day was coming. It just came a little sooner than expected," she said, surprised at how confident she sounded even as her heart broke.

"I just wish... Maybe you could come to Tokyo," Graham blurted out.

She averted her gaze when she saw the regret at this hastily spoken statement cross his face. He obviously hadn't meant to invite her to Tokyo.

"Maybe," she murmured.

"I mean it, Charlie," he said, using his thumb to lift her chin until she met his eyes. "I want you there. I can show you all of the great things about it. We can travel. We can go all over Japan."

"Maybe," she repeated then looked at the water.

"Charlie—"

"Let's enjoy this night together," she said, interrupting him once more to allow him a graceful way out.

He was silent for a moment then abruptly stood and pulled off his shirt. He unbuckled his jeans and pulled them down. Charlie surveyed his muscled legs and the bulge in his briefs before she remembered that they were outside. It was isolated, but they were still outside.

"Graham," she said, giggling. "Someone will see you."

"Believe me, anyone who comes up here will be too focused on your gorgeous body to look at me."

"I am not taking off my clothes."

He pushed down his underwear and Charlie gulped. He was already half-erect. He walked towards her totally unashamed. He knelt in front of her. His desire washed over her in waves and her center clenched as if sensing his impending presence.

His voice was deep as he whispered, "I want to remember you naked under the moonlight." It took her several seconds to tell herself to stop holding her breath. She glanced around the clearing once more and he smoothed back her hair. "No one will bother us, Charlie. They'll see my truck and they'll leave. This place has always been about first dibs."

Charlie bit her bottom lip then looked at him again. When would she ever be in this situation again? A gorgeous man who wanted her naked on a moonlit night. She smiled then slowly pulled off her tank top. He smiled and continued to watch the show.

She tried to be as confident as he was as she stood and slowly unbuttoned her jeans. She gulped as his gaze moved over every inch of her. She pushed the jeans down over her hips. His gaze focused on her underwear. He grinned up at her and motioned for her to take them off.

Charlie crossed her arms over her breasts and looked around the edges of the clearing once more.

"I'm a prude, aren't I?" she asked, laughing.

He stood and kissed her. "An adorable prude." He fingered the lace-covered strap of her bra. She didn't move as he held her gaze and reached around to unclasp the garment. He eased the straps off her shoulders, gently pushing down her crossed arms in the process. Her breasts spilled into the cool night air, her nipples instantly beading.

"Now, for my favorite part," he whispered, his hands on the edge of her underpants.

She released a breath as he slowly pulled her underwear off and down her legs. His hands moved up her legs then around to her behind as she stood fully naked in front of him.

Graham then took her hand and led her into the water.

"It's warm," she gasped in surprise. She continued to walk down the slope until the water came to just above her breasts.

Graham stood in front of her. Any amusement in his expression had disappeared as he regarded her closely.

He whispered her name like a prayer as he pulled her towards him and kissed her. He was slow and gentle. Sweet. Except her emotions were too raw for slow and gentle. She wanted him to be out of his mind, to remember always that she had done that to him.

She trailed her hand down his chest to touch his now fully engorged penis. She caught his gasp of surprise with her mouth. She massaged the length of him, and his body jerked against hers.

"Charlie, baby, please…I want to make this last," he pleaded.

She ignored him and pulled him to her mouth again. Her movements became more insistent as she sought to discover the elusive taste of him in his mouth. She knew she would never discover it, but she tried just the same. She pulled his bottom lip into her mouth and suckled, then she slowly released it, latching on for one small extra moment.

Graham's heavy breathing filled the clearing and his hands had become like a vise on her waist. She loosely wrapped her hand around his length, unable to fully close her fingers.

He stared at her for a moment then muttered, "One day I'm going to take my time making love to you."

"But not today," she said hopefully.

"Not today," he replied, with a grim expression.

Charlie grinned, even as he practically carried her out the pool. He laid her on the blanket and was on top of her in seconds. He gave her no respite, no chance to catch her breath. His hands were everywhere. His tongue was everywhere. His tongue dipped inside of her center and she screamed his name. His tongue plunged inside her repeatedly until she was writhing and shaking her head, unable to handle the feelings.

He cursed again then plunged his length into her at the same time his mouth latched onto hers. Charlie tasted herself on him. She clung to his back, moving with him, as he moved inside of her. It was a perfect rhythm, as if they had done this one hundred times before, rather than twice.

She arched against him and he plunged faster, barreling into her, no longer in control. Charlie screamed his name as she hovered on the edge, the feelings pulsating out of every point of her body. Graham dropped his head to her and moved harder and faster. It was too much.

She screamed as she fell over the edge into the weightless, terribly perfect abyss. He plunged into her a few more times than gave a hoarse cry before he collapsed against her.

Charlie's heart continued to pound against her chest as she took several deep breaths. Sweat and water glistened over Graham's chest and face, as he grunted and looked down at her. She traced each of his features with her finger, running along the hard planes of his face.

He kissed her once, twice, soothing, bringing her back to herself. Then a long, erotic kiss that promised a new beginning instead of an ending. His hand tweaked her right nipple then he nipped it gently. She gasped into his mouth as she felt his still-submerged hardness harden inside her again, as her own body responded again. His kisses grew more demanding, eating her, his hands were doing wonderful things to her sensitive breasts. He was fully hard, and he began to move inside her once more.

Incredibly the butterflies returned to their spiral. Charlie was too hoarse and exhausted to cry Graham's name. Instead, she moaned and squeezed her eyes shut as she dug her fingernails into his shoulders. Graham whispered hoarse words of lust, and maybe love, as one of his hands trailed down to play with her pulsating knob.

Graham shuddered inside her for the second time that night, and this time, Charlie followed suit seconds later. The last shudder wracked his body and then he stared down at her with wonder and fear in his eyes.

"What have you done to me?" he whispered, speaking more to himself than to her.

Charlie averted her gaze from his and stared at the star-filled night sky, uncertain how one acted after something like that. Tears filled her eyes because she knew that things would never be like this with anyone else. Not even the poor fool Bradley Anderson, who she would compare every night to Graham. Bradley didn't deserve that. And neither did she.

Now that Charlie knew what was possible, she wasn't going to settle for anything less. Maybe one day she would find another man who made her feel like Graham did. Maybe.

Graham made a move to pull out of her. She groaned in protest, but he pressed a kiss on the tip of her nose and whispered, "I'm crushing you."

"Never," she said, shaking her head.

Graham smiled gently, but moved off her. He pulled her on top of him and stared at the same stars that she now watched.

He stroked her hair for a few moments, as if she really was precious to him, before he said, quietly, "I didn't use protection. That was stupid."

"I'm a big girl. I could have stopped you at any time."

He ignored her dry remark and said, "If anything... Call me if anything happens because of this night." She was silent and his hand wrapped around her tighter. He growled, "Promise me, Charlie."

"I promise."

He smiled then kissed her ear. "I'm going to miss you, Charlie."

She didn't answer because Graham didn't need to know that she was going to miss him every day for the rest of her life.

Chapter 22

Charlie screamed as the shower curtain in her bathroom was ripped open the next morning. She covered her breasts with her dripping wet washcloth and stared in shock at her two sisters, who stood in the morning light of the bathroom. Identical expressions of annoyance and anger were on their faces.

Charlie wiped water—and a few tears that she had spilled over Graham—from her eyes and screeched, "What are you doing?"

"Get dressed," Kendra snapped. "We need to talk."

Quinn pursed her lips then pulled the curtain back into place. Charlie took as long as possible to finish showering. She dried herself off as slowly as possible and then spent about five minutes brushing and flossing her teeth. The last thing she wanted to do was talk with her sisters, especially when all she could think about was Graham. She had vowed last night not to settle for anything less than what she shared with Graham, but in the harsh light of day, she realized that she didn't want anyone else. She wanted Graham. And she would never see him again.

Charlie dressed, then went to find her sisters. They waited on the front porch. Kendra was pacing the length of the porch, while Quinn actually sat on the porch steps. Since Quinn was wearing a white skirt, Charlie knew that she was upset.

Both women turned at the sound of Charlie stepping onto the porch.

"You and Graham?" Kendra shouted, throwing up her hands in disbelief. "When the hell did that happen?"

"You said you didn't want to be in the bet," Quinn said, accusingly.

"And Graham… He made us do all those things, eat all of those horrible things, as a joke," Kendra snarled. "He is going to pay for this. I can't wait to wrap my hands around his neck."

"Why did you tell us you didn't want to be in the bet, Charlie?" Quinn demanded. "You lied. You should have competed with us fair and square, instead of sneaking behind our backs."

"And night before last… You weren't working. You were with Graham," Kendra continued ranting. "You slept with him. Don't even bother to deny it. You slept with him, and didn't tell us."

"You slept with him?" Quinn asked, her eyes growing

wide as saucers. "But, you don't…I thought… Aren't you a virgin?"

"Of course, she slept with him," Kendra told Quinn, with a "duh" tone. "No man kisses a woman the way Graham kissed her in our kitchen, unless he has slept with her."

"Charlie," Quinn said, a disappointed and worried tone in her voice. "I told you what he was like. I hope you're not expecting a relationship with him."

"Enough," Charlie said, holding up her hand. Her sisters actually listened to her and stopped talking. She took a deep breath then said softly, "I'm in love with him."

Quinn sagged against the porch, while Kendra stopped pacing to gawk at her.

"What?" Kendra whispered, horrified.

"I'm in love with Graham." Charlie wrung her hands together as tears filled her eyes. "And I'll never see him again. He's leaving day."

"Today?" Quinn repeated, as she slowly rose from the porch. She grabbed Charlie's arms and said, with a dramatic sigh, "Oh, Charlie, I know exactly how you feel."

"You do?"

"Sephora went through this exact same thing with Prince Dexter of Amtaria, a small island off the coast of Italy. See, she loved him, and he loved her, but their love was impossible. He was pledged to marry another," Quinn said, in that loud stage voice she drifted into whenever she spoke about Sephora. "The writers wanted to have Prince Dexter break his vows, defile his honor, ruin his country and have him move to Diamond Valley with Sephora. And I told them—no. No. Prince Dexter was too honorable and Sephora—God bless her—values honor and duty above all else. If Prince Dexter broke his vow to marry Lady Lucinda, the very thing that made Sephora love him would have been destroyed."

Quinn ended her dramatic speech with tears in her eyes and a downcast head.

Charlie extracted her hands from Quinn's grip and exchanged glances with Kendra.

Kendra spat out, "What in the hell are you talking about, Quinn? This is Charlie's life, not some stupid soap opera. She's in love for the first time in her life, and I'm sure she doesn't want to be compared to Sephora and one of her thousands of lovers. The woman shouldn't even be able to walk with the number of men who have been between her legs."

Quinn sniffed and said, stiffly, "I was just trying to help."

Kendra rolled her eyes in irritation then turned to Charlie. Her tone gentled, but she was her usual no-nonsense self. "You have to know that you and Graham will never work. He lives in Japan, Charlie. He's a single, wealthy, gorgeous Black man. No kids. No ex-wives. No record. He's probably one of the last eligible Black men on this planet. Believe me. He's not settling down any time soon."

"I know. I know," Charlie said, slightly annoyed. "Everything you two are saying…absent the Sephora reference…I've told myself a million times. I'm not stupid."

Quinn's expression changed, as she said softly, "We never thought you were stupid, Charlie."

Charlie walked away from Quinn to place some

distance between them before Quinn tried to grab her hands again. She willed her tears not to fall, but it was a losing battle. With Graham leaving, her sisters always fighting and the knowledge that she would never see them again after this weekend, it was too much.

"I love Graham, and I know that I'm probably just a diversion for him. But, that doesn't stop my heart from breaking. And I don't need you two to tell me that. I just need you two to for once act like sisters and just be there for me."

Quinn's own eyes filled with tears as she nodded. "Of course, Charlie. Anything you need. We just didn't know…" Her voice trailed off and she looked to Kendra for help.

"We're sorry," Kendra said, gently. "Just tell us what you want us to do. We'll be here for you."

Charlie wrapped her arms around herself then wiped at her eyes. She took several deep breaths then said, "Graham will be stopping by on his way to the airport. I don't want him to know anything about this conversation. Understand?"

"We won't say a word," Quinn said at the same time as Kendra said, "Understood."

Charlie turned to the road as she heard the sound of a truck engine, except it wasn't Graham's truck. She didn't know who the black pickup belonged to until it came to a stop in front of their house and Boyd Robbins stepped out of the cab. Alma scurried from the passenger seat.

Charlie withheld her groan. She could not deal with Boyd right now.

"Good morning, ladies," Boyd said, tipping his cowboy hat.

"Mr. Mayor," Kendra greeted coolly. "How can we help you?"

Boyd walked onto the porch and leaned against the railing, as if he had every right to be there. "I'm not one for game-playing. I've fought in two wars and any number of conflicts defending this great county and not once did I play a game or allow anyone to play games on me. I had too much respect for my opponent to do that."

Charlie glanced at Kendra, who shrugged at her unspoken question. Neither of the women knew what in the world Boyd wanted.

"I was going to talk to you girls at church on Sunday, but none of you bothered to show up," he said, and there was a note of censure in his voice.

"I was sick," Quinn volunteered. Kendra sent her a silencing look.

"We need to talk about why you girls are here," Boyd said, bluntly. "I know—the whole town knows—that you're here because you have to be here. You can't get your inheritance without being here. Isn't that right?"

Kendra stepped forward, anger on her face. "What are you talking about?"

"I'm talking about what the future holds for Sibleyville and the Sibley girls. Your grandfather was a bastard. I'm sure not even you girls would disagree with me on that. When the town was weak, he came in and bought up everything. He owns everything. You girls own everything."

Kendra crossed her arms a smug smile on her face. "Then I would think you'd be a little more nice to us."

Boyd laughed, but to Charlie it didn't sound pleasant. "The problem is, Kendra, I now own you girls."

Kendra snorted in disbelief. "I highly doubt that."

Boyd smiled again and walked across the porch to stand toe to toe with Kendra. Charlie instantly went to her sister's side, while Quinn flanked her on the other side. Charlie knew that Boyd would not hit Kendra, but then again, the man was half insane.

"I know what your inheritance is if you remain in this house for two weeks," he said, bluntly

"I don't believe you."

"And I know that this town inherits everything if you don't stay in this house," he continued, ignoring Kendra. The sisters exchanged glances, but remained silent. Boyd sent them another stiff smile as he said, "I see I now have your attention."

"What do you want?" Kendra demanded.

"I wanted to give you a choice. Something Max never did," he said, flatly. "If, you three remain in this house, you'll each receive $5,000—"

"Five thousand dollars," Quinn exclaimed in outrage. "I can't even pay my mortgage with that."

"He means a month," Kendra said to Quinn then looked at Boyd and asked, hopefully, "Right?"

Boyd shook his head then said, "On the other hand, if you leave the house, the town gets the notes, and I'll pay you each $10,000. Double what you'd get from Max. It's a win-win situation for all involved."

"What happens to the town if we stay for the full two weeks?" Charlie asked.

"It goes to a trust that no one knows anything

about," he answered. "I've always said that I like the devil I know."

"I don't believe you," Quinn cried. "Grandpa Max would not do this to us. Five thousand dollars, when he was worth millions? We'll be the laughingstock of the country."

"No, it makes sense," Charlie said, quietly, while wrapping her arms around herself. She smiled to herself. "Grandpa Max left this town with $5,000 in his pocket. He wants to give us the same start."

"That is preposterous," Kendra exclaimed.

"He's evil," Quinn declared. "Pure evil."

Boyd ignored their cries and turned to Charlie, sensing that she was the only one still in control. "You girls have about six days left. You get the double the money if you leave before then. The offer goes off the table in an hour."

"How do we know you're telling the truth?" Charlie asked, suspiciously.

"You don't," Boyd said, simply, then added, "But you knew your grandfather. Doesn't this sound like some bullshit he would pull?"

When Charlie had no answer, he smiled then said, "Good day, girls. You have one hour to think about it. I'll be at my office in the town hall."

He tipped his hat again, as if he hadn't just left them in shambles, then walked down the porch. Alma stood in the same spot where she had stood and looked as horrified as the three sisters. "Alma," Boyd ordered from the truck.

Alma startled, then hurried down the steps. Charlie watched Boyd's truck exit the driveway then turned to her sisters. Kendra looked shell-shocked, while Quinn looked on the verge of bursting into tears.

"What am I going to do?" Quinn whispered, as she slid to the steps again. "I have no money, no home, I have nothing."

"What?" Kendra said, turning to Quinn, surprised. Quinn ignored her and buried her face in her hands.

"You have me," Charlie said, firmly, sitting next to Quinn on the steps.

Quinn looked at Charlie then laughed dryly and rolled her eyes. "No offense, Charlie, but you're just as screwed as Kendra and me."

"If Boyd is right, then we're not screwed. We're loved."

"Charlie, I can't take your optimistic crap right now," Kendra snapped angrily.

Charlie stared calmly at her two sisters then said, "I've been trying to tell you guys that I finally figured out why Grandpa Max did this. It wasn't about the money. It was never about the money. It was about us, the three of us. He saw how far we had drifted apart, and he wanted to bring us back together. He wanted us to be sisters again. And it worked. If we hadn't spent this time together, we wouldn't have known how much we need each other, now more than at any other time in our lives."

Kendra looked warily at Charlie, and her voice held a warning, as she said, "Charlie—"

"Quinn, Kendra lost her job," Charlie said, ignoring Kendra's curse, as she stared into Quinn's wide eyes. "She got in some trouble at work, and she may not be able to work as a stockbroker again."

Quinn looked at Kendra and whispered, "But, you love being a stockbroker."

"And, Kendra, you were right. Quinn's contract is not being renewed," Charlie said, looking up at Kendra, who had beads of sweat on her forehead. "She fell in love with a con artist, who stole all of her money."

"Thanks, Charlie," Quinn muttered, dryly.

"I'm sorry, Quinn," Kendra whispered, her expression concerned, as she sat on the steps on the other side of Quinn.

Charlie took each of her sisters' hands in one of hers. "Grandpa Max gave us a gift. He wanted us to make it on our own, like he did, except he made sure we had something that he didn't—family."

Charlie's vision blurred with tears as she noticed the tears freely falling from Quinn's eyes, and Kendra's own tear-filled eyes.

"What should we do?" Kendra asked, sounding uncertain.

"We're going to stay here for two weeks, and we're going to come up with a way to salvage our lives and our careers," Charlie said, firmly.

"What about the town?" Quinn asked. She shrugged in defense when Kendra looked at her, surprised. "It's not the absolute worst place in the world, and some of the people are nice."

Charlie smiled as Kendra shook her head in disbelief. "Even though everyone in this town seems to have hated Grandpa Max, I don't think he hated this town. For him, it was a place where he remained Max Sibley, not the millionaire, but just the man who was starting out, before all the heartaches and sadness twisted him into the man we knew. I don't think Grandpa Max would turn this town over to anyone who would destroy it."

Kendra wiped at her tears then nudged Charlie, as she asked, "You're not even a little upset? We thought we were going to be millionaires. All of your problems at the museum would have been over."

Charlie stared into the distance for a moment, and Graham filled her thoughts. If she had never come to Sibleyville, she never would have met him. That was worth more than five thousand dollars. Having loved someone was priceless.

She squeezed her sisters' hands as she whispered, "Not even a little."

"Thanks for driving us, man," Theo said to Wyatt, as he sat in the back seat of Wyatt's sports utility vehicle. "Let's get this show on the road."

Wyatt sent Graham an amused look then sat behind the steering wheel. Graham rolled his eyes then placed his own luggage in the SUV trunk. Theo didn't have to act so damn cheerful that they were leaving. Graham had been in a bad mood all morning: while he packed, while he put on a suit for the first time in six months, while he showered, while he ate breakfast with his parents, who had been strangely silent. Graham had tried to deny it, but he knew the reason why. Charlie.

He didn't want to leave her. It was that simple. Graham Sibley was in love, and it was the most awful, terrifying thing in the world. And, paradoxically, it was the only thing in the world that made everything else better.

"This is the last suitcase from your room," Lance said, walking out of the house with a large carry-on. Now that Lance didn't have to pretend he was injured, he was lifting and carrying things that a few weeks ago would have caused him to warn of a second heart attack.

Eliza followed behind her husband, her eyes filled with tears and a tissue wadded in her hands.

"Mom," Graham groaned, even as he accepted his tenth hug of the morning from her.

"I know, I know," she sniffled. "I just got so used to having you around. It was nice."

"Mom, you'll forget about me by tomorrow, as you sit gossiping with your quilting circle," he assured her, patting her back.

Lance shoved the suitcase in the trunk then slammed the door closed. He gently extracted Eliza from Graham's arms and shook Graham's hand. His eyes were strangely bright as he said, "Thanks for everything, son."

Graham ignored the man-code and wrapped his arms around his mother and father. "I'm going to miss you guys, too," he said, truthfully.

When he pulled away, his mother was fully crying again, and his father looked choked up himself. Graham swallowed a lump in his own throat. He definitely hadn't planned on it being this hard. It had been quite an adjustment living with his parents again after being on his own for so many years, but now that he was leaving, he knew that he would miss the dinners, the constant questions from his mother about his social life, the constant orders from his father about the farm.

"We should get going, Graham," Theo called from inside the SUV.

"We'll see you at Lance's exhibit in Los Angeles," Eliza said to Graham, attempting a wobbly smile.

Graham's smile fell as he thought about Charlie. He didn't know if he'd be able to see her that soon. Not when his feelings were so fresh. He couldn't be in love with her. Not Charlie. She wasn't his type, she would never leave Los Angeles and Graham wasn't leaving Tokyo, and even though he didn't believe in all that hocus-pocus, that wasn't how it was supposed to happen. It wasn't love at first sight. And he wanted his chance, just like his father and Red.

"Are you going to stop by and tell her bye?" Lance asked, quietly.

Graham didn't have to ask who his father was talking about. "I said bye last night."

Lance stared at him for a moment then said, quietly, "I know you don't believe in all that love-at-first-sight stuff, but I thought you should know that sometimes, it takes a while to realize that it was love at first sight."

Graham shook his head, confused, but Lance only smiled and took Eliza by the hand. He waved to Theo and Wyatt then dragged Eliza back onto the porch.

Graham hesitated. He wanted to ask his father what he meant. He wanted to demand an explanation. Were the stories not true?

"Graham, we're going to miss our flight," Theo said, a note of impatience in his voice.

Graham waved to his parents then sat in the passenger seat. Wyatt started the engine, but didn't move.

"Where to?" Wyatt asked, staring at Graham closely.

Graham looked at his best friend, wondering if Wyatt also knew something that Graham didn't. Something Lance had tried to tell him.

"The airport, of course," Theo said, from the back seat. "That's why you're here, remember? Been spending too much time around the formaldehyde, Dubya?"

Wyatt ignored Theo and continued to stare at Graham. Graham cleared his throat then said to Wyatt, "I have to see Charlie."

Wyatt grinned and started driving. Theo groaned from the back seat then said, "Graham, our flight—"

"I have to see her, Theo. I can't explain it, or…maybe, I can, but I can't leave town without talking to her."

"She's not there," Theo said, flatly.

Graham turned in the seat to stare at Theo. His body went cold and his palms sweaty as he said, carefully, "What are you talking about?"

"She and her sisters left an hour ago."

Wyatt asked, "How do you know?"

"Boyd offered them $10,000 a piece to leave town before their two weeks were up," Theo explained, reluctantly. "Somehow, Boyd found out that if the Sibley sisters left town, then the town would inherit all of the notes and deeds that Max Sibley had acquired over the years. If the sisters stayed and actually fulfilled the conditions of the will, they would only receive $5,000 a piece. It was an easy choice for them."

Graham turned back in the seat and stared blindly at the highway. Charlie had left without seeing him. He loosened his tie and rolled down the window, even though the cool air of the air conditioning blasted in his face. It wasn't enough. He needed air. He needed something.

He knew Charlie was in love with him. She had to have been, but she had still left. Without one word. He had been so wrapped up in his own feelings that he hadn't even stopped to consider hers. And apparently hers hadn't been that strong, since she had left as soon as she had been offered a better deal.

Graham shook his head in disbelief. He had been played. He inwardly cursed, even as his heart broke. If this was love, he wanted no part of it.

"See," Theo said, as they rode past the Sibley house. "No one's home."

Theo was right. Kendra's Jaguar was not parked in front of the house, the windows were shut. The house looked empty.

"Do you have her phone number?" Wyatt asked Graham.

Graham shook his head, dumbly. He didn't even know where she lived.

"Maybe it's better this way, Graham," Theo said, quietly. "You two had a good time. Leave it at that. You told me from the beginning that she wasn't your type. It's easy to fall for someone when you have no other options. As you know there are plenty of options in Tokyo, especially when you can tell a woman that you're the vice president of Shoeford Industries—"

"Shut up, Theo," Wyatt snapped at Theo. Theo bristled, but wisely remained silent. Wyatt glanced at Graham. "You can get her number, Graham. You can go the museum. She'll be easy to find."

"No," Graham said, speaking for the first time since Theo had broken the news. "Theo's right. Charlie and I had a good time, and that was it."

Wyatt groaned in frustration and said, "She's a good woman, Graham. You're not going to find a woman like that again. Just call her—"

"She made her choice, and I'm going to honor it," Graham said hoarsely, then opened his briefcase. "I have some work to do."

Wyatt sighed, but kept his gaze on the road. Graham stared at the papers Theo had given him, but couldn't see anything. At least, Charlie had not had to put up with him making a fool of himself over her.

Chapter 23

"Ten hours remaining, ladies," Quinn said, excitedly.

Charlie exchanged amused glances with Kendra, but otherwise did not comment as Quinn continued to string lights around the living room.

The Sibley sisters had done it. They had survived two weeks together in the same house. Charlie wouldn't have traded this time for anything else in the world, but then there was Graham. She put on a brave face for her sisters, but late at night alone in her bed, Charlie cried. She hadn't thought it would hurt this badly, but it did. Like Sephora had said in one episode after her third husband had left her, "Love hurts."

"We should receive a call from Max's lawyer on this telephone at precisely 12:01 a.m.," Kendra said, while checking the cell phone that the same lawyer had given to them at the reading of their grandfather's will two weeks ago.

Charlie looked from Quinn's excited expression to Kendra's then forced a smile. She should be excited, too. Five thousand dollars was nothing to sneeze at. Plus, they had stuck together. Grandpa Max would have been proud.

And she would find someone else. It had taken her twenty-eight years to find Graham, but there would be another Graham. She remembered his smile and tears filled her eyes. She admitted that there would never be another Graham, but maybe there would be someone. Whoever it was would not be Graham, but since Graham had made no attempt to get in touch with her since leaving, she could only accept that she had been right. There was no future for them. And, even though she wanted to hate him, she couldn't. She had had two wonderful nights with him. No matter what Kendra or Quinn said, Charlie knew those nights had meant something to him, too.

Someone knocked on the door, and Charlie stood, expecting Lance or Eliza, who had dropped by with news about Graham every day, as if to torture Charlie. But, since those nuggets of information had been the only thing that had kept her moving forward, Charlie waited for their visits the way a kid waiting for Christmas morning.

Charlie opened the door and gasped in surprise when she saw Alma Robbins. Alma. She heard her sisters' similar gasps of shock from behind her.

"Alma," Charlie said, recovering. "What are you doing here?"

Alma's voice was just as frail as she was, as she said, "I'm probably the last person you want to see, but I have to atone for Boyd."

Charlie realized those were the most words she had ever heard the woman speak at one time.

Kendra walked to Charlie's side and glared at Alma. She snapped, "Boyd should atone for himself."

Alma shot a fearful look at Kendra then asked Charlie hesitantly, "Can we talk alone?"

"Of course," Charlie responded then motioned for Alma to follow her into the kitchen.

Alma gratefully sank into the chair at the table, while Charlie stood at the sink, uncertain how to proceed. She hadn't thought Alma was capable of breathing without Boyd stuck to her side. Alma glanced around the kitchen, apparently in no hurry to break the awkward silence.

"Would you like some water or juice?" Charlie asked, since Alma didn't seem on the verge of speaking.

"Oh, please," Alma said, eagerly.

Charlie grabbed a glass from the cupboard then pulled Kendra's pitcher of fresh-squeezed grapefruit juice from the refrigerator. It tasted awful, but considering that Kendra was a health nut, Quinn didn't eat and Charlie had eaten all of her food from her last trip to Bentonville, there wasn't much that was edible in the refrigerator.

Charlie set the glass on the table in front of Alma then took the chair across the table from her.

Alma took a delicate sip of the pink juice and audibly choked, but through a sheer force of will managed to swallow it and even to smile.

"It's horrible, isn't it?" Charlie said, sympathetically.

"No, it's not," Alma responded, politely. She looked around the kitchen once more. "You all have done a remarkable job on this place. I never thought anyone could live here, but it's clean and very nice."

"We had a lot of help from the men in town. They came over one day and made this place livable." Charlie waited as Alma once more tried to pretend to like the juice. More silence followed. Charlie finally asked, "Alma, what are you doing here?"

Alma finished the whole glass in one gulp, as if for fortification, then blurted out, "Boyd lied. If you all remained in this house for two weeks, Max had set up a trust for the town. No one would have to worry about their farms or ranches. The trust was for our benefit. But, Boyd tried to make you girls leave early because if you did then he was promised that he would have direct control over the town property that Max owned."

"I don't understand," Charlie said, confused. "Who promised him that?"

"Graham's friend from Tokyo, Theo... He found out the conditions of the will. The bank that would have owned the town if you girls had failed, belonged to a company under the Shoeford Industries' umbrella. Graham, of course, had no idea. Theo approached Boyd at our house a few nights ago, and told Boyd that if he got you to leave early then he would make certain that Boyd was in control of the trust."

"Why?" Charlie choked out. "Why would Theo do that?"

"I don't know." Alma shook her head as tears filled

her eyes. One veined hand went to her thin lips as she held back a sob. She finally recovered enough to speak, "Boyd has done a lot of things during our thirty-five years of marriage that have made me weep. But, doing this to you girls and twisting the gift that Max left the town… I couldn't sit by and allow that. Max wanted you to love this town, without any pressure. And I know you do, because how could you not?"

Charlie opened her mouth then promptly closed it. She didn't know what to believe or even who to believe anymore.

"Boyd is not a bad man," Alma continued in a soft voice. "He just loves this town, and he wants to protect it."

"By blackmail and threats and lies?" Charlie demanded, angrily.

"Don't judge him too harshly." Alma smiled then stood, a fearful expression crossing her face as she glanced at her watch. "He'll be home soon. I'd better go."

Charlie stood, too, and said, begrudgingly, "Thank you, Alma."

"What are you going to do?"

"I don't know."

"Oh…I hope I didn't make a mistake coming here," she said, sounding close to tears.

"No, I needed to know the truth." She suddenly became nervous, as she added, "And Graham needs to know the truth, too."

"I thought you'd be the perfect person to tell him," Alma said, with such confidence that Charlie wondered if Alma had done some eavesdropping of her own. "I don't know why Theo wants to keep you two apart, but that's impossible when a Forbes man picks his future wife."

Charlie laughed, embarrassed. "You believe that myth?"

"It doesn't matter what I believe. It's only what you and Graham believe that's important."

Alma smiled once more then walked out of the kitchen. The swinging door hadn't even swung closed before Kendra and Quinn rushed inside, nearly running into one another.

"What did she want?" Kendra demanded, crossing her arms over her chest.

"Theo doublecrossed all of us," Charlie explained. "He's the one who told Boyd about the conditions of the will. He's probably the one who gave Boyd the money to offer us since I doubt Boyd has $30,000 lying around to throw at us."

"Theo," Kendra gasped. At her sisters' concerned looks, she cleared her throat and said, "I just…I don't see what he has to gain from manipulating us."

"I think the correct question is what did Theo have to gain by getting Graham back to Tokyo?" Quinn murmured. "Theo came to town for the precise reason of dragging Graham back to Tokyo for the vote for the vice presidency. Once Graham is made vice president, Theo is then promoted and becomes one step closer to being vice president himself. Maybe Theo saw the direction of Graham's feelings for Charlie. Maybe Theo correctly deduced that Graham wouldn't leave Sibleyville if Charlie was still here, and that if Graham wasn't present for the vote, Graham's future would be gone and so would Theo's. Theo had aligned himself with Graham at the company. If Graham doesn't become vice president, Theo has made enemies, and he'd be exposed. Theo would have thought that his only recourse was to make certain that Graham got on that plane, fully focused and ready to battle."

Charlie's mouth gaped open as she stared at her suddenly brainy sister.

Kendra laughed in amazement and said, "When did you become *Murder, She Wrote*?"

"I keep telling you guys that Sephora has taught me a lot. Three years ago, there was a dinner party at Sephora's mansion, and a murder took place. We spent the next four months on air locked in the mansion unraveling the murder. While the script was fabulous, I spent four months wearing the same hideous purple dress and you know that purple has never really been my color."

Charlie stared at Quinn for a moment longer, once more asking herself how they could be sisters, then she turned to Kendra and said, "If Quinn is right, then I have to talk to Graham as soon as possible. I have to tell him the truth about Theo. The vote is tomorrow. If Graham becomes vice president, and promotes Theo, he'll… It won't be fair."

Kendra stilled as she stared at Charlie. Hard. "You mean, you have to talk to him as soon as possible on the telephone, right?"

Charlie stared from Kendra to Quinn then she sighed in resignation. "If he'll accept my calls."

Quinn squared her shoulders and said, "The telephone won't do. Charlie has to go to Tokyo."

"Like hell," Kendra spat out, angrily. "We have nine and a half hours left in this shithole. It may only be five thousand dollars, but it's my five thousand dollars."

"Calm down," Quinn said, annoyed. "She won't be able to find a flight until midnight anyway. The more important question is how is she going to afford a last-minute flight to Tokyo."

Charlie groaned then raked her hands through her hair. "There goes my five thousand dollars," she moaned.

"Just wait, Charlie," Kendra tried. "You can call him from Los Angeles, or we can tell Eliza and Lance. They can call Graham and tell him everything. Or there's email, or express mail, or—"

Quinn interrupted, urgently. "She has to be on the first flight to Tokyo that we can find."

"Why?" Kendra demanded. "She doesn't need to fly halfway around the world to tell him something that can be resolved in a 5-minute phone call."

"She has to go to Tokyo," Quinn insisted.

"Why?" Kendra repeated, enraged.

"Because she is in love with him," Quinn said simply. "It's not about the promotion, or even that snake-in-the-grass Theo. It's about Charlie. She loves Graham, and as Sephora would say, 'If you can't act a fool over love, then what can you act a fool for?'"

Kendra narrowed her eyes at Quinn and demanded, "When did you become a romantic? You don't even believe in love, or so you've proclaimed a million times."

Charlie gasped. Quinn looked pointedly at Kendra, who groaned then muttered, barely audibly, "You can have my share, too."

Charlie's heart began to pound against her chest. Her palms grew sweaty. She was the pragmatic one. She couldn't just fly to Tokyo to see a man, who'd be shocked—though not she hoped, that appalled—at seeing her. He hadn't said that he loved her. He'd never given any indication that he loved her. She could be making a fool of herself. An idiot for love, like an old song from the forties or fifties.

Charlie suddenly smiled, causing Quinn to clap excitedly and Kendra to throw up her hands in surrender.

"Between the three of us poor slobs, we might even be able to afford a first-class ticket to Tokyo," Kendra muttered.

"No," Charlie gasped.

"Kendra's right," Quinn said, nodding. "You can't fly to Tokyo in coach. It's inhumane."

"We're going to be all right," Quinn said, firmly, then planted her legs and held her arm out, her fist closed.

At her sisters' strange looks, she sighed in impatience and continued to wait. Charlie laughed as it hit her what Quinn was doing. The three sisters had touched fists when they were children to be like superheroes. She immediately touched her fist to Quinn's. Kendra rolled her eyes, but Charlie saw the small smile tug at the corner of her mouth before she too joined her fist.

"All I have to say is Graham better be worth it."

"He is," Charlie answered. And neither of her sisters questioned her.

Chapter 24

Graham scanned his office to make certain that he had left nothing behind. His office, or his former office, was empty now. Every scrap of furniture was gone, the paintings on the walls were gone, even his name plate was gone. Graham crossed the grooves dug in the carpet by his furniture and stood at the floor-to-ceiling windows that gave him a bird's-eye view of Tokyo. The buildings, the people, the excitement. Graham would miss it, but not enough to stay here, when his entire life was back in the United States.

Graham sighed and stuck his hands into the pockets of his slacks. He had been back in Tokyo for one week, but it had only taken him one step off the plane to realize what a mistake he'd made. He shouldn't have left Sibleyville. More specifically, he shouldn't have left Charlie.

Instead, he had thrown himself into his job. Campaigning. Trying to rectify the damage from the past six months. And, in the end, it had worked. Graham had been offered the vice presidency, and he had turned it down. He had apologetically told the board that he just wasn't cut out for the job. Not anymore.

The door to the office swung open and Theo stormed inside. Judging from his flushed vanilla skin and blazing brown eyes, Graham knew that he didn't have to tell Theo what had had happened.

"I see you've heard the news," Graham noted mildly.

Theo frantically glanced around the office as if willing the furniture back into place. When that didn't happen, he finally turned to Graham. "What have you done?"

Graham shrugged and glanced out the window once more. "I quit."

Theo flinched as if he had been struck. "Please tell me it's a joke."

"It's not a joke, Theo. They offered me the vice presidency, and I told them that while I am flattered, I wanted a job that would allow me to have roots closer to home."

"You idiot," Theo roared, stalking across the room towards Graham. "You've ruined everything!"

Graham remained calm since he had expected Theo to take the news hard. "You're a good consultant, Theo. You don't need me to advance."

"Of course I do. Kent knows I was aligned with you. He'll do everything in his power to make certain that I'm punished for that. I can guarantee my next assignment will be in Idaho or somewhere equally as awful."

"A stint in Idaho will do you good," Graham teased.

The glare Theo sent in his direction should rightfully have cut steel. Graham took pity on him and said, "I put in a good word for you with Shoeford. You'll be up for your own vice presidency within the next three years."

"It's not going to be enough. I didn't go to the same fancy schools as you and the others. I don't have that pedigree. They don't treat me the same way they treat you. I will be shoved aside when you leave."

For the first time, Graham saw Theo's insecurity. It made sense since Theo spent most of his time trying to convince people that he was so confident.

"You may not have the degrees, but you're one of the best consultants in this company. You have nothing to worry about, Theo," Graham assured him. "You just have to be patient."

"Patience? Where has that ever gotten a Black man in corporate America?" Theo shook his head in disappointment then said, "You could have gone far, Graham. They were comfortable around you. They think I'm going to steal their Mont Blanc pens. I can't believe that you let a woman ruin it all."

Graham's tolerance quickly ended as he growled, "Leave Charlie out of this."

"I thought if you knew she didn't care for you, you would stay here where you belong," Theo said through clenched teeth.

"What are you talking about?" Graham asked, confused.

Theo took a deep breath then straightened his shoulders. He looked Graham square in the eye and said flatly, "I found out the conditions of her grandfather's will and I told Boyd to bribe her to leave early, so that you wouldn't have the chance to see her before you left and you wouldn't have the chance to ruin your—and, coincidentally, my—life."

Graham didn't know his fist flew until the pain of it connecting with Theo's face sent a razor-sharp pain through his arm. Theo flew backwards, falling flat on his back, as blood squirted from his nose.

Graham's anger still was not appeased. He stood over Theo, his hands curled into fists, waiting for Theo to rise so he could pummel him. Theo wisely remained on the floor, raising to his elbows to feel his nose.

"You bastard," Graham snarled. "Why?"

Theo didn't look angry so much as resigned as he said, tiredly, "You two weren't going to see each other after you left Sibleyville anyway. I just sped the process along."

"Why?" Graham demanded in a louder voice.

Theo pulled a cream-colored handkerchief from his inside suit-jacket pocket and held it to his nose. He finally answered, "I knew you were starting to feel something for her, and I knew that you would do something stupid, like not come back to the office so you could spend time with her. I couldn't allow that to happen. I knew you'd regret it, and I would definitely regret it. So, I told Boyd what I knew, and he did what he could to make her leave early. The funny thing is…she wasn't gone when we drove by her house. I didn't find out until later that they didn't take Boyd's deal."

"I was right, Theo. You'll have no problem climbing the corporate ladder," Graham said, coldly.

"I did it for your own good," Theo screamed.

"You did it for yourself."

"Helping your career helps mine. That's not my fault."

Graham stared down at Theo and once more contemplated pummeling him into a black-and-blue mess. Instead, he realized that he had other more important things to do. Like flying back to California to find his woman. It was not too late. It couldn't be.

Graham stepped over Theo and walked toward the door.

"Where are you going?" Theo demanded, scrambling to his feet.

Graham stopped at the door then glanced at Theo. "I'm going home."

"You won't last two weeks in Sibleyville," Theo sang out. "You'll miss the excitement, the thrill. You can't trade all that in for farming soybeans in Smalltown, USA. You'll be back, Graham."

"I wasn't talking about Sibleyville," Graham murmured then walked out the office.

Graham ran through Los Angeles International Airport, plowing through conversations and ignoring the resulting curses directed at him from irate travelers. Graham didn't care. He was on a mission. His red-eye flight from Japan had gotten in an hour late, and he had exactly ten minutes to sprint across the football-field-sized terminal to reach his flight to Bakersfield, where he would then rent a car and speed to Sibleyville. It was a circuitous route, but it was the only one he could get on such short notice.

Graham motored through another group of people and then ran down an escalator. If he missed the flight, he would have to wait until afternoon for another one, and Graham didn't want to wait. He couldn't wait. Not anymore. His body burned with the desire to see Charlie, to hold her, to love her. So what if it hadn't happened at first sight. It was just as real, and it was going to last just as long.

Graham glimpsed his gate ahead and almost stopped running in relief when he noticed the line of passengers walking onto the plane. He was not too late. Because his attention was distracted, he didn't notice the person to his right running in the opposite direction. At the last moment, just before impact, Graham saw the person. He closed his eyes as the two collided. The other person fell to the ground in a tangle of luggage, arms and legs.

Graham caught himself on one knee before he fell fully to the ground himself. His luggage, however, slammed to the ground with a loud noise that caught the attention of most of the people in the terminal. He heard several gasps from onlookers and then the feminine moan of pain coming from the person he had run into, who was flat on her back a few feet from him.

Graham cursed. He didn't have time for apologies and manners. He had to get on that plane. He glanced at the gate again, noting that only two people remained in the passenger line.

"Lady, are you okay?" he asked, quickly, as he gathered his bag and stood.

Then Graham looked down. Time stopped. He stopped breathing. He would later swear that the earth stopped moving on its axis. Because it was happening. A Forbes man was falling in love at first sight.

Beautiful brown skin, dark shoulder-length wavy hair, warm brown eyes and a beautiful mouth that could make a man give up everything—including a big promotion in Tokyo. Even in her rumpled travel clothes, he could tell she had a shape like an hourglass, curved in all the right places, soft and vulnerable. At that moment, Graham fell in head-over-heels, crazy, unreasonable love. At first sight.

"Charlie," Graham whispered.

Charlie blinked up at him, as if she wasn't quite certain she trusted what she saw. Graham instantly reached down and pulled her to her feet. She still looked a little dazed. He framed her face with his hands, her soft skin under his fingers, as it was meant to be.

"Charlie," he whispered again, not remotely embarrassed that he said her name with a reverence he would have once found comical.

"Graham, what are you doing here?"

"I'm going back to Sibleyville."

"Why?"

He smiled because she really didn't know. "Because you're there, Charlie, and I want to be wherever you are."

Tears filled her eyes, and Graham hoped and prayed they were happy tears and not tears of sadness. Then her hands covered his and she squeezed them.

"But, the promotion…Tokyo?" She gasped suddenly and said, "Theo—"

"I know about Theo," he said, gently. "He did it because he wanted to make sure I went to Tokyo. He thought I wouldn't go because of you, and he was right."

"Graham, no," she whispered, horrified, as her hands

dropped to her sides. "I don't want you to give up anything for me. You deserve that promotion. I have to stay in L.A. for now because of the museum and my sisters, but you and I will work something out. We love each other and that's all that matters."

Graham smiled and gently wiped away her falling tears with the pads of his thumbs. "Didn't you hear me, Charlie? I want to be wherever you are. I have to be wherever you are because without you nothing else matters."

For the first time, she smiled at him. "This is crazy," she whispered.

"This is love," he murmured, right before he covered her lips with his own. And he was home.

Her arms wrapped around his waist, and she pressed against him, her body welcoming his. Her mouth was soft and sweet, and she allowed him to express all of his frustration and longing. Each kiss only whetted his appetite for more. If he had anything to say about it, the two would not be doing any more traveling that day.

He finally pulled away from her, then noticed that there was clapping around him. He glanced around and noticed a group of people watching them and applauding. Charlie ducked her head in embarrassment. Graham bowed then shouldered her carry-on bag with his and grabbed her hand.

"Let's get out of here. Do you have a car waiting outside or something?" he asked.

She sent him a strange look then said, "I wasn't going home. I was going to see you. I was coming to Tokyo."

Graham's heart stopped and he stared down at this amazing woman, who for some reason loved him. He wanted to kiss her again, but decided that if he did, he would not be able to stop this time.

"I'm sorry about the will," he said, softly. "I know you were expecting a lot more than what you got."

"I love you, Graham."

His heart squeezed at her softly spoken words. He stuttered, "I love you too, baby, but the museum—"

"The museum will survive. It always does. Somehow."

"What about your sisters?" he asked, hesitantly.

"They'll survive, too." Charlie smiled, then wrapped her arms around him. And Graham realized that out of all the places in the world he had been, no place had ever been more right.

Epilogue

Six months later

From her perch on the second-floor balcony, Charlie scanned the gallery of the Max Sibley African-American Art Museum. The museum was packed to capacity for the grand opening of Lance Forbes's "African-Americans in the West" series. Men in tuxedos and women in glittering dresses mingled, their laughter and indecipherable conversations drifting up to Charlie. Waiters moved amongst the guests offering trays of champagne and finger food.

A fair amount of cowboy hats and cowboy boots were in the crowd, since half of Sibleyville had driven down for the opening. Lance and Eliza were beaming in a corner of the museum as they spoke to a gaggle of reporters. Lance looked handsome and slightly bald without his Chicago Cubs hat. Wyatt was in attendance, standing at the bar, looking across the room at Quinn, who looked slinky and gorgeous and seemed to be purposely turning her back on Wyatt. Kendra also was in the museum somewhere, probably hiding in an office, afraid to run into anyone she knew, but at least she was there.

The museum itself had never looked better. It had been repainted last month and new track lighting had been added to better display paintings. Sometimes Charlie wanted to pinch herself to make sure she was awake because her life had changed so drastically in the last six months.

Graham had moved to Los Angeles and started his own financial company. The two had lived in her small apartment for a few weeks until Graham had found a gorgeous house close to the beach. The house also had a small cottage in the back that Quinn had moved into because, frankly, she had nowhere else to go even though none of them mentioned that. Kendra had returned to New York, but Charlie hoped it was a matter of time before Kendra came around, too.

With Graham's contacts, Charlie's museum was opened to a whole new world of donors. All she needed was an introduction, and her passion did the rest. She soon had donations flooding into the museum, which had made this night possible. The new money and round of wealthy donors had brought more headaches, but they were headaches any museum director would love to have.

Charlie smiled as Graham spotted her from the

ground floor. He looked dangerous in a black tuxedo. Even from that far away, she could feel his intensity and love for her. She glanced down at the sparkling diamond engagement ring on her left ring finger. He had given it to her one week after moving to L.A. Now she felt as if it had always been there.

He ducked under the rope cordoning off the stairs that led to the balcony and administrative offices and walked up the stairs. She watched him the entire way, sighing to herself. She didn't even try to hide how his nearness made her feel like a schoolgirl. And even six months later, the feelings hadn't faded one iota.

"Why are you up here hiding out when you should be down there accepting accolades for a job well done?" he murmured, while pressing a kiss to her cheek.

"I just wanted to enjoy the view for a moment," she replied.

Graham followed her gaze down to the crowd. "You did a good job, Charlie."

"We all did a good job," she corrected. "Your mother and your father were invaluable in putting this together. Even Kendra and Quinn helped out."

"Not to mention good ol' Grandpa Max," Graham added, with a smile.

Charlie grinned and repeated softly, "Not to mention good ol' Grandpa Max."

Good ol' Grandpa Max. Her grandfather's crazy will had given her everything. She had gotten her sisters back. And she had found Graham, the man who made it all worth it. The money Grandpa Max had left her was long gone, but as he had intended, it was only the beginning.

The fourth title in the
Forged by Steele miniseries...

USA TODAY bestselling author

BRENDA
JACKSON

riskyPLEASURES

Unable to acquire Vanessa Steele's company, arrogant
millionaire Cameron Cody follows Vanessa to Jamaica,
determined to become the one temptation she can't resist.
But headstrong Vanessa is equally determined to prove that
she's immune to his seductive charm!

Only a special woman can win the heart of a brother—
Forged by Steele.

*Available the first week of April
wherever books are sold.*

KIMANI
ROMANCE

www.kimanipress.com   KPBJ0120407

Some promises were just made to be broken...

Other People's Business

Debut author

PAMELA YAYE

Stylist Autumn Nicholson looked like the kind of uppity,
city girl L. J. Saunders had sworn off. And Autumn wasn't
interested in casual flings, especially with a luscious hunk
who'd soon be leaving. But fate, well-meaning meddling
friends and a sizzling, sensual attraction all have other plans....

*Available the first week of April
wherever books are sold.*

What happens when Prince Charming arrives...
but the shoe doesn't fit?

THE *Glass* SLIPPER PROJECT

Bestselling author
DARA GIRARD

Strapped for cash, Isabella Duvall is forced to sell the
family mansion. But when Alex Carlton wants to buy it,
her three sisters devise a plan to capture the handsome
bachelor's heart and keep their home in the family.
The question is...which of the Duvall sisters will
become the queen of Carlton's castle?

Available the first week of April
wherever books are sold.

KIMANI™
ROMANCE

www.kimanipress.com   KPDG0130407

Sometimes love is beyond your control...

Bestselling author

ROCHELLE ALERS

The twelfth novel in her bestselling Hideaway series...

Stranger in My Arms

Orphaned at birth and shuttled between foster homes as a child, CIA agent Merrick Grayslake doesn't let anyone get close to him—until he meets Alexandra Cole. But the desire they share could put them at the greatest risk of all....

"Fans of the romantic suspense of Iris Johansen, Linda Howard and Catherine Coulter will enjoy this first installment of the Hideaway Sons and Brothers trilogy, part of the continuing saga of the Hideaway Legacy."
—*Library Journal*

Coming the first week of April
wherever books are sold.

ARABESQUE®

www.kimanipress.com

A searing and unforgettable novel about secrets,
betrayals…and the consequences of one's own choices.

Acclaimed author

PHILLIP THOMAS DUCK

APPLE
BROWN
Betty

With her brother Shammond having turned into a career
criminal and her family life in shambles, Cydney Williams
leaves her hometown of Asbury behind to build a new life.
But she soon discovers that the ties that bind us can also
define us.

**"His writing is emotional and touching, while at
the same time dramatic and powerful."**
—*Rawsistaz Reviewers* on
PLAYING WITH DESTINY

*Coming the first week of April,
wherever books are sold.*

sepia™

Visit us at www.kimanipress.com   KPPTD0410407

CAN I GET an *Amen*
AGAIN

JANICE SIMS • KIM LOUISE
NATALIE DUNBAR
NATHASHA BROOKS-HARRIS

Follow-up to the ever-popular
CAN I GET AN AMEN...

The sisters of Red Oaks Christian Fellowship Church
are at it again—this time there are some new members of
the church looking for love and some spiritual healing...

Coming the first week of April
wherever books are sold.

ARABESQUE®

www.kimanipress.com

KPCIGAAA0670407